...nge, author of The...

"In this dark and twisted thriller, nothing is what it seems; but Pollock's greatest triumph is the portrait of a psyche at war with itself."
The Guardian

...ceptional. It's funny, bleak and emotionally brutal, ...nd had me permanently on the edge of my seat."
...on Courtenay Grimwood, author of *Moskva*, *The Last Banquet* and *9Tail Fox*

...)azzling. It's as though Escher and Schrödinger had collaborated on a thriller."
...R. Carey, author of *The Girl With All The Gifts*

"Smart, complex and dizzyingly twisty."
The Bookseller

...evelatory about mental health, ingeniously constructed and a thrilling ride."
***The Sunday Times*, Children's Book of the Week**

"A dazzling, dizzying rollercoaster of a novel, about memory and family and other things you can't completely trust. ...way."

Also by Tom Pollock

White Rabbit, Red Wolf

HEARTSTREAM

TOM POLLOCK

WALKER
BOOKS

For Lizzie, the most amazing wife-slash-genius

First published in Great Britain 2019 by Walker Books Ltd
87 Vauxhall Walk, London SE11 5HJ

2 4 6 8 10 9 7 5 3 1

Text © 2019 Tom Pollock
Shatter effect image © 2019 Ihor Svetiukha / Alamy Stock Vector

This book has been typeset in Fairfield, ITC Avant Garde Gothic

Printed and bound by CPI Group (UK) Ltd, Croydon CR0 4YY

British Library Cataloguing in Publication Data:
a catalogue record for this book is available from the British Library

ISBN 978-1-4063-7818-4

www.walker.co.uk

MIX
Paper from
responsible sources
FSC® C020471

1
THE KINDNESS
OF STRANGERS

CHAPTER ONE

Amy

The coffin starts moving in mid-sentence. The conveyor belt must not have been oiled in a while, because the vicar's every fourth word is interrupted by a squeal that sounds like an unhappy cat being dragged by its tail down a blackboard.

"And so, Lord, we" – SCREEEEEEEECH – "commend thy daughter" – SCREEEEEEEEECH – "to thine divine mercy…" – SCREEEEEEEEECH

Despite the Reluctant Feline Symphony the vicar keeps his rhythm, his delivery unflustered. I guess he's had a lot of practice.

People die all the time, I remind myself for the thousandth time. *And the world doesn't stop.*

The vicar drones kindly on, and the box containing Mum inches closer to the fire. I don't know what to feel. No, that's not true. I know what I *ought* to be feeling:

Grief.

Desperation.

Despair.

That's what a good daughter would feel. Fuck good, that's what a replacement level human *being* would feel. Unfortunately, the only feeling *I* can muster is a nagging anxiety that all the tea the vicar poured into me before the ceremony will overcome my bladder's valiant rearguard defence before I can get out of here. If I do pee myself, Charlie will think I did it on purpose; he's already convinced I'm an incurable drama addict. I try to probe for deeper emotions, but it's like prodding your tongue at the dentist's. I'm numb.

Which is hardly going to make for compelling content, is it? says a nasty little voice in the back of my head.

Don't think about that.

I'm cold, even though the bright July sunshine is streaming in through the stained glass. A church on a sunny day should be for a wedding, not for … this. Shivering, I sneak my phone out of my pocket and my trembling fingers almost drop it. The screen shows 11:37. I glimpse my lips reflected in the glass: they're blue.

Huh, I must still be in shock. She died a week ago, Amy. Get over it already.

My thumb twitches on muscle memory. I pull it back just in time. I swear – *I swear* – I only took my phone out to check the time. Now that I'm thinking about it, though, the three oval fabric patches on the back of my head – one behind each ear, and one at the top of my spine – have started to itch.

Forget it. You promised you wouldn't. Not today. Charlie would never forgive you.

I glance along the pew at him. His mascara's already drawing shadow stalactites as it runs down his cheeks. He catches my look, and tries to smile at me. I smile back.

The day of his mother's funeral is a terrible time to break a promise to your little brother.

Which is why I won't, I tell myself. *I won't I won't I won't. I.*

Won't.

Then why, the nasty voice in the back of my head says, *did you decide to wear the hat?*

The wide-brimmed black hat is, I realize, the reason my patches are itching. They normally breathe pretty well, but between the felt and the high turned-up collar on my dress they're getting stifled. I *could* take the hat off, but then everyone in here would see the coin-sized neuroreceptor pads stuck to my skull.

Come to think of it, the nasty voice enquires, *if you aren't going to stream, why did you even put them on this morning?*

Shut up.

But the voice is right, of course. I thumb the Heartstream icon on my phone. Not to stream — that's the promise. I won't stream — but it won't do any harm just to check my...

Oh. Shit.

15,733 notifications.

My spine ices up when I see the number. Careful to keep the phone below the edge of the pew, I skim the first few. A lot of them, as always, are delightful. Messages of support and love: *We're with you, Ame; we love you, Amy. You're so strong, Ame; you're so brave, Ame. Chin up, girl, you can do this.*

But for every one of those, there are ten like the one from BeckerBrain4Life:

> 👤 Please, please, please let me feel! I'm so lost right now. I don't know what I'm going to do without Mum!!

Mum. I recoil from that word. I want to snap back, all caps – *SHE WASN'T YOUR MOTHER*. But that's the point, isn't it? As far as BeckerBrain4Life is concerned, she might as well have been.

I keep scrolling, everywhere the same phrases.

> 👤 Let us feel.
> 👤 You owe us.
> 👤 Let us feel.
> 👤 We need closure.
> 👤 Let us feel.
> 👤 Let us feel.
> 👤 Let us feel.

My hand starts to shake harder, so hard that the text on the screen blurs and for an instant *feel* reads as *feed*.

The conveyor belt squeaks and rattles and stops. The incinerator doors slide shut, sealing Mum inside. The doors have flowers and cherubs painted on the outside.

Let us feel, the notes beg. But there's nothing *to* feel. Maybe my followers are right. Maybe I *do* owe them an ending, after everything I've dragged them through. But I don't have one to give. I grope behind the immediate physical urgency of my aching bladder, trying to define my emotions, but there's just numbness, a howling, windswept *nothing*.

The vicar's stopped talking, and I hear a muffled *whump*. My mum, up in smoke, like so much condemned paperwork. She smiles up from the photo on the altar, her tight curly brown hair framing her face. The picture is from a picnic about eight years ago, but Mum basically didn't age until the disease kicked in.

What is *wrong* with me? Feel something, Becker, anything: *your mum is dead!*

But I can't. I think I'm broken. Sitting here in church with my full inbox and my empty heart with every single person I love in the world crying, and me with tear ducts a cactus would be proud of. It's staggeringly lonely.

And loneliness has always been my kryptonite.

I thumb the icon in the top-right corner of the app, the cutesy one of a blue heart giving off radio waves. The patches heat up behind my ears.

A couple of seconds later, the responses start to roll in.

👤 Thank youuuuuuuuuuuuuu!!!

👤 Literally crying here, in floods. Thank you, Ame!!!

👤 OMG the numbness!!!

👤 So intense, so truthful!!!

I feel sick.

A creak of wood to my right draws my attention and Charlie runs for the door, stifling a sob. I didn't see him check his phone. Did he see me break my promise?

No, idiot, he's upset because they just incinerated his mother; get over yourself.

I push past Aunt Juliet and go after him. Dad's also halfway out of his seat, with that look of well-meaning, semi-engaged concern he wears for everything from a broken egg in the carton to treating a major burns victim when he's at work.

"It's OK; I'll get him," I mutter as I pass. "You stay with the guests."

"You're such a good big sister." He puts a fond hand on my arm.

I don't reply. The patches on my head are so hot they're almost burning me.

Outside, the midday sun forces me to squint; the church's gravestones, trees and railings become a glare-drenched blur. I peer around me.

"Charlie?" I call. "Chucklemonster?"

"Don't call me that," a voice says from behind the door; at least that's what I think it meant to say. Blotted by sobs, it comes out as: *"D-uhn't c-c-ull m' tha-a-a-."*

"Whatever you say, Chuckerigar." I push the door closed and there he is, the spikes of his hair awry from where he's been pulling at it, mascara bleeding all over the white collar of his shirt.

"Chuckerigar? What even *is* that?"

"No idea, Chuckifawoodchuckcouldchuckwouldchuck, I just made it up."

He snorts through his tears, and for a second I think he's going to smile. "It's j-j-j-just," he begins, but then another sob chokes him.

"Hey, hey, I know. I know." I pull him to me and just hold him there for a while, feeling his skinny little chest expand and contract against mine. He sobs again, and my stomach twists. I can't bear hearing him in pain, I can't *bear* it, yet – and it's a hateful thought, but I can't *quite* bury it quick enough – I kind of envy him it too.

The irony is, Charlie would make an amazing streamer. He feels everything so vividly. My grief, by contrast, hangs over me like a piano on a fraying rope.

"It's OK," I tell him. "It's OK."

"Nuh-nuh-nuh…" he begins.

"No, fair point, it's not OK," I concede. "It's not in the same galaxy as OK. If OK was a star it would take decades for its mediocre light to reach us. But, still, it is what it is and I'm here in it with you, and I promise you, I won't let you be alone with it. OK?"

He clings tighter to me, burrowing his face into my shoulder. After a while his grip slackens and I let him pull away. He blinks tears back, smiling at me through his freckles. Charlie's like a miniature version of our father. The spitting image of Dad at that age, that's what everyone says. People say that kind of thing about boys.

Of course, fourteen-year-old Dad would never have left the house wearing enough slap to equip the Moscow State Circus for a month.

"How on earth did you manage to get make-up on your *ear*?" I ask him, smearing it away with my sleeve.

"Oh, I reckon earscara could be a thing." He poses, framing his face with his palms. "Dani says I have very sexy ears."

"Do feel free to keep your girlfriend's fetishes to yourself."

He sniffs back his tears and grins at me. He holds up his hand, and we interlock our fingers.

"Thanks, sis."

"It's what I'm here for."

"I know, that's why…" He tails off.

"Charlie?" I prompt him, but he doesn't answer.

His smile is still in place, but I realize he's not looking at me any more. He's staring past my shoulder and his hand squeezes mine so tight the knuckles pop.

"What?" He doesn't sound angry; he sounds baffled, and that's worse. "What are *they* doing there?"

I turn to follow his gaze, and feel my heart plunge.

There must be three – maybe even four – hundred of them. Most of them wear white T-shirts emblazoned with a crappy charcoal drawing of a bird, the lines of the avian stick figure all wobbly because the sixteen-year-old girl who drew it was so upset her hand was all over the place. To be fair, you can't blame me for the shoddy artwork: it was the day we found out Mum's disease was inoperable.

That T-shirt, plus the fact that they all have the same haircut – a close crop to allow the patches maximum contact, same as me – makes them look like inmates of the same goth prison. A lot of them have dark circles under their eyes. I'm not surprised. This bunch must be the hard core; they'll have been keeping up with everything I've been putting out since last Thursday, which means they won't have been sleeping much recently.

"Amy!" A willowy boy in the front rank calls out. "What do we do now?"

I pull myself free of Charlie's grip and walk towards them. I feel light with horror. I *hate* that they're here and, in an appalled flash, I realize I'm still streaming, so *they know* that's how I feel. None of them seem to mind, though, if they've noticed. They're looking at me hopefully.

"What now?" the boy demands again when I reach the railings. He's so tall he looks like he should bend in the breeze. "What do we do now?"

I spread my hands helplessly. "I wish I knew."

"But..." he stammers. "But..." He doesn't seem to know how to finish the sentence.

I look around at the other faces; a bunch of them are crying, or have been recently, reddened eyes staring at – or through – me in shock.

You knew what this was, I want to say. *I never lied to you. I never forced you to follow me, to stream off me. Go work it out for yourselves – that's what I have to do.*

I want to be cold, but I can't, because – in a way – they just lost Mum too.

"Look," I begin, "thank you, all of you, for—"

"*YOU FUCKING VULTURES!*"

I whirl around. Aunt Juliet is stalking towards the church

gate, her handbag raised over her head like a medieval chain mace. (Having carried it for her earlier, I know that handbag would make a tremendous weapon. It weighs as much as a baby elephant.) Dad bobs along in her wake.

"Is nothing sacred?" she yells. "Christ, this is a house of worship, you spiteful toerags – show some respect!"

"But, Juliet—"

My aunt bears around to bring the speaker – a small round girl with glasses at the left of the crowd – within her field of fire.

"Who's that? Who told you my name? Who gave you permission to use it? Who the hell are you, you little snot rag? This is a *private. Family. Funeral.*" She spits every word separately. "You miserable shit-heel tourists. No one invited you!"

"But … with respect, Mrs Rice … she did."

I freeze. The tall boy's finger is levelled at me.

"Hey," I protest, "that's not true. I never said—"

But I never get to finish my sentence, because, even while still sniffing back tears behind me, Charlie moves like a viper. An awful look of suspicion on his face, he darts forward and yanks the black hat off my head. The patches on my head hiss slightly, starting to cool as they're exposed to the air.

"I didn't," I begin. I want to say *I didn't mean to.* But that's not true. It's not like I slipped this morning and fell into a bucket of neuro-conducting headwear.

Dad and Aunty Jules are gaping at me. Their expressions are almost identical: *How could you be so stupid?* That's bad enough, but it's nothing compared with the look on Charlie's face.

"You promised." He says it so quietly I can barely hear him.

He drops the hat on the grass by a gravestone and runs off, towards the church. I make to go after him, but Dad's in my way, his placid smile belying his strength as he holds my arms.

"Give him a sec, eh, love?"

I look back over my shoulder. Four hundred faces look at me from above four hundred crow T-shirts. I kill the stream, but still, from every one of them I see my own regret reflected back.

There's no sign of the family car when my taxi pulls up outside my house. When Dad "suggested" I take a cab back on my own "just to give your brother a little space", I didn't argue. It was an hour's drive home through London traffic and I think Charlie's betrayed glare would have flayed me alive by the time we arrived.

While I was in the car I tried to take my mind off it by catching up on Lance Yalta's stream. Lance may be a ludicrous bronzed man-child with purely decorative biceps, but he's the biggest thing on Heartstream for a reason. His last update was 8 p.m. St Lucian time, which I guess is where he is with his yacht. Rumour has it the yacht was free – the sponsors can't get enough of him.

I hit the little purple "playback" icon, and felt my patches go warm as 7 gigabytes of Lance's recorded emotions pulsed into them from Heartstream's servers. A wave of contentment washed over me. I felt the Caribbean sun on my bare skin, the fresh-salty scent of the ocean tingling in my nostrils. I didn't *see* the sun glaring, or hear the soft lapping of the waves – Heartstream makes bandwidth space by leaving sight and sound out since regular VR does them better – but that did mean my eyes were open to see a gaunt-looking streamer in a crow shirt in tears by the side of the road; and all of a sudden, Lance's sun-drenched smugness felt like an unforgivable waste of time. I killed the playback. That's the problem with Heartstream. It can give you pretty much any feeling, but it can't take even a single one away.

I thank my driver, crunch my way up the path, slam the door behind me and dump my keys on the hall table.

"Dad?" I call, just in case. "Charlie?" But there's no response.

The house swamps our meagre handful of pictures and rugs the way hand-me-down clothes swamp a toddler. A year after we moved in, there are still boxes. Our life was already on pause when we arrived.

I remember the first time I came to see it, walking through the shell of a home with the fawning estate agent, ticking off items on my grim mental shopping list.

Proximity to a specialist hospital – check.

Doorways wide enough to get that massive mechanized bed through – check.

Bathroom on the ground floor for when the stairs become too much for her withered legs – check.

Other people get to hunt for their first house looking for a garden for the dog.

I dump my bag on the hall floor, kick my shoes off and exhale. "Home sweet home."

Now, the place seems quieter than I've ever heard it, quieter than when I wandered around it in the middle of the night and the only sounds were my own breathing and the creak of the floorboards under my feet. I wonder what's missing...

Oh.

I get it. Some stupid obstinate part of me was expecting to hear Mum's voice greet me as I came through the door. And all at once, the pain of it is overwhelming, raging up through me like I've got a hurricane bottled in my lungs.

I try to walk it off, but eventually I have to sit down on the bottom stair and watch tears run off the end of my nose to spot the parquet flooring. I fight for breath after hitched breath, forcing myself to study the interlocking wood panels until the air comes easier.

I guess it makes sense that it hit me here rather than at the graveyard. After all, it's not really her presence in the little flower bed where they'll bury her ashes that I'm mourning – it's her absence from everywhere else.

"Come on, Ame," I say aloud through gritted teeth. "The wake's about to start. There's like five thousand tonnes of coleslaw you need to peel the cling film off." Admittedly not the deepest mantra in the world, but repeated seven times it manages to get me on my feet.

As I head towards the kitchen, a sound finally does split the silence, a familiar hissing. Someone's boiling the kettle.

"Dad?" I call again. "Charlie?"

Have they been here the whole time? Again there's no answer. It can't be them anyway. I would've seen the car out front. Gooseflesh plucks at my skin, but it's too late – I've already pushed on the door.

"Would you like a cup?"

The woman beside the stove is wearing a down jacket despite the heat. She pours boiling water into our Alice in Wonderland teapot. She's got the buzz cut all streamers have, so close it's hard to tell what colour her hair is. At first, I think she's my parents' age, but then I realize she's only maybe in her early thirties, it's just the way the skin hangs dark under her eyes that makes her appear older. She looks like she hasn't slept in *weeks*.

"I'm sorry I couldn't make it to the funeral, but I didn't really think it would be appropriate, and there was *so* much to do here."

She potters fussily around the kitchen pulling out crockery. There's a Tesco bag on the table and she unpacks a box of iced buns and sets two of them on a plate. The platters and platters of sausage rolls, biscuits, finger sandwiches and home-made coleslaw we put out for the wake this morning are still on the counter, a supply dump awaiting a grieving army. She doesn't even touch the cling film covering them.

"I figured everyone likes iced buns." She ambles over and pushes the plate at me. "Cake, Amy? I got them for you."

20

It takes me a second to force words past the incredulous horror that's blocking my throat. I don't know who this woman is, but her buzz cut tells me why she's here.

"This is *way* over the line," I burst out. "This is my *house*! You can't *be* here!"

She blinks at me; her eyes turn down at the corners, baffled and a bit hurt. I feel like I just shouted at a puppy.

"It's only a cup of tea." She raises the plate again. "And I brought my own cake; I didn't want to presume."

Outside, a car growls up on the gravel.

"That's my dad, and my little brother," I tell her desperately. "You *cannot* be here when they come in. Look..." I fight to get my voice under control. "I know today's been tough if you've been streaming off me, but I just can't help you, not right now. I mean, she was actually *my* mum, OK? Charlie's already flipped out once today, and if he sees a random streamer in here he's going to *lose it*."

She just stares at me with those shadowed eyes.

I drag in a deep breath. "Look, I'm sorry to do this, but if you don't leave, right now, I'm going to call the police."

"Oh," she says, deflating like I've just told her it's going to rain on her birthday. "Oh well, I'm sure they'll be along sooner or later anyway."

Car doors slam outside. Feet crunch on the path. I freeze midway through reaching for my phone. "Wait, what?"

With an apologetic expression on her weird, youthfully wizened face, she unzips her jacket. For an instant, I think, *Did you rob a DIY store?* Through the zip, wires sprout, and

I glimpse tubes of transparent liquid next to glass canisters of nails and ball bearings. At first my brain refuses to recognize it, it's just so *incongruous*, but then it clicks into focus. I've seen enough obsessive rolling twenty-four-hour news reports to recognize a bomb.

"I just wanted to see you," she says. "Before the end."

CHAPTER TWO

Cat

"FIVE!"

Eighty thousand screams coalesce into the countdown.

"FOUR."

"THREE."

"TWO."

"ONE."

Four rectangles of light shine on the pitch-black stage: backlit screens. Inside each rectangle, a silhouette of a boy, perfectly still. Every curl of their hair is as familiar to me as my own (Lord knows I've spent more time looking at their faces than at mine). Giant LED screens on either side magnify them. My eyes ache and I can feel my corneas drying, but I don't blink. I don't want to miss this.

"ZERO."

There's an instant's rushing silence: eighty thousand fans all drawing breath.

Whump. The pyros detonate, the screens drop, the lights dazzle my eyes, and the boys explode forward onto the stage and into the opening bars of "Saturday 3 a.m. Forever".

"Three a.m. running out into the street now, feelin' like I'm dreamin' but I'm not asleep now. You're the one…"

Nick holds his mic out to us and with one voice we all roar back. *"YOU'RE THE ONE!"*

"Hearin' church bells chime as I kiss you forever. We'll be stoppin' time cause I know that you'll never not be the one."

"London!" Ryan urges us, as if we need the encouragement. I already feel like my throat's about to tear, but I strive to scream louder.

"NOT BE THE ONE!"

Ryan's delighted grin rewards us, and his fingers twirl out a short solo, an improvisation I've never heard him do before. He's using the black Stratocaster with the flames from the "Cybersex" video.

"Have you ever heard him do that before?" Evie screams into my ear, yanking on my shoulder to bring my head down to hers.

"No!"

"Me neither! This is the best day!"

Evie's got seven years on me, but her grin is so little-girl-thrilled it's impossible not to grin back. She dances wildly, a five-foot-nothing tornado in black. I just bob and sway, but despite knowing the rhythm as well as my own heartbeat, I can't quite get my feet moving in time to it.

"Yeah, yeah, yeah, yeah, yeah, yeah, you're the ooooooone!"

With a thunderous drum solo from Dion, "Saturday" ends and the riff segues straight into the intro to "Teenage Petrol". Evie shrieks in delight, this being her favourite song of all time. She hauls me back down to her level (for a human being roughly the size of a milk carton, she's phenomenally strong – must be all the yoga and terrifying green stuff she drinks) and together we belt out the words:

"Burnin' in my veins like teenage petrol, You do things to me I just can't control."

The music ebbs and flows and we ebb and flow with it, the crowd flexing and surging like one huge muscle. At every chorus, we all rush forward and my excitement crests to panic as the bodies crush in on me.

"Grab my hand!" I yell to Evie.

"What?"

"Grab my hand, so we don't get separated!"

She laughs. "You're such a *mum*, Cat." She ignores my proffered hand and throws her arms up over her head, grooving hard to the drums in the bridge.

"And, baby, fire up my ignition tonight!"

The song ends and the lights go up.

"London!" Nick calls out to us. "It's good to be home!"

We roar our love back.

"Ow!" I feel five needle points of pain in my forearm. I look down. Evie's perfectly manicured talons are clamped onto me.

"Did you see that?" she hisses.

"See what?"

"They just did a close-up on Ryan's hands."

"So?"

"He's wearing purple nail polish."

I gape at her.

"Bullshit."

"I swear on Nick's mum's life, and you know how much I love Nick's mum."

I do. Judging by her Instagram, Judy's lovely.

"I'll bet you my right kidney Nick's wearing it too. What with them having Puffy out on stage at the Manchester gig, they're *definitely* sending us a message."

I'll be honest, three months ago, when the whole of RickResource was interpreting the presence of Nick Lamb's childhood stuffed puffin as a symbol of his undying love for his lead guitarist, I was sceptical, and I really, *really* wanted to believe. But this? Purple nail varnish when the band's breakout ballad was "Lover in Purple"? It's hard to believe that isn't deliberate. I feel my heart stutter.

"Can you imagine?" Evie goes on. "If they just came out and announced it? Right now? Better, if Nick just walked over and *kissed* him. I think everyone in this stadium would immediately die. Like, *that's it – I'm out; I've peaked*. It would be a massacre. Sheer ecstasy as a weapon of mass destruction." Her voice swells into a shout. *"RICK IS REAL!"*

It's picked up like a war cry, echoing through the stadium. Not everyone here's a Ricker, not by a long shot, but there's at least a pocket in every block, every tier. There must be five thousand of the community here, at least. Soon we're all chanting it.

"Rick is real! Rick is real! Rick is real!"

Ryan looks ready to play, but then he takes his fingers off the fretboard and just bows his head. He looks like he's soaking it up, enjoying it.

"RickisrealRickisreal!" Louder and louder, faster and faster, until, breathless, we trip over the words and collapse into more screams and applause and laughter.

Evie looks a little smug. I wonder what the other Rickers here would do if they knew that the chant was started by Teenage Petrolhead herself, but it looks like they'll find out, because she's got her phone out filming it. Later she'll post it for her sixty-five thousand Twitter followers, taking credit.

I look around, taking in the armies of Rickdom. The vast majority of the Everlasting's fans are girls, and I know a lot of them are older than they look. Most of the crowd is in tour merch, but there's a pretty big overlap between the ones holding up home-made banners declaring *Rick is Real* and *Ryan + Nick = Forever,* and those who've made a bit more of an effort. I see a stunning black-haired girl wearing the grass skirt from the video for "Honolulu Legend", and another young woman in a home-made version of the catsuit Ana Alia wears in "Cybersex". Next to me, Evie is sexy as hell in the short little belted mac from "Rainin' You", so it looks like she might not be wearing anything underneath. And I...

I'm wearing a stifling white mohair coat that I found in a charity shop for a fiver, home-made hooves made out of cardboard, tinfoil and nail polish, a mane made from a tattered mop and even a half a Tipp-Ex-painted coconut over my nose, because my favourite song is "White Horses".

"It's *cuuuuuuuute*, dubs," Evie crooned to me back in her cavernous kitchen, when we were getting ready. (She calls me *dubs* because my handle, Wild White Horse, compacts down to WWH, and *double-you-double-you-h* compacts down to dubs. Evie's mouth is like a flesh and blood zip file sometimes.)

She even spray-painted my rucksack to look like a saddle. "Details matter," she told me. Apparently, the fact it's my only rucksack and now I have to walk around at school taking jokes about "offering rides" matters less. She snapped a pic of us and stuck it on her Insta before we left. Fifteen hundred likes, but the comments mentioned only her.

Nick spins his mic by the lead a couple of times and catches it. "So, London, guess what? We're filming the tour DVD tonight. And it's a good thing too, because you all look *incredible* out there."

Another blitz of gleeful screaming and Nick revs up into the intro to "Cybersex".

The tour DVD? Oh shit, now I think of it, there *were* some signs up over the entrances saying something about how by being here we were consenting to being filmed, but in my excitement I barely registered them. I am suddenly acutely aware of the hemisphere of tropical fruit elastic-banded to my face. *Please let the cameras not land on me,* I think. I can't bear being the focus of attention. It makes me squirmier than a caterpillar under a magnifying glass on a cloudless day.

It'll be fine, though, right? It's not like it's random.

Everyone knows the producers find the hot girls in the crowd. Tall and blonde, or tiny, dark and perfect like Evie, not great galumphing gingers built for all the sports girls don't get paid to play.

I'm so caught up worrying about Coconutgate that I almost miss the big swell into the chorus.

"You got me spending all my time, searchin' high and low online, looking for you-ooo-ooooooo."

Nick's voice surges effortlessly through the octaves and, as though it was an invitation, the crowd surges forward. I feel my feet come off the floor and my hips tilt and no no no no no NO!

"Put me down!" I yell. "Put me down. *Eviiiiiiiiiie!*"

But no one can hear my panicked cries over Dion's crash cymbal, least of all Evie who's getting down in a world of her own. There are hands under my shoulders, hands under my arse, bearing me up. I kick and flail but I can't dislodge them. I wash forward and back on the crowd, inexorably borne closer to the stage, laid out like the centrepiece of a ceremonial feast. *You've just tripled your chance of being in the DVD,* I think, as the hideous mohair coat rides up to show my appendix scar. I *have* to get my feet down. I shove my bum backwards, and I begin to tilt towards the right way up, but now a hand grasps my arm, pulling me up up up …

… onto the stage.

The song's finished. All I can hear is the torrent of blood in my ears. I look down at the hand holding my forearm. The perfectly manicured nails are painted purple. In disbelief, I raise my gaze to be confronted by a smile that's graced seventeen music videos and approximately one point nine billion magazine covers, not to mention all the posters that surround my bed.

"Nice costume," says Ryan Richards into the mic. A ripple of laughter echoes through the stadium. I've never been more grateful to have my face covered. I start to blush; the blush becomes a burning; the burning becomes a nova. I must be visible from space. *Running a stadium tour on a budget? Save money on lighting by publicly humiliating Catherine Canczuk at your next gig!*

"Hey!" Ryan says sharply. "I mean it. It's a great costume; it's cool."

The laughter stops like he's thrown a switch. A moment's chastened silence, and then a chant rises up.

"'White Horses!' 'White Horses!' 'White Horses!' 'White Horses!'"

"What's your name?" Ryan proffers the mic.

I start to tremble. Briefly, I consider lying. "C-C-Catherine," I mumble. "Cathy. Cat."

"You like 'White Horses', Cat?"

Concentrating with every fibre of my being, I manage to convert my tremble into a kind of nod. "M'f'v'rite."

"Can we do 'White Horses', lads?" Ryan calls over his shoulder.

Dion, twirling his drumsticks, rolls his eyes. Stef ostentatiously looks around, anywhere but at Ryan, whistling and tuning his bass. But they're both smiling. It's biologically

30

impossible for a human being with working hormones to refuse Ryan Richards. Nick plonks himself down on an amp and grabs an acoustic. Ryan sings this one himself.

"I dreamed last night, I rode a white horse, rode a white horse to the ocean."

He offers the mic to the crowd and the response is full-throated and strong.

"And the white-crested waves, they crashed in the caves, but there was never a sound of you."

It might be a slightly obscure album track, but it seems like everyone here knows every single word, and I'm embarrassed and grateful and terrified and *great*, now I'm crying and I'm definitely going to be on the DVD let alone like five thousand YouTube videos and I can't breathe through the coconut but I'd rather die than take it off and let them see my face and oh *Christ*, I love my fandom.

And then I just let myself drift on the ocean of their voices:

"I rode my white horse to a secret city, the streets were paved with stars, but wherever I ride, I know I'll decide to stay wherever you are."

As the final strains of the song fade, I come back to myself. A single paralysing thought pierces the blissed-out fog around my brain.

Oh hell.

Evie's going to be pissed.

I cast around frantically, trying to find her, trying to read her expression in the crowd. Out of the corner of my eye,

I spy a U-shaped curve of black ink peeking from the cuff of Ryan's shirt.

OK, I think. Yes, it's low, and it's selfish, but that might *just* be my way out. With a brief spasm of guilt, I pull out my phone and snap it, just before Ryan turns round and offers me his hand like he's helping me out of a carriage at a ball. I step down from the stage, fighting the urge to cower from the gazes of the fans around me. I push through the crowd until I find myself back beside Evie. Her smile could slice bone china without breaking it.

"Holy shit," she says. "You lucky bitch." She sounds playful, but there's a hardness in her eyes. It should have been her, she's thinking. *She* looks cute. *She* looks sexy. *She* wouldn't have needed three tries to say her own name. I swallow back the apology that automatically forms in my mouth. Instead, I hold out my phone and the picture of Ryan's forearm.

"Evie, *look.*"

Irritably, she lowers her gaze. "What am I looking at?"

"Ry's got a new tattoo."

She stares at the screen and I know she's thinking what I thought when I first saw it.

"Is that the top of a padlock?" she breathes.

I'm not sure when the padlock became the official online symbol of Ryan and Nick's love for each other. It started out as a dumb three-point turn of a pun: Pad short for Paddy, short for Patrick, long for Rick – as in "Locked in Rick" – but soon #Padlocked and Padlock emojis were everywhere in the fandom.

Evie just stares at me. I thumb the AirDrop button and the picture wings its way to her phone. A pre-emptive peace offering.

"You don't want to post it yourself?" She sounds suspicious.

"You've got way more followers. You're Teenage Petrolhead – it'll mean more coming from you."

She doesn't need a second invitation. Less than a minute later Breaking: Ryan defies management injunction to get intimate ink #Padlocked #RickIsReal appears on Twitter and RickResource. I check four minutes later during "Camden Town Blues", and it's already got over a thousand retweets and #Padlocked is trending again. Evie's smile is back. She jumps and throws her arm round me and we both lean back and holler *"Rick is real!"* at the top of our voices, and the knot in my chest loosens because, after a rocky moment, we're friends again. I belong.

That's the thing people don't get about the fandom. They think we believe Ryan and Nick are a couple because the idea of two hot boys together is a turn-on, or because it's some kind of weird way of exerting control over them. But it's not *about* the boys. Not really. Believing in Rick is what gets us up in the morning; it's what tells me who'll be a good friend; it's what makes a joke so funny we'll snort tea over it, all the funnier for the fact that civilians don't get it. It's what makes us a community; it's what makes us *us*.

It's the most precious thing in the universe.

"London!" Nick hollers at the end of "Lover in Purple". "Thank you very much! Goodnight!"

I groan. It can't have been two hours already.

We stay and scream for yet another encore (they've already done two) but this time the stadium floodlights come up. A ripple of disappointment runs through the crowd, but eventually we begin to drain towards the exits.

Evie grins at me. She's soaked in sweat, but model-in-a-sports-bra-advert sweaty, not drowned-squirrel sweaty the way I suspect mohair, jumping and the heat of eighty thousand packed-in bodies have made me. "Best night *ever*."

"Best," I agree.

She shows me her phone: the padlock tattoo tweet is up to eleven thousand RTs. @RickofTheLight, another big-name fan, has @-ed Ryan's and Nick's official accounts into the thread, begging them to confirm, saying their love story is the only thing she lives for.

"Come back to mine," Evie says. "We'll get pizza and work the thread."

It looks like my five minutes of fame are forgiven. She's beaming, full of the anticipation of the all-nighter to come combing the replies, finding and amplifying the best theories, chatting about the fics we could write around them. It's tempting. Some of the best nights of my life have passed that way.

"Sounds good…" I stop in my tracks, patting the back of my rucksack. "Shit."

"What?"

"My purse. I think it must have fallen out of my bag when I got yanked up onto the crowd."

Evie shrugs. "Well, it's gone now." She could lose a dozen of her designer purses and it wouldn't bother her. In percentage terms it would just be a rounding error; and anyway, she'd only buy more.

"It was a birthday present from Mum; she's gonna *kill* me. I have to go back and try to find it."

Evie eyes the flood of exiting fans with scepticism. "Good luck."

I wince. "Don't wait for me."

Evie laughs. "Don't worry, I won't. You sure you're staying?"

"If I want my grounding to end before the menopause, I have to at least *try*."

"More pizza for me, then."

Evie lets the tide carry her towards the exit, and after a couple of moments she's obscured by jostling bodies. As I turn back towards the stage I hear a delighted cry – *"Omigod, you're Teenage Petrolhead?!"* – and I know she's having a good time.

I make a show of scanning the ground for my fallen purse, sweeping my phone's torch like a searchlight, but I'm moving far too fast to look properly. With the anticipation fizzing in my stomach, it's all I can do not to break into a flat-out run.

As it is, with my head down, that run leads me into what

feels like a brick wall draped in high-vis polyester.

"Exit's that way, miss," the security guard rumbles, pointing back over my shoulder. He has a voice like a passing train.

My throat is parched, my hands are moist and I need to pee, but I just about manage to croak one word: "Padlocked."

He stares at me for a long moment.

It hasn't worked, I think. *This was all some kind of joke.*

But then he rolls his eyes, sighs and stands aside. "Behind the curtain, then first left," he says, "then second door on the right."

"Thank you!"

"Whatever."

I mount the steps at the side of the stage, and push through the black curtains. Ahead, under a scaffolding lattice, a corridor opens like a mouth. I hurry into it, fuelled by a mix of anxiety and anger and need. Am I too late? Did I not push through the crowd fast enough? Is there someone else now? My skin itches with it.

A skinny woman rushes past, lanyard flying, but she doesn't challenge me. A hallway opens on the left, and I follow it. I pass one unmarked door on my right, but then there's nothing but a seeming eternity of blank corridor. I'm losing heart for the second time in as many minutes, before I see a bend in the hallway ahead of me and, just around the corner, a second door.

I raise my fist and, tensing my legs to flee into the bowels of the stadium if the wrong person answers, knock.

The door swings open. He smiles at me. Not the magazine-cover, music-video smile, his real one. He's stripped off his shirt, and I feel a little quiver in my inner thighs as I take in his chest and shoulders, still shiny with sweat from the stage lights. I can see the whole of the new tattoo on his right forearm now too: not a padlock, but an infinity loop. "For eternity," he'd told me. "I never want to be irrelevant." I'd laughed at him for that, shocked at myself for being so bold. How could *he* ever not be relevant?

"I was waiting for you."

I don't think I'll ever get tired of *that* voice saying those words.

"I can't..." I realize I'm gasping; I must have rushed more than I thought. "I can't believe you—"

But I don't get to finish my sentence, because Ryan Richards stops it with a kiss.

CHAPTER THREE

Amy

I remember the first time someone from the Internet scared me.

At my mother's bellowed insistence (you never would have known she was working with one and two thirds of her lungs) I'd taken a weekend to check out potential universities. It was a mad scramble, up to Edinburgh via Durham and then back down through York and Leeds to Bristol, all in two days, a blizzard of forms and pamphlets and unfamiliar faces, trekking up and down massive Victorian halls, past statues of monumentally mustachioed Victorian men who'd endowed this or that college with uncountable sums of money they'd plundered from equally uncountable numbers of people they'd conquered in the name of, well, Victoria.

I felt like a zombie as I got off the train at Temple Meads station. The shafts of sunshine slanting through the glass roof dazzled me, and I had to squint. There she was, conspicuous by her stillness among the colourful blur of bodies and bags and chatter.

I'd had my share of online hate, of course; show me a woman with more than five hundred followers, and I'll show you a woman who's been showered with spiteful shit by toerags with anonymous accounts. I'd had pictures of burning buses and bleeding babies posted in my feed whenever I'd had the temerity to voice any sort of opinion in public, but none of that had *scared* me, not bone-deep-chill-in-summer scared me, not the way this anxious-looking girl with her purple buzz cut and her too-thick eyeshadow did.

I knew she was there for me, even before I heard her call.

"Amy!"

I remember the moth-wing flutter in my chest as I tried to smile at her. I asked her how she'd known where I'd be – I hadn't posted about my trip on any of my accounts – and she told me all about the detective work she'd done, the way she'd mined not just my feeds, but Charlie's too. Her guesswork based on the time of year, the calls she'd made *pretending to be me* to the train company to reconfirm my tickets, even down to the seat and the carriage. She beamed proudly, wanting me to be impressed, expecting gratitude for her dedication.

"Since we're friends…" she said.

I fought to keep my voice even, toeing a tightrope between stern and gentle as I explained how she'd overstepped. I eyed her thinness; I remember being scared of what she might do to herself as much as to me if I tipped her too far. But all the while, I was panicking inside. *Oh God, they can get to me. They can get to me here, in the real world, in my jeans and travel sweat and exhaustion, in my family and in my skin.*

There have been others since, but it's that first girl's eyes I recall now, eager, anxious, begging me to notice her and approve. The woman in my kitchen could be that girl's aunt, or her older sister: the expression is exactly the same.

Of course, it does make a *bit* of a difference that instead of a ragged Ramones T-shirt, she's wearing a bomb.

A swell of sound through the window – feet crunching the gravel, then Dad chatting and Charlie laughing (*laughing*: Dad's a miracle worker with him, always has been) – snaps me out of it.

I spin on my heel and sprint for the hall. Blood thunders in my ears. My throat closes up. At every step I expect the blast, the heat, the ball bearings tearing into my skin and fat and muscle, the concussion wave to break my bones and pluck me off my feet and hurl me into the wall. My panicked face swells in the windowpanes set into the front door as I bear closer. I'm fractured into an insect's view by the bubbled glass.

The sound of the key sliding into the lock is like a gunshot.

The door opens a crack as I reach it. I feel the air from outside on my fingers as they curl around the jamb, and – just for a split second – I think, *Pull, open it, get out, run; it'll only take a second.*

But I don't have a second. I see the woman's blurry shape advancing behind me in the glass, and even with the distortion I can tell she's reaching into her coat. I shove my weight against the door and it clunks shut.

Dad utters a startled yelp as he staggers back. "Amy? What on earth—"

"Dad, RUN!" I scream. "THERE'S A WOMAN IN HERE WITH A BOMB! TAKE CHARLIE AND RUN!"

He freezes, but only for a heartbeat, then through the bubbled glass I see his blurred shape spin. He grabs Charlie's smaller blur by the midriff, lifts him bodily off his feet and then sprints back down the path, tie flying out behind him.

He didn't even hesitate. Is that sick feeling in my stomach relief, or betrayal?

Muddled by tears, shaky with adrenaline, I glimpse a hand hesitate over mine. She seems to think better of the gesture, and pats me on the shoulder instead. I go rigid as a prey animal at her touch.

"I'm glad you handled it that way." I look over my shoulder. There is sympathy in her eyes. In my line of work, I see a lot of sympathy, and hers is the genuine twenty-four-carat kind. "That can't have been easy."

I just stare at her. What does she expect me to say?

"That's fair. You're right; I'm sorry." Her hand emerges from her coat, not with a button, or a lever, or a trigger, but with a small roll of shiny metallic tape.

"Excuse me," she says. Easing past me like we're on the Tube at rush hour, she unrolls the tape and presses it to the

41

gap between the door and the frame, running it from the bottom right along the top and down the other side until it's completely sealed. It's only then that I notice lengths of the same tape running along the skirting board either side of the door.

"There," she says. Her shoulders visibly relax, and she straightens, like she's just put down a heavy backpack. "That's the circuit complete."

The circuit?

I look again at the rats' nest of wires poking out of her jacket. In among them, I can't help but notice, there's now a little green light that wasn't there before.

I feel my skin dry out. I think I'm going to be sick. I follow the line of tape along the skirting board with my eyes. It disappears through the near side of each doorway, and re-emerges on the other side.

She follows my gaze and nods. "Smart girl," she says approvingly. "It's basically like wire. One continuous loop running through every room in the house. Now that the circuit's complete, if you break it, it sends a radio signal, and…" She delicately avoids saying what the signal does, but her eyes flick downwards to the bomb vest.

"So," I croak. My throat feels like someone has grated it. "You've sealed off—"

"Every external door and window." She smiles shyly. "It was a full morning's work. A bit of a scramble to get it all done, but I knew I had at least a couple of hours."

"What? What do you … what, you mean you…" I tail

42

off. The horror I feel must show on my face, because she grimaces.

"Sorry," she says. "Yes, you posting the funeral time was a bit critical for this whole thing to work."

All the air goes out of me. I put my back to the door and slide down it, staring up at this skeleton of a woman with her bomb and her apologetic smile.

"You left the front door open." My voice is hoarse, my throat raw from screaming.

"Well, you had to get in. Not much point without *you*."

"What would you have done if I hadn't got home first? If it had been Dad, or Charlie?"

The smile slides from apologetic to plain wretched, but still stays on her face. It's like she wears that smile as a shield – the worse news she has to deliver, the harder she clings to it. She reaches casually into her jacket and pulls out a small black snub-nosed pistol. I recoil against the door.

"Only if they refused to leave you," she says, like that's supposed to reassure me. She frowns. "Not that that proved to be an issue – your father scarpered like his feet were on fire. I can't help feeling that's a pretty shabby way to treat your only daughter."

I can taste something sour and bloody, like I've bitten my cheek. "He was protecting Charlie."

"Oh, I'm sure he was." Her voice is mild, but there's a hard edge to it, a set to her face, and just for an instant I think, *She's angry – no*, furious. *Furious at him for leaving me.*

Is she relieved she didn't have to shoot him, or angry she

43

didn't get the chance? The knot in my guts ties itself tighter at the *chaos* I'm seeing in her. *This woman – if the gun and the bomb and the iced fucking buns weren't proof enough – is completely insane.*

"What do you want?" It comes out as a weak whisper.

She doesn't reply, just tilts her head and looks down at me.

"Is it money?" I ask. "Take whatever you want."

She looks around the hall at the height of the ceiling, the old wood frame of the mirror, the broad sweep of the lawn through the door's window glass.

"Well, it's kind of you to offer, but no. I'm not after money."

A high-pitched whine carries through the glass, then modulates downwards. I feel the skin on the back of my spine pucker: sirens.

The movement is casual, but the gun is now pointing at me.

"The first thing I want from you, Amy, is your phone."

My phone?

I crouch and reach slowly into my handbag where it lies abandoned by the door. My hand touches my phone, and on sudden inspiration, I press my finger down to unlock it, tap the Heartstream app, and hit *broadcast*. It takes less than a second; the motions are so familiar I can do them blind. Any info I can get outside has to be good, right? My patches are pressed on right up against my hairline at the back, and are near enough the same colour. With luck, she might not even have noticed I'm still wearing them. Just in case, I lift my chin to look her in the eye, burying the little pad on my neck below the level of my high collar as I relock the phone, pull it clear of my bag and pass it over.

"Unlock it, please."

I obey. She takes it, squints at the screen, then at the gun, then back at the phone, and backs up a few paces. "Stay there a minute," she orders, then types one-thumbed, occasionally looking up at me. I can see her lips twitch as she tries out words.

"How's this?" she asks. *"Hi Jeremy, you don't know me. But I've got your daughter. Please don't worry – we're both safe and I have no intention of hurting her, but I do have a bomb and have wired every external door and window to the detonator, so if you could tell the police that storming the place is a bad idea, that'd be great. Kind regards."*

I look at her helplessly. "What do you want advice on, your grammar?"

"By all accounts he's a good guy. I don't want to worry him."

I think that's wiring the stable door with explosives after the horse has bolted, don't you? I think, but it's a bit much to vocalize staring down the barrel, so I stay silent.

She shrugs, hits *send*, and I hear the *whoosh* of the message disappearing. The sirens get louder and louder. I'm used to screening them out as they swell and then ebb, rushing to someone else's emergency. Now, they're parked outside, rattling the windowpanes.

"Oh, damn." She tucks my phone away inside her jacket, turns on her heel and heads back towards the kitchen. "The tea will have stewed."

Dazed, I just stare at her retreating back. She turns and beckons with the barrel of the gun.

"Come on, Amy, we've got a *lot* to talk about."

CHAPTER FOUR

Cat

"I can't believe you did that."

"What?"

"The nail thing." I zoom the phone camera in on Ryan's nails, but the purple varnish has long since been scrubbed away. "I didn't tell you about purple theory so you could use it to mock us."

He leans back against a concrete pillar. The clock on his phone screen says 02:43. I imagine the thousands of fans in thousands of bedrooms around the world after he posts this, poring over images from Google Maps and Yelp and Land Registry, cross-referencing it with the band's tour schedule and confirmed sightings, trying to find this exact stairwell in a car park behind an Asda in Streatham where this nineteen-year-old demigod once chose to manifest. I wouldn't put it past them. Seriously, all MI5 needs to do is recruit the Everlasting fandom and buy in a warehouse full of Red Bull and no terrorist would ever be safe again.

It's why Ryan and I never come to the same place twice.

"It was just a bit of fun!" he protests. "Besides, whose idea was it to take a picture of *this*" – he pushes his sleeve up to show the infinity loop – "and tell them it was a padlock?"

I flush. "That's different. It was an emergency."

"Oh, really? What was emerging?"

"Evie was mad at me."

"She was?" The perfect mouth gapes in mock horror. "And you didn't call the police? Or the army? Or the *pope*?" He flicks his fringe out of his eyes with a dramatic jerk of the head and continues in his forties film star voice. "You crazy, courageous, beautiful fool, Canczuk. Don't you dare take your life in your hands like that again: don't you know I love you?"

My stomach tingles. *Don't you know I love you?* He's always doing that, saying serious things in a jokey voice or jokey things in a serious voice or sexy things in a sexy voice, wrong-footing me, making me blush. In fact, in the three months I've known him, he has become remarkably adept at manipulating the Catherine Canczuk colour chart. Right now, judging by the heat in my face, I'm way past Pardon Me Pink and into Spontaneous Human Combustion Crimson.

"You don't understand. Evie can be … intense. Still, I didn't expect it to get as much traction as it did."

"So there were a lot of tweets, were there?" he surmises. "About Padlockgate?"

I avoid his gaze. "How did you know we called it that?"

"I love our fans, and God knows they're phenomenally

48

creative in many ways, but naming things is not one of them."

They're, I note, not *you're*.

"But were there?" he presses. "Tweets, posts, theories, videos, all that?" His smile is eager; he finds this stuff *fascinating*. I feel a twinge of guilt, treating Rickers like zoo animals, but I can't refuse that smile, and to be fair, if they were here, none of them could either.

"Thousands," I admit. "Evie's got a big audience."

He shakes his head. "Crazy. The whole thing's crazy." Then he must see my expression, because he steps towards me, rests one hand on the small of my back and pulls me into a kiss that stops my heart.

"Hey, it's OK," he says, putting his forehead to mine. "It's like you said: this whole thing's not really *about* Nick and me, right? We're just an excuse for you all to come together, make friends. You're a community, a tribe."

I nod. I may have held forth at embarrassing length on this last night while sprawled across his chest.

"Well then, you've done them a favour. Gotta add kindling to the campfire now and then. Can't have the stories the tribe tell getting cold. Speaking of which…"

He leans over the banister, and I follow suit. The bare concrete of the stairwell dwindles into the darkness below like a throat.

"I really don't think this is a good idea," I say.

"Will you just relax? I know what I'm doing."

"Really? You've done this before?"

"Sure."

"Ry?"

"Sort of."

"Ry!"

"Well, OK, no. But I've watched this parkour vid on YouTube, like, six hundred times."

I laugh, but my palms are sweating as they grip his phone. "Seriously, if you're going to break your neck in a dumb stunt over a stupid bet, does it have to be *me*, aiding and abetting?" I try to pass him his phone back, but he closes his hand around mine.

"It absolutely does."

I try to protest, but he holds up a hand. "For two reasons. One – everyone else I know who could film me doing this has a significant financial stake in me *not* breaking my neck over a stupid bet."

I have an I-love-you stake in you not breaking your neck over a stupid bet is what I just about manage to avoid saying out loud, because unlike him, I don't have a funny voice that can make those three words after just three months *not* sound like the words of a crazy stalker. This dream universe I've somehow found myself in feels as fragile as a wine glass, like the wrong word in the wrong tone could shatter it.

Instead I sigh, and ask, "What's the second reason?"

He leans forward and kisses me again. Again, my heart stops. I need defibrillation; seriously, being with this boy is bad for my health.

"I won't break my neck. You're here. You're my guardian angel."

I first met Ryan Richards in the waking, non-fictional flesh ninety-four days ago. I'd run out of the house in the middle of the night, my throat raw from shouting. I'd had yet another argument with Mum over whether seventeen was old enough to try and find my dad. Come to think of it, I actually used the word *Dad* to refer to him, which was why Mum was crying. Christ, Cat. You know better than that.

I slung my leg over my bike and just pedalled, street lights strobing over me, pushing my muscles until the burn eclipsed everything and the wind in my face chilled my tears to the point where I could pretend they were just sweat and not tears at all.

I was heading to the Dance Hall. If, now I've said *Dance Hall*, you're picturing some kind of sweatbox full of lithe bodies and backflips where I could forget the strictures of my uptight uptown upbringing in the lubricated embrace of a south London Patrick Swayze … I wish, but forget it.

For one thing, my upbringing was not so much uptown as down-suburb; for another, my signature move at discos is the sit-in-the-corner-and-hope-no-one-looks-at-me; and for a third, no one has pulled on their dance shoes in anger in the Dance Hall for a long, long time.

It was built as a ballroom in the thirties and got a German bomb through the roof in the forties. In the fifties, sixties, seventies and eighties, they tried to turn it into a bingo hall, a cinema and a block of luxury flats. But they failed, and so it remains the Dance Hall.

Inside, the walls are covered in fifty-foot murals of gentlemen in Fred Astaire tails and ladies in elegant gowns, their faces blasted by time and Luftwaffe shrapnel. Sometimes I talk to them. Bit pathetic, I know, but it is what it is. It's been sealed off by developer-branded hoardings the whole time I've known it, but work never starts. It's my own place, frozen in time. My secret city.

Except that night, as I pulled my bike to a screeching halt by the fried chicken shop over the road, a man was squeezing his way out from between the hoardings. I felt momentarily scandalized, then absurdly jealous. I wondered how many other people were praying in this private chapel of mine.

If anyone in the community ever heard this story (please God never let that happen), they'd make me turn in my RickResource credentials for not recognizing him, but it was dark. I only saw him from the back, he had his hood up, and I couldn't see any of his face. He set off at a diagonal across the street, towards a junction about fifty metres away.

Just then, a rumble roar filled my ears. I looked round in time to see an eighteen-wheel lorry swinging onto the road behind us.

"Hey!" I called after him. "HEY!" But he didn't look back, didn't show any sign of getting out of the way of the twenty tonnes of clattering articulated death rolling towards him. His head was nodding gently. *Oh shit,* I remember thinking. *He's got earphones in.*

And so I started to pedal. I cursed myself for riding there

so fast, so angry, for burning my legs out. *Come on, Cat; come on, Cat; come on, Cat. MOVE!*

Panting and swearing, I managed to dredge up a bit of hypothetical pre-emptive anger at myself at the prospect of failing to reach him in time. The roar of the wind mingled in my ears with the roar of the lorry as I sped up, and *now* I hear the screech of brakes but it's too close, too loud and he'll never stop in time and my entire world is basically the back of a hoodie stretched over a pair of shoulders which, while nice, are probably not *quite* hot enough to die for, but oh well, too late to pull out now, and then *oof!*

The world shuddered. We collapsed in a tangle of limbs and spokes and heaving lungs as the wheels rumbled past, inches away.

"Holy … whoa! Thanks."

I knew the voice instantly. I stayed face down on the pavement. I was hallucinating; I had to be. I didn't dare look up, even when he gently pulled me to my feet. Gaze directly at the sun and you'll go blind.

"You saved my life," said the disembodied voice of Ryan Richards.

My heart lodged in the bottom of my throat like some massive cork. I scrambled for something cool to say, something likeable and diffident. *A hero? Oh, I wouldn't say hero. You would, would you? Well then, who am I to argue?*

But what I actually said, as near as I can remember, was "*Fneeeeeeep?*"

He laughed, and it was that laugh that gave me permission

to look up. I realized I'd never heard a sound like it before. All the interviews of him I'd watched, and I'd never heard him laugh like that, so deeply, genuinely delighted.

"I'd buy you a drink to say thank you, but I don't think anywhere'll be open at this time of night. Wanna come back to the flat?"

I shook my head, not in refusal, obviously, but in reflexive disbelief. He offered me his hand, and I felt my blood fizz as he turned my forearm gently over.

"Ouch." He winced. A bloody graze covered half of it, like a giant's thumbprint. I hadn't even felt it. "Come on," he said. "Back to mine at least so we can get this cleaned up. Else you'll be waiting for hours at A & E."

"Mnnehhh?" I managed. Maybe I actually *was* concussed. I didn't remember hitting my head, but I reckon the presence of a pop star is equivalent to four solid blows to the cranium.

"I was being oblivious. You saved my life. Can't let your reward be you getting hurt while I'm fine and dandy, can we? I couldn't live with myself."

He took me back to the aeroplane-hangar-sized duplex the band were renting while they were in London. Where, I need to be clear, we did *not* make out and have wild, fic-worthy sex. Not then, because that first night I still would have sworn blind that Ryan Richards's boxer shorts were a sacred ark whose contents were for Nick Lamb and Nick Lamb alone.

A conviction that lasted right up until the point when

a ravishing blonde girl who I'm fairly sure I last saw in the video for "Rainin' You" came out of Nick's bedroom in a T-shirt that barely skimmed her bum.

Her name was Nikki de Venn. She was lovely, sat with me in a kitchen that looked like a cross between a spaceship and a piece of Danish abstract sculpture while Ryan fetched first aid supplies.

"So Ry brought you here?" She said it so casually, mixing herself a Martini in a silver shaker. (I say it was a Martini like I know what supermodels drink. Look, it was clear and she put olives in it. It could have been engine descaler for all I know.)

"Um … yeah, I guess. You?"

"Nick. We're trying to keep it quiet." She leaned over the bench conspiratorially. "There are these fans the guys have got. They're convinced Nick and Ry are boning each other and every girlfriend either of them gets is a management plant."

"Ha ha ha," I laughed weakly. A pair of embarrassment-fuelled fireballs ignited behind my cheeks, but she didn't seem to notice. Maybe her engine-cleaning cocktail affected her observation skills.

"One girl, Anna? They found out her address and sent a pair of clippers to her house, because she was a beard, get it? I bet they didn't stop laughing for a month, but she was *terrified*; she had to move."

I felt like I'd been punched. I felt like my heart had fallen out of its place in my chest and was rattling around in my abdomen with all my other organs. I remembered Anna Carpenter and the clipper gambit. I'd sat in Evie's bedroom fielding identifying info from the WhatsApp group, while Evie used it to comb through the data from the LinkedIn hack for her address.

"Want a bit of friendly advice?" Nikki asked.

"Um ... sure?"

"Keep a low profile. I know you shouldn't have to and it seems like caving, but trust me, you don't need the aggro."

"Oh..." I said. "Ryan and I aren't ... *together* like that; we just, I just... He brought me back here to patch my arm up."

Nikki winked at me, her outrageously long lashes meshing and demeshing. "Yeah," she said. "Just like that."

"Where's the patient?" Ryan boomed from the doorway, holding up a length of gauze and a bottle of TCP. "Dr Richards's clinic is open."

Nikki disappeared back into Nick's room with her drink. Ryan started to clean and bandage my arm. I winced at the sting of the antiseptic. He winced at my wince.

"So," I said, when the silence got too heavy. "What were you doing at the Dance Hall?"

And what do you know? Ryan Richards is a London nerd. He'd heard about the Dance Hall on Londinium, a Tumblr I followed before my dash filled up with all things Rick and nothing else. He made a point of going there whenever band business brought him to town; we'd just never overlapped before now.

We didn't talk about the band, not once. Instead we

nattered about how the city's best museum wasn't the Science or the BM, but the old operating theatre above St Thomas's Church, and how like time travel it was, walking into Goodwin's Court, with its gas lamp fittings and its bulbous bay windows bowing like the sails of a glass ship. I felt a dormant part of me wake, a kind of delicious pins and needles of the soul. I couldn't remember the last time I talked to someone this intently and it not be about the Everlasting.

What's more, I don't think he could either. I've spent months racking my brain trying to work out what this imperial prince of pop sees in me, and I still don't know, but this is the best I've got. When he looks me in the eyes he *doesn't* see a pop star reflected back, just a nineteen-year-old London nerd. The way we met wasn't stage-managed and PRd and airbrushed the way he's used to. It was pure serendipity. I think he found that refreshing.

Slowly, throughout that conversation, a realization set in. *Rick wasn't real.* I hadn't let it go, not in my bones, not even when Nikki slipped back into the Lamb master bedroom to continue what was almost certainly – judging by both of their ab muscles – really athletically challenging sex, but I let it go then. Because if Ryan Richards could be as invested in my home town as I am, and if I – who knows the name of his childhood hamster and the birthdays of all his roadies off by heart – could have no inkling of that fact, then clearly neither I, nor anyone else on RickResource, knew him at all.

I felt his fingers sneak in between mine. Warm and strong and certain. Rick wasn't real, and I didn't mind in the slightest.

I looked down. Our interlinked hands were in shadow, but my bandaged forearm was drenched in red. My first thought, addled, but not concerned, was, *Huh, my graze is bleeding through.* Except the red wasn't blood; it was the sunrise washing in through the floor-to-ceiling windows.

It was morning.

"Shit!" I yelped, scrambling up from the bench.

"What?" Ryan barked, just as alarmed.

"I've been gone for *hours*. My mum will be freaking *out*." I scrambled for my phone. It was on silent. Shit. Thirty-four missed calls. "Shit shit shit *shit*."

"Divide and conquer," Ryan said. "You call her; I'll call a cab."

Mum started yelling as soon as she heard my key in the lock, but then she saw the bandage and she went all quiet.

"I fell off my bike," I explained. Her face was a colour I'd only previously seen on geese and bathroom tiles. "I went to Evie's; she patched me up. It's only a graze, honest."

"You don't go to Evie to patch you up," Mum said, folding me into a tight hug. "That's what I'm for." Her tone turned puzzled. "Did you lose Evie's phone number or something?"

"What? Why? I..." I tailed off, looked down. Inked neatly on my bandage was an eleven-digit mobile phone number. There was only one person who could have put it there.

Two days later, we had our second meeting; a week after that, our first kiss. I couldn't believe it was happening as our lips met. To tell the truth, I still can't.

But now we're here.

"You sure you want to do this?"

"No choice," Ryan says. The scrape of his trainers on the concrete echoes as he backs away from the stairwell to give himself a run-up. "Do you know how many views Nick got for that lip-sync thing? Eighty-seven million. He's set the bar pretty high."

"So? Surely, after the first couple of million, it's all just numbers? Kind of a wash?"

He turns to look at me, the pop star perfection of his face made ghoulish by the car park fluorescents. His expression says, *Wow, you don't understand* at all. I think of the Möbius strip tattoo. *I never want to be irrelevant.* I wonder what he'll do when the world moves on, and the band drifts apart. He'll find something. The Everlasting might not live up to their name, but Ryan will, I know it.

"OK, fine, how high do you want to go, then? How many pairs of eyes can you possibly want on you?"

He smiles. "You can always add one more."

And with that he runs, head-down at full tilt. I swear and just about manage to juggle his phone into position so it's covering the stairwell, hitting *record* just as he vaults the banister. To be fair to him, he really *does* seem to have studied some parkour for this. He zigzags down the first

59

four levels with apparent ease, springing from banister to banister like a squirrel on speed, but on the fifth—

"Ryan!" I shriek as his fingers miss their grip and he drops the last two storeys like a stone. I plunge down the stairs, sweating and huffing, heart like an alarm clock behind my ribs. *Omigodomigodomigodomigod I killed Ryan Richards.*

I crash through the emergency exit at the bottom level. A hacking, wheezing sound emerges from his crumpled form. I'm two steps away, 999 already punched into the phone in my hand, when I realize he's laughing. I crouch beside him. His face is the pale green of over-diluted Fairy Liquid and his arm is bent in one too many places, but he's laughing.

"Tell me..." he begins, and then winces and gasps for breath, reaching for the phone with his good arm. "Tell me you got that."

CHAPTER FIVE

Amy

It was our ritual, our stolen half-hour before Dad and Charlie were awake. Before the early morning hush was broken by the clunk of the pipes, the stomps on the floorboards and the volleys of sleepy shouts – "Honey, where are my keys?" "What did I do with that file?" "Charles Michael Becker, have you showered? Well? Have you? No, just deodorant doesn't count; and no, you can't have chocolate for breakfast" – Mum and I would have tea.

"What is it?" she asked, dropping into her chair while I, like always, perched on the edge of the table, chewing the split ends of my hair.

"What's what?"

"Whatever's had you looking like a family of hedgehogs has taken up residence in your underwear for the past week."

"Mum, don't talk about my underwear; it's weird."

"Up until two years ago, I still bought your underwear."

"Those two years make a difference."

"I was the alpha and omega of your lingerie world."

"Not getting any less weird."

"And you're not getting any closer to answering my question. What's up?"

I hesitated. "Someone at school."

Mum blew the steam off her tea. "I see. And is your relationship with this person administrative, amorous or purely adversarial?"

"A little from column b; a little from column c."

She perked up; she liked hearing about my love life. "What's his name?"

I squirmed; every muscle south of my solar plexus tensed up. But if I chickened out, I'd have to lie, and where the fuck would that end? I sucked in a breath, let it stream out of me and, trying to ignore the way my toes were tingling, said, "Christina."

"Oh." She blinked, sipped her tea. "I guess those two years really do make a difference."

"Mum..."

She looked baffled, lost.

I could feel the backs of my ears heating up. I knew it would go like this. I battled the urge to shout. "It's my—"

"What about Bradley? And wasn't there a Timmy?"

"Jimmy, Mum. No one called Timmy has ever been more than eight years old."

"Ah, well, there was no point in me learning his name, was there? Scruffy boy, pimples, clearly wasn't right for you."

She lapsed into an expectant silence. Waiting for me to fill it.

"Christina kissed me," I said. "Well, I kissed her. We both sort of kissed each other."

"So, what's the problem with that?"

I didn't realize it at the time, but her asking that question was the moment when everything in me relaxed ever so slightly. "She's decided she likes boys."

"Well, so do you. Or at least if you don't, I imagine it would come as news to young Johnny."

"Jimmy, Mum."

"Ah yes, of course."

"And Christina's decided she *only* likes boys."

"I see. And you?"

I stared down into my Hufflepuff mug, closed my eyes and let the steam wash over my face. "I kinda think I only like Christina."

And I started crying into my tea, as much out of relief as sadness, and she hugged me and told me that I only liked Christina right now, but there "were plenty more boys and girls in the playground" (her words – I honestly think she thought of us as eternal eight year olds), and then Dad woke up and stomped downstairs in his shirt and pants, and I told him, and he just looked confused until Mum said very loudly and slowly that if Christina ever came to her senses they'd love to meet her, and he shrugged and asked Mum where his trousers were and that was it.

I was out.

"How do you take it?" the interloper in the bomb vest asks, as she boils my family's kettle and sets out two of *my* Hogwarts mugs.

She pauses for a moment, considering, and then selects the Mad Hatter teapot that I gave Mum one birthday. Mum loved Alice in Wonderland. We used to squabble over whether that or Potter was better. I gave her the teapot as a kind of peace offering, and the Hogwarts mugs arrived on my birthday in kind. The stranger pours hot water into the pot and then studies the wall clock in intent silence until three minutes have ticked around. All the while the sirens shriek in through the window glass.

"Sugar?" she asks. "Or just milk?" I don't answer. "Just milk," she guesses, and adds it. She passes the Hufflepuff mug across to me, keeping the Ravenclaw one for herself.

She sits down in Mum's chair. I want to tear out her fucking eyes.

"Would you mind if I had a sandwich?" she asks.

"You're the one with the detonator."

She makes a face, as though reminding her of that was in bad taste. "Fair point." She takes a crustless cheese and tomato triangle from the food for *my* mother's wake, and carefully reseals the cling film. She bites, chews, swallows. Brightens. "Did you make these?" she asks. "They're delicious. What's the recipe?"

"Cheese. Tomatoes. Bread." I glare at her, but if she notices my sarcasm, she doesn't seem to care.

"I forgot to have breakfast," she goes on. "It's always the small details that trip you up, isn't it? The plan for today looked good on paper, but you don't know until you try it."

"So this is your first time threatening innocent people with a bomb?" I ask, flatly.

"Oh, I wouldn't quite say that. But I've never done it like this before." She finishes her sandwich and carefully reseals the cling film. "Do sit down," she says. "Please."

I shuffle over and drop into the chair opposite her. My legs are numb. My sweat-soaked dress sticks to my stomach where the table edge presses it into me.

"Now, tell me, how's school?"

"You want to talk about *school*?" My voice is flat, but I'm unbalanced, teetering between fear, fury and bafflement.

"Of course I want to talk about school. I want to talk about everything!" She looks at me like she's the luckiest human being on earth. "How's Charlie?"

I feel my gut cramp up. *Charlie?* "He's OK." *He's not in here with you.*

"Do you like it? Having a brother?"

I curl my fingers into the wood of the table. Her tone is as pleasant and vague as an afternoon nap. I start to shiver; I can't help it. Her expression comes over concerned.

"Here," she says, pulling one of Charlie's silk scarves from the back of his chair where he'd left it. "Or, if you show me how, I can turn the heating on."

"I'm not cold," I say, but I accept the scarf anyway; slung

around my neck it covers the patches better than my collar does. My teeth are starting to chatter and I have to grit them to get the words out. "I … I … I'm scared."

For a moment she looks confused, then she follows my gaze to her bomb vest like she's forgotten it's there.

"Of *course*," she says. "Of course you are. I know exactly how you feel. I'm sorry about this." She gestures to the vest. "But you understand, I know you do. I'm sure *all* your fans tell you this, but I see so much of myself in you." She squeezes her mug between her palms and hugs it to herself. "I'm scared too," she confides.

My leaden guts sink a little further. I think of the woman's nervous prattling, the spoon's out-of-control rattle against the inside of the mugs as she stirred in the milk.

The fact that she's sealed up every exit, not just for me, but for herself.

I'm scared too.

I stare at her bomb vest. Her *suicide* vest. The wires on it curl like nooses.

I'm loath to generalize, of course, but I'd be lying if I said that self-destructive feelings weren't a little more widespread among my Heartstream followers than in the general population. And I'd be a hypocrite if I pretended I didn't understand why.

"Did you…" I ask the question in spite of myself. "Did you lose someone?"

Her voice is very solemn as she answers. "Oh yes."

"Do you…" I stammer. I'm not sure if it's fear or fury that

makes the words tangle in my teeth. "Do you want t-t-to talk about it?"

She looks astonished, then delighted. "That is *so*, so kind of you! I'd be thrilled to. Later. When we've got to know each other better."

"Got to know each other? I don't even know your name."

She smacks her forehead. "What a numbskull I am! See, like I told you, small details." And then, ridiculously, she's seized my hand and is pumping it up and down like she's a small child who's expecting chocolate milk to squirt out of my nose. "I'm Polly!" she announces. "It's a delight to formally make your acquaintance."

My phone starts to buzz and skitter across the tabletop. A withheld number is calling.

"That'll be the police." She lifts the phone and answers it in one movement. "You can wait," she snaps into the mic with a voice like a whip crack and hangs up. It starts to buzz again, immediately, like an angry electronic hornet. She rolls her eyes conspiratorially, mouths *honestly*, switches the ringer off and stashes the phone in one of the pockets of her high-explosive outerwear.

She stands up, smooths out her front and offers me a hand, beaming at me like I'm a mischievous Austrian schoolchild and she's a singing fucking nun.

"Do you know, Amy, I've read *everything* there is to read about you, but I don't know you half as well as I'd like. It's such a thrill to be in your home, I don't mind telling you. Would you mind giving me the tour?"

I don't take her hand. She looks crestfallen, but she goes to the door anyway, and beckons me after with the pistol. My reluctance evident in every muscle, I rise.

"That's it!" she says delightedly. She turns and exposes her back to me with deliberate care. "Now, I'm trusting you, because I want you to trust me. But please don't do anything, you know, *cinematic*, like trying to hit me with a vase, or tampering with the tape on the windows. I'm wearing what I'm reliably informed by the best reviewed bomb-making site I could find is enough explosive to level Big Ben, and I only need to press a very tiny button. So even if the blast didn't get you, the falling masonry would. And I'd hate that." She turns to face the wall, and in *exactly* the same tone says, "Ooh, this is a *gorgeous* picture: do tell me about it!"

Polly passes through the house like the Queen on a state tour, taking the same polite interest in the pile of crusty, ancient wellington boots in the downstairs loo as the grand bookcases in Dad's study, or the figurine of a belly dancer on the hall table that he bought from a junk shop on Portobello to keep me quiet when I was five. Any time she encounters a piece of paper – insurance quotes, medical bills, even old birthday cards – she studies it intently before putting it back down with a small sigh that could just as easily be contentment or disappointment. We pass through the small study where Mum ran her IT consultancy before she got too sick. Polly doesn't say a word, but tucks Mum's old laptop under her arm. She's put the gun back into her pocket, and it stays there, but the bulk of her bomb vest is all the threat she needs.

The little green light taunts me from by her breastbone.

When we reach my room upstairs, her demeanour changes. She pauses in the doorway, then enters with very small, eager steps, like a pilgrim, hesitating to enter the sanctum that is the culmination of her journey. I feel a greasy unease, like I'm being pressed up against a sweaty body on the Tube, as she runs her fingers over my early charcoal cartoons of Nicky the Sticky Crow, and then rubs her fingertips together, savouring the residue. "These are extraordinary," she gushes encouragingly. "I've loved them since I first saw them on your Instagram. Are you going to go to art school?"

"I hope so," I say quietly, eyeing her bomb vest. And then, in the hope that reminding her I'm a living breathing human being with a family might encourage her to not, you know, kill me, I add, "Charlie's the really talented one, though; he barely even needs to practise. We always hoped we'd get a chance to be there together. Me as a final year and him as a fresher."

"Right." She looks awkward. "Well, I hope so too."

She takes my books off the shelves and comments approvingly on the Terry Pratchett and the Frances Hardinge. I feel myself tense as she rifles through my drawers, and pulls out a thin black pair of knickers.

"Racy," she says, and frowns. "You mustn't let them rush you into it, you know."

"What makes you think I need rushing?"

She flushes, drops the pants back in the drawer and bustles past me, her ear passing close enough to me that my breath stirs the tiny hairs. I glance at the empty wine bottle with a candle shoved in it by the bed, and for the briefest of seconds I think I might be able to smash it over her head.

But then I think *I only need to press a very tiny button*, and how could I guarantee, in the split second between waking and unconsciousness, that she couldn't?

And she's out on the landing again, and the moment's gone.

"Your parents are across the hall?" she asks. I nod. She makes a happy noise in the back of her throat. "I'd be delighted to get to know them. Amy Becker's mum and dad, imagine!"

I'd be delighted to get to know them. This creepy woman says it like she's my girlfriend and I've invited her home for tea.

She ambles into Mum and Dad's room and rifles through the closet. She paws through the contents of the old box files on top of the wardrobe. She runs my grandmother's pearls through her fingers, picks up the little scrap of red fabric I clung to for comfort as a baby. Mum spent *years* trying to wean me off that; she just casts it aside like a dirty tissue. With each new fragment of my family's life she handles, I can feel the anger building hot and violent in my chest. Weirdly, I can see the same emotions flitting over her face. Her nostrils pinch, her skin tight around her skull. It's almost like *she's* still streaming off me, but she can't be – her stubbled scalp is bare.

She lifts another handful of Mum's jewellery, and

alongside my anger a stitch of something else snags my chest – hope.

Revealed from underneath the tangle of beads and chains is a black oblong: Mum's old phone.

We never cancelled the contract, I think, my heart suddenly beating faster. It's probably dead, but there are chargers all over the house.

Polly freezes, and I freeze too, belatedly staring at my hands in case my eyes have given me away. Polly's fingers go limp, dumping the jewellery back on the dressing table, hiding the phone. Her gaze is fixed on my parents' wedding pictures. She holds up a shot of Mum, smiling and radiant, backed by soft-focus summer trees.

She hesitates, an almost *mischievous* expression on her face, then she crosses the room in three quick strides to the wardrobe, flings a bunch of Dad's suits onto the bed and with a bark of triumph comes up with the ivory bolero Mum wore to her wedding. She tries to tug it on, *over* the bomb vest. A smouldering coal in my stomach explodes into flame as I hear the seams rip.

"STOP IT!" I yell at her. "JUST STOP IT!"

She freezes guiltily, like an animal that's been caught going through the bins, and I freeze too, watching for any sign of her hand twitching for the bomb trigger.

"Oh … sorry," she mumbles. "I just… Sorry."

She replaces the torn bolero on the hanger, and even tries to pull the dry-cleaning plastic back over it, but gives up when it gets tangled in the wire.

"Sorry," she says again. She's blushing, hard. Head ducked, avoiding my gaze, she bustles out of the room.

I wait for a call, a threat, a demand that I follow and show her the tourist highlights of the fucking attic, but none comes.

She's left me alone.

I scramble over to the dressing table and claw the jewellery and photo frames out of the way. I've probably only got a few seconds, but if I can just hide the handset somewhere on me, then the next time her guard drops I can...

But I falter, my hands slowing as they pick through the pearls, moving the perfume bottles out of the way. I peer into the dusty ravine of cobwebs between the dressing table and the wall, in case it's got knocked down there, but it hasn't.

I stand, blinking and swallowing, my stomach hollowing out. I search one last time, but in vain. I was sure. I was so *sure* I saw it.

But Mum's phone is no longer there.

CHAPTER SIX

Cat

Like always, I check my reflection in Evie's fancy brass door knocker before I press the bell. I changed out of my school uniform in the loo of the McDonald's on the high street, and while my outfit doesn't make me glamorous exactly (it's a denim skirt and a vest top, not eye of newt and the finger of a birth-strangled babe), I do at least look a little more mature, more presentable. Even now, three years after I was first summoned by Evie to her four-bed mansion on the edge of Clapham Common, this still feels like an audience.

Back then I only knew her as Teenage Petrolhead, at once world-renowned and anonymous. She'd linked to a fic of mine on her Tumblr, the main one, with over half a million followers, and my dash had erupted, like unpronounceable-Icelandic-volcano-ground-all-aircraft erupted. I was elated. I felt like my future had finally arrived.

I was still responding to comments at breakfast when

I got her DM and I'd barely slept. I read it and sprayed milk and Frosties halfway across the table. She'd invited me round for tea.

It's surprising how little has changed since. Back then, maybe my throat was a little drier, maybe I trembled at a slightly higher frequency, but the sweat's still slick on my hand and I've still skipped a lesson to be here. Biology. I'm barely keeping my head above water in it at the moment, but I've never refused an invitation from Evie. I'm terrified they'll stop coming.

"Horse Girl!" Evie's delight greets me before the door's even fully open. She's wearing pyjamas like always. It's one of our unwritten rules: I dress up for Evie; she doesn't dress up for me. This time they're pink with little yellow hippos on them; she looks like a giant piece of pick 'n' mix. Her make-up is immaculate, though. I've never seen it not.

Also like always, she's got a cigarette dangling from the corner of her mouth. Long-buried embarrassment drags itself from its grave just long enough to kick me in the stomach as I remember the first words I ever spoke to Teenage Petrolhead in person.

"Your parents let you smoke in the house?"

"Parents? You're adorable. How young do you think I am?"

In the morgue, I will still be cringing at the memory of her laughter.

"It's freezing," she says, hauling me back to the present doorstep. "Get your gangly backside in here." She shuts the door and presses her back to it. In a conspiratorial whisper she asks, "Have you seen it yet? The video?"

A momentary, panicky instinct tells me to deny all knowledge, so I start to say *no*, realize too late that that would be impossible to believe, and wind up saying, "Noooooo doubt. No doubt. I have, yes. Of course. I have indeed seen the video."

She stares at me. "What was *that*?"

"I haven't slept much," I tell her, which is at least true.

"And when you don't sleep you turn into a character from a Gilbert and Sullivan operetta?"

"A what?"

"Never mind." She waves it away. "What a muppet! I can't believe he broke his arm."

"I can. Ryan's entirely made of thumbs and ego. Remember the time he tried fire-swallowing at the gig in Dublin and his hairspray went up?"

We were both about thirty feet away and barely had time to scream before Nick tackled him to the ground and smothered the flames with his jacket. It took less than two hours for the still shots of Nick Lamb lying on top of Ryan Richards to become the most used profile pic on Twitter.

"And he had to get that crew cut?" Evie laughs. "Yeah, I remember. RickisLife held a week-long wake for his quiff on her blog, but I thought he looked hot shaved."

I shrug. "I don't really think of him that way."

She reaches up and tucks a strand of hair behind my ear and I fight the urge to go rigid. Her eyes settle on my face. "Uh-huh. Come upstairs."

Despite having this palace all to herself, Evie does all her work in her bedroom. To be fair, though, you could fit the entire floor plan of our Tooting maisonette in Evie's bedroom and still have room for a 747 and a game of cricket, so it's not like it cramps her style. Unlike in my room, the posters of the Everlasting on the walls are framed, signed and precisely spaced. The wall above the bed is dominated by a massive oil painting of Ryan dipping Nick back into a Hollywood golden era kiss. She commissioned it from an artist in the fandom who's been able to live off her paintings since Evie featured her on her Instagram.

Where my room is a snowscape of drifts of dirty laundry, empty crisp packets and half-eaten fruit burrowed away like hibernating creatures, Evie's converted loft space is meticulously tidy. The gigantic bed is made. The Mondrian patterned rugs are perfectly parallel to the floorboards. I suspect she'd even conform to the cliché of the pens lined up on the desk – except, of course, Evie doesn't keep pens out on her desk; she keeps them in a rack in her drawer. "A place for everything, and everything in its place," she likes to say.

A year back, she went through a bad patch. She started cutting herself again – the first time, she said, since she was my age. I was the only one in the community she told. I was so proud. I took her to the doctor's, sat with her in the waiting room. I saw the cuts. They were all *exactly* the same length, like a bloody barcode on the inside of her upper arm.

She drops herself into the desk chair. The polished

surface in front of her is covered in half a dozen iPads, each of them showing a different photo of Nick or Ryan, each of them captioned with a different Everlasting lyric. She likes to be able to move them around to get the sense of it. Later, she'll splice the two she chooses together so they're looking into each other's eyes and post it to RickResource.

Evie is good at the Internet. Which I suppose means she's good at people, because what else is the Internet made of? She has a perfumer's instinct for the exact blend of cruelty and sex and cute and flirtation that will make an image splash onto social in a cascade of reaction GIFs. You know how when there's a really big poster campaign for some movie or perfume or something and you can't turn a corner without seeing it? When Evie posts a GIFset or an image spread it's like that, but online. And I *live* online.

That's why I'm so flattered when she turns to me and says, "I just can't get it working. The closest I can come is these two, but there's something not there in Ryan's expression. Help me."

I look at the photo of him on the tablet. He's gorgeous, obviously, and he's got this little smirk at the corner of his mouth that could inflict a swoon at a hundred yards, but she's right: it doesn't fit. That's Ryan's face when he's pleased with *himself*, not looking at anyone else. The caption Evie's chosen is from "Saturday 3 a.m. Forever": "We'll be stopping time…"

An idea takes me. There's an expression Ryan gets when he's really into something, a kind of yearning mixed with a premonition of loss, like it's already slipping away. It's ... well, it's an expression I usually only get to see when we're in bed together, but still, I have seen it in *one* other context.

"Here," I say, pulling up the image search. "Try this."

Evie stares at it for a long time. In the picture his eyes are intent, his fringe slick with sweat and curled to one side, his mouth slightly open as he wills the moment to go on. He's gazing at the crowd as they sing his lyrics back to him. He's devastatingly beautiful.

"I thought you didn't think of him that way," Evie says softly.

"I don't!"

"Uh-huh. The speed you found that, you've looked it up before."

I don't reply, but she presses. "Probably more than once. Possibly on your phone with your left hand because your right was 'busy'?"

I feel the blush enter my cheeks like a volcanic eruption.

"You *do!*" Evie levels her finger like the Witchfinder General. "All this time you've been claiming you were devoted to Nick and Ryan's true love, and meanwhile you've had your hand shoved down your pants while you dreamed about getting in the middle of it. Honestly, Cat!" She presses her hand to her cheek. "What would the fine people of RickResource say?"

"I ... I didn't. I haven't," I stammer like my jaw is falling apart. "I ... I ... I ..."

"I'm *kidding.*" Evie bursts out laughing. "Honestly, Horse

Girl, you're so strait-laced. Your virginity's the problem. You take sex way too seriously. We need to get you laid – that'll get you over *that*."

"Yeah." Honestly, I deserve a medal for how much effort I put into this laugh. "One hundred per cent extra virgin right here – you could make oil out of me."

"I'm not going to drum you off RickResource for *fancying* Ryan. I mean, he is seriously gorgeous." She says it with a wicked smile, flouting the law with a queen's freedom.

She draws herself up to her full height, so I only have to bend *almost* double to receive her kiss on the cheek. "Thanks for finding the photo, and your secret is safe with me. Although, if you don't want the rest of the fandom knowing that Ryan brings stormy weather to your lady parts, you might not want to write such knicker-ignitingly hot stories about him."

I'm momentarily baffled. "I… What?"

"I read the draft you sent me. Not only did the sex bit make me thirstier than a cactus, but the way they met was *adorable*. Honestly, dubs, it's your best yet. The best Rickcute I've ever read."

Mt Blush gathers itself into a second eruption, this time in pleasure. I'd conservatively estimate that Rickcutes – stories in which Ryan and Nick meet in a cute way (like all societies, Rickdom makes its own language out of the origami of its forebears) – make up sixty per cent of everything on the fic side of the community, so that's quite the claim. Neither Ryan nor Nick has ever told the story of how they met. Rickdom's taken that as a kind of challenge, as if we can divine it through the medium of twenty-thousand word "short" stories.

"The whole thing's gorgeous," she says, pulling it up on the iPad. "Them sharing the same passion for that bombed-out dance hall, but never meeting each other? Nick knocking Ryan out of the way of that lorry? *We can't have you being hurt and me being fine; I couldn't live with myself.* I mean, seriously, dubs, you could have lit London for a night purely off the power of my swoon. Wouldn't it be amazing if that actually *was* how they met?"

Look, I know what you're thinking. *I know* it's crazy, but at the same time, sometimes the urge to tell Evie about Ryan swells so much in my throat I can barely breathe past it. I feel like a cat with a hairball, like I have to cough up *Hi, E, nice jim-jams, love the GIFset, and oh, by the way, the secret love affair that is the basis of our friendship and the entire community that you basically rule is a lie. I know because for the last three months I've had an all-access pass to one of the lovers' boxer shorts* all over her carpet.

Writing the fic was a compromise, putting my boastful confession in a code I pray she never, ever breaks.

Still, it's hard to describe the deliciousness of the chill I feel, hearing my and Ryan's origin story coming from Teenage Petrolhead's glamorous lips.

"Post it now," she insists. "I wanna see the reaction."

I pull out my phone and obey. Evie immediately reblogs it, adding: Seriously, peeps, this story. THIS STORY!!!!!

The speed with which my fandom flocks to the new hot thing never fails to take my breath away. Within ten minutes there are a hundred notes, in half an hour a thousand, most in all caps.

- 👤 OMG YAAAAAAAAASSS!!!!
- 👤 THIS IS PERFECTION.
- 👤 I'M LITERALLY CRYING, THIS IS SO WONDERFUL!!!

The black string of notifications under the original post grows like an insect in a time-lapsed nature documentary. More and more, every time I refresh. Evie looks on like a proud parent at graduation, as if she's given me this incredible opportunity.

- 👤 THEY ARE SO MEANT TO BE.

Is that a twinge of guilt I feel? Maybe, but maybe it's just relief, to have our story vindicated by so many people I love and trust.

At first, the responses are universally positive. But it's the Internet's law of gravity that when any post gets big enough, it will inevitably draw some bitter little asteroid into its orbit.

- 👤 Oh my Christ bitch, do you really have nothing better to do? Ryan and Nick are NOT TOGETHER. Get a fucking life, you sad whore! 😂😂😂😂😂

I look up from the post. Evie's over by her desk, fussing with Photoshop on her massive desktop screen. My thumbs are sweaty as I fumble for the delete button on my phone. If I can just get rid of it before she sees it—

"Oh, well then." Evie pronounces each syllable as calmly

as if she's spelling her own name. "Fuck. You. Bitch."

She spins round in her chair. She has an iPad in her lap.

"Evie…" I begin. "It's fine. It's just someone being a twat online. It's nothing."

"Just because it happens online doesn't make it nothing, sweets. Online is where we live, you know that. What's the username?"

"They don't have one. It's an anon."

She makes an irritated noise in the back of her throat. "Of course it is. Cowardly turd. What's the exact time they posted the comment?"

"Look," I say. "If you want to wade in, flame them, whatever, obviously that's fine, but…"

"That's exactly what they want. Attention is these people's fondest wish. I'm just going to get them to reconsider that aspiration."

"Evie, please."

"The exact time, Cat. You're my friend; I'm not going to let this cretinous cockroach crotch talk to you like that."

I hold her gaze, pleading without speaking, but her eyes are like granite. "The *time*, Cat."

I give it to her. She opens a Gchat window and pings it along with the URL for my story to a friend of hers who works for Tumblr's user experience team. Eleven beats of my frantic, panicky heart later, she has the anon's IP address and the name of a baking blog they maintain on the same platform: Diary of a Cake Fiend. Apparently our troll is called Nat.

"Ooh, look," she purrs. "She's still online, and her DMs are open."

Which is when she really sets to work: thirty seconds to find a particularly enticing picture of a home-made cherry Bakewell on the troll's blog. Another minute to google a cherry Bakewell recipe on a more famous food blogger's Tumblr, screencap it and paste Cake Fiend's picture over the original one. Three minutes to set up the fake URL www.yummyyasmine.tumblr.com, and another two to comb Cake Fiend's previous posts for someone she seems friendly with, and screencap *their* user pic.

In seven and a half minutes exactly, Evie's ready to pull the trigger.

Holy shit babes! she types into the message field, having installed the pirated user pic and name onto the burner account. You didn't tell me Yummy Yasmine was featuring you! You've really hit the big time!

She pastes in a compacted link and hits *send*. "Pay dirt," she mutters with satisfaction.

"What?" I ask.

"She clicked. Now she just has to try and log into our fake Tumblr page with her *real* ID and password, and bam!" She claps her hands together, little-girl delighted in her pink hippo PJs. "I own her. Now, I wonder if she uses the same email and password for her Facebook? Oh, she *does*. Well, isn't it just Christmas Day all of a sudden?"

I try to protest, but the Facebook profile of one Natalie Amani is already open on Evie's enormous desktop.

"Photos?" she muses to herself. "No, she doesn't have any private folders. *Messages*, on the other hand… What do we reckon the odds are that this articulate person reuses her vocabulary?"

I stand helpless behind her as she combs Natalie's message files for the words *bitch* and *whore*. She squeals with delight to find the people they're used to describe also in her friends list.

What's on your mind, Natalie? The cursor blinks next to the prompt.

"Well, since you ask, Mr Zuckerberg," she says sweetly, and begins to type.

Dear Friends, I thought you might like to know what I really think of you…

I try one last time. "Please, E, I don't mind."

"*I* mind," she says firmly. "She wasn't just insulting you. Calling you a bitch, well, you can let that slide if you want, but come into *our* space, denying Nick and Ryan's love? That's an attack on all of us."

Her eyes were granite hard. *That*, her gaze implied, was sacrilege.

"A place for everything. And everything in its place." She hits *post*. "And your place, Natalie, is in the bin."

I picture the face in Natalie Amani's smiling profile photo running with tears as she pleads with her friends. The first comments appear under Evie's post and I turn away without reading them. My phone buzzes on the desk. Evie passes it over, too engrossed in her handiwork to look. I open the message.

I'm delirious. I can't stop thinking about you.
Come nurse me. The drugs they give you for
a broken arm are awesome btw – Rxx

"Who is it?" Evie asks.

For a second I can't answer; it feels like I've got a conker, spiked husk and all, shoved in my throat.

"Cat?" God help me, those brown eyes are trained on me now. "What is it?"

"Just Mum," I finally manage to croak. "She wants me home."

CHAPTER SEVEN

Amy

I'll never forget, as long as I live (although with the maniac and her bomb across the hall that feels like less of a commitment than it used to), the night I decided to start streaming.

Everyone else in the house was asleep, and I should have been too, but the clock on my wall was too loud, shaving seconds off Mum's life, and there wasn't anything I could do to stop it. It had been an exhausting day. The first day she couldn't use the loo without help. She'd had an accident; I'd cleaned it up. I didn't mind the mess, or the smell; it gave me something to do, a fig leaf of usefulness. Head down. Do the job in front of you. Be of service to those around you.

But her *face*…

Mum's stricken expression had barely been able to command the muscles under her skin, and, like a distant storm, I'd felt something inexorable batter at the fortifications of practicality I'd built up in my head.

Every day of your life, you teach yourself to believe that the people you love are more than just bodies. Their hair changes and their skin wrinkles and they gain and lose weight, but it doesn't matter – it's still *them*, right? But then the disease comes, and it mocks your faith that they're more than flesh as it shuts them in, and shuts them off.

Dad had work in the morning, so the baby monitor was in my room. I lay awake, watching it. When her moans came over it, the static made them ghostly, like she was already gone.

She was in the back study we'd converted into a bedroom. I crept downstairs and opened the door as quietly as I could. She was so small, sprawled half in, half out of the bed. At some point she'd rolled half over the edge of the bed, and she wasn't strong enough to get back in. I rushed over, but when I put my arms under her and tried to pull her up she cried out.

I let go like she was made of burning hot metal. "Mum, what is it?" I whispered. "What did I do?"

But she couldn't answer. She wasn't properly awake. The drugs they'd given her – that *I'd* given her – were tethering her somewhere down beneath consciousness. There were half a dozen bottles clustered on the bedside table. The doc had prescribed them in a batch; the nurse had brought them all round. "Give her as many as she wants," she'd said, like it was kind, like it was a mercy we should be grateful for that, next to the disease, any damage an overdose could cause her would be immaterial. I could see her struggle against the chemicals, scrabbling to make herself understood, squirming and making little sounds of distress.

Suddenly I thought, *What if the medicine doesn't stop the pain? What if it only stops her telling me it hurts?* I watched, helpless. She was like a drowning woman, anchored just below the surface of the sea.

"Mum?" My whispers became more and more frantic. "Mum, what should I do? What do you want me to do?"

But she couldn't speak. She couldn't wake. All she could do was mumble and moan and hurt. I thought about waking Dad, even waking Charlie, but then what? They'd be just as alone with this as I was.

So I took her, and I hauled and I dragged and I manhandled her back into a position where I told myself that maybe she'd be a little more comfortable, and every time she whimpered I wanted to curl up around the wound it made in me.

And then when she was back in bed, I took the bottle of pills, ground one up under the base of the glass the way the doctor had shown us all as we'd lined up like amateur med students, swept the powder into her water glass, diluted it, and put it to her lips.

She slurped at it, craning her neck forward, eager as a baby.

I sat there for a while, stroking and crooning and shushing her until she seemed to calm, then I sat a while longer. This, I realized, was as good as it was going to get. There was never going to be a "better", ever again, just more and more nights like this, until…

All the air went out of me. I picked up the pill bottle. It felt such a natural fit in my fist. I shook a handful of the little white tablets into my palm, and it still felt abstract, like an experiment, like *I wonder what happens if…*

It wasn't until half the pills were in my mouth that my throat tightened and I realized what I was doing.

I choked, spat and the pills cannoned off the bedpost. I threw the bottle down and it rolled under the bed. I stood there, gasping and panting. What the fuck was I doing? Charlie was sleeping not ten feet above my head. *Charlie.* Had I really been ready to check out on him? On Dad? Ease my pain by doubling theirs? *Jesus Christ, Amy. You're a piece of work.*

That was when I knew I wasn't coping. I was only pretending to cope. People treat you like that's the same thing, but it's not. I fled the room, my stomach roiling with self-disgust. I couldn't be alone any more.

The patches arrived the next day.

I descend the stairs as quietly as I can, and push open the door to the makeshift bedroom, almost like Mum's still in it and I can still disturb her. It's been stripped, of course. Just a wardrobe, a bedside table with a lamp on it, and a bare mattress sitting on a frame. The silver tape around the window frame glints in the sunlight, and I feel a brief flare of fury that Polly's desecrated this place.

The room's emptiness reinforces the sense of the house being a film set – established for principal photography on

Amy Becker's Mother Dies By Inches and It Pulls Her Family Apart Like Pizza Cheese and then just as rapidly cleared out.

Aunt Juliet's shrill voice echoes back to me from some point over the endless preceding months: "How *dare* you? How dare you turn this into some kind of sordid reality television show?"

I shiver. The muscles in my neck and jaw tense. I've not been in this room since she died. I tried. I even volunteered to be the one who went through the wardrobe and shoved her clothes into bin bags, who hoovered up the last few fragments of herself she left as dust on the floor. It was a bloody-minded challenge to myself: *I will not be afraid.* But I was, and when it came to it I couldn't go through with it. Dad had to do it instead.

I was afraid, and I still am.

Holding my breath as though what lingers in the air is a smell, I cross the floorboards. My skin feels blistered by the atmosphere in this room and I desperately want to bolt, but I think about Dad, about Charlie.

Are you ready to check out? I ask myself again. *Ready to ease your pain by doubling theirs?*

No? Good. Then do something about it.

I crouch down beside the bed frame. I grope behind the near leg under the valance. The pill bottle's still there.

I pour out a handful of pills and set them on the table. I use the base of the lamp to crush them. A moment's panic: I've got nothing to gather the powder in, but then I see the valance has one of those big papery labels on the hem with washing instructions on it. A few seconds' work with my teeth tears the fabric. I collect the opiate dust in the label, fold it up into a little envelope, tuck it inside my bra, then I all but run out of the room.

Back in the kitchen, Polly's sat bent over the table. Two phones rest on the wood in front of her: mine, and Mum's hooked up to a charging cable.

"Oh, there you are," she says, smiling vaguely at me. "Look at this – you're so *adorable*." There are tears in her eyes.

I glance at the phone. She's looking at my baby pictures, Dad beaming into the camera holding me while I cling to my little red cloth. As I watch, she swipes, and now the one on the screen is of me in a fluffy yellow chick costume, still clinging to the cloth. When I was thirteen, Mum had threatened to break into the school intranet site and make that photo the landing page if I didn't tidy my room.

For some unknowable reason, Polly cooing over that photo in particular enrages me, and I stifle an urge to stave in her head with her mug.

You've got a job to do, Amy, I tell myself. *Survive.*

I pick up my own mug, take a gulp and make an exaggerated face. "Cold," I announce, too loudly.

She looks distraught. "Shall I make another pot?"

"I'll do it," I offer. To my own ears, I sound suspiciously eager but she just beams at me, as delighted and unguarded as a little girl.

"That's so *nice* of you!" she exclaims.

"How do you take it?"

"Normally just milk," she says, patting her stomach, which is ridiculous because you could break this woman up and use her for coat hangers. "But this time I'll treat myself to a couple of sugars."

I nod and collect her mug. I pour them both out in the sink and put the kettle on. Sweat stipples the nape of my neck. I glance back at her; she's looking at me with that proprietary fondness I saw back when I made the mistake of watching fan vids. I make a show of scratching my chest, close to my bra strap. It suddenly feels necessary to give every limb and digit an excuse to be where it is.

"Itchy?" she asks, her face a sympathetic frown. "I've got a tube of cream somewhere, for my rashes. Want some?"

"No, it's OK. I'll just scratch it."

She shrugs. "It's your boob."

The second her eye flits back to the phone, I make a dart for the pill fold. The paper slips between my sweaty fingers and my heart lurches, but I just manage to cling on with my fingertips, tilting the stream of powder towards Polly's cup.

The kettle boils and I fill the teapot, crushing down my desire to pour it instantly. I remember how intently she watched the clock when she brewed the tea. Maybe she's one of those people who is super-pernickety about their tea. I need to make this the single most irreproachable brew in the history of English afternoons. If she won't drink it because it's too weak, I won't get another chance.

Every second of the three minutes I leave the bags to

brew feels like it takes six months, but she's completely absorbed in Mum's phone. I pour the tea, adding as much sugar as I think I can get away with to disguise the flavour.

"Oh, look!" she exclaims. "There's one of you as a little platypus!"

She holds up the phone, making cooing noises. She looks at me for comment. I'm suddenly aware of how unnatural my silence feels.

Tea goes with conversation, Amy. Make some fucking conversation.

"I used to be cute." I offer a self-deprecating shrug.

"You were lovely then, and you're lovely now," Polly insists, accepting the mug from my hand.

I cast around for something to keep the conversation going. I try desperately not to stare at her mug. My eye lands on the two phones. Mine and Mum's.

"Do you not have a phone?"

"Why do you ask that?"

"You needed mine to message my dad."

Her lip quirks. "Sharp girl," she says approvingly. "No, I don't. Can you guess why?"

I squirm a little. I'd intended this to be small talk, but it's growing like it ate a Mario Mushroom. Still, there doesn't seem to be a graceful way to switch to another subject.

"Because if you'd sent the message from your own phone, the police would be able to use it to find out where you bought it, work out who you are."

She smiles, nods her encouragement. "Keep going."

"They'd try to hack it. Then they'd know everything about you."

Dates, locations, people we contact the most, and least, the friends we value most and least. Things you won't admit to yourself, or plain can't remember. Hacking someone's phone tells you more about them than reading their mind.

"The less certain the police are about me," she says calmly, "the slower they'll move. I'd like to extend our time together."

"Why?"

She smiles shyly. "Because I'm your friend, Amy." She utters a little laugh, and plucks at the front of her bomb vest in a way that almost makes me throw myself under the table. "And from where we are, I'll understand if it takes a little time for me to prove that to you."

My eyes settle on that deadly little green light. "Friends don't kill friends," I say.

She makes a pained face, like I've said something hopelessly naive. She lifts her mug and sips.

"Oh, honey," she says. "Of course they do."

CHAPTER EIGHT

Cat

My phone buzzes. It's Evie.

You seen this?

Below her text, a link, and below the link, a preview pane of the gossip site headline:

POP PRINCE'S SECRET
LOVER? PHOTO EVIDENCE!!!

It's like someone's plugged a hoover into my lungs. I'm airless, paralysed. I don't even know how I manage to thumb the link.

But we were so careful.

For a moment, I don't understand what I'm seeing. The picture under the headline is Ryan. He's walking down a street, Chelsea by the look of it, past black iron railings and fancy red-brick boutiques, but he's alone. Not even a telltale scrap of ginger hair snapped through a window to give me away.

Then my eye lands on the circled part of the photo they've blown up. It's the bag Ryan's carrying, one of those square card ones with rope handles that they give you in fancy shops. It's glossy black, with one word printed in silver on the side: *Lustgarden*.

Has boy band royalty Ryan Richards been buying lacy lingerie for a lusty lady??? the top line of the article asks breathlessly. To help address this vital query, the site's picture editors have included several shots of models clad in a variety of Lustgarden's finest wares, including a bra that costs as much as a house, and has roughly the same amount of structural engineering built in. They've even written in tiny print underneath: *Artist's impression: is this how Ryan's lady love looks?*

"Sorry, boys, not quite," I murmur as I begin to breathe again. "You got the knickers on the third girl right, though." Lacy purple ones. I'm wearing them now, and they prickle like *murder*.

Another message from Evie swoops in.

Get round here.

What's the big deal? So
he went shopping.

Just get your arse round here, Cat. I'm
not kidding. I need your help.

"It's everywhere!" she groans at me the second she opens the door. Her eyes are puffy. It looks like she's barely slept, and…

"Jesus Christ."

"What?" Evie snaps.

"You're not wearing make-up. Should I be buying tinned food?"

"When did you get hilarious?" she says flatly, and I press my lips together. It's a good question. I guess the relieved euphoria from not seeing myself in the photo still hasn't worn off; it's making me reckless. "Upstairs, now," she orders. "Help me. We need damage control."

In Evie's world, you control damage by dealing out damage of your own. Each iPad is open to a different platform: RickResource's main forum, plus the Everlasting fic and sightings subthreads, plus Twitter, Tumblr, Instagram and Snapchat. Each is a window on to a field of scorched earth.

- 👤 Fuck you for believing it.
- 👤 I will destroy you.
- 👤 It's a management set-up, you cretin.
- 👤 You're betraying the community and you know it.
- 👤 You're weak. You're letting the boys down. They need us to believe in them.
- 👤 I will destroy you.
- 👤 I will destroy you.
- 👤 I will destroy you.

Most of her interlocutors bail on the thread after a brief exchange. I don't blame them. The majority of the people she's talking to live on other continents, but Evie has that particular Internet skill of being able to imply in just a few words that she would be willing to part with time, sleep and international airfares for the pleasure of stabbing you in the face.

You're crazy, TP, one of them complains. A goddamn madwoman.

Oh, we're all mad here, she snaps back. If you aren't then, wow, are you in the wrong place.

"It's not just the pap shot," she explains, dropping herself into her desk chair, and absent-mindedly wishing a fiery death on a fellow fan's entire family. "They're referencing a source close to the band saying he's been seen with some mysterious girl."

My throat dries. "That's all they said? A mysterious girl?"

"That's the lot."

"Vague," I say as dismissively as I can. "Anonymous. It's a management ploy, just trying to spin it."

Evie smiles wanly. "You know that, and I know that, but it's giving it juice with the anti-crowd, and some of the weaker Rickers are wobbling. We need to push back; we need to make it visible. I don't want Nick or Ryan seeing this and thinking we've given up on them. With all the pressure management are putting on them to break it off, we're their bulwark. They need us to keep the faith."

I manage to hold her gaze. "Yeah, I know."

"We need to stamp on this."

I can't help but agree. Rumours about Ryan's love life

are more common than bad YouTube covers of his songs, but he's usually linked with some other celebrity. This speculation about the most famous fringe in pop dating an unnamed random has the uncomfortable ring of real reporting; we need to kill it until it's dead.

I think for a second, and then pull out my phone, crack open my own Twitter and write: Don't know what the fuss is about re Ry's latest shopping trip. Everyone knows R&N play with gender. Peeps assuming it's a pressie for a girl – your heteronormativity is showing, not to mention how boring you are in the bedroom.

I sign it off with a hashtag #Knickers4Nick and post it.

A few seconds later I hear a snort from Evie. "Nice, dubs," she says, and I feel a glow at her approval.

"Hang on." Evie sits bolt upright in her chair. "Horse Girl, you're a genius! I don't know why I didn't think of that."

"Think of what?" I say, suddenly wary.

"Give me a sec." She's hammering away at her keys. "I bet *someone* on RR lives near there … *yes.*"

I look at her screen. She's got a message app open to someone called GetRickorDieTryin'. I just see the bubble Get receipts before she tabs back to Tumblr.

"What are you doing, E?" I press, trying to keep the anxiety in my chest from bubbling up into my voice.

"This Ricker I know only lives a couple of doors down from that knicker shop. She loves me. Basically wants to be me. I've sent her up there to nose the place out. See if she can get some deets."

I feel a prick of heat in each earlobe, sharp enough to re-pierce them. I frantically try to think of a plausible reason to ask her to recall her spy, but my mind is a howling wasteland. Evie, oblivious to my distress, sets her rage cannon back to auto-fire and returns to Twitter. I sit, sweating, waiting out the interminable minutes with nothing to say.

One of the iPads pings. Evie studies it in silence. "Fucking got you!" She punches the air.

"What?"

"When I told her to get receipts, I guess she took me literally. She actually charmed the staff into showing it to her." She grins, holding up the screen. It shows a photo of a credit card receipt in Ryan's name, showing the purchase of the Petra lace brief in imperial purple. I feel my stomach tumble at the price – briefly I wonder if the reason the damn thing's so uncomfortable is because it's made out of platinum wire – but it's the final detail on the receipt that Evie's triumphant finger is trained on: the size.

"You were dead to rights, dubs. He definitely bought them for a guy. No way he'd be getting them that big for any of the waifs the press try to peg him to."

I let my breath out slowly. Never in my life have I been more grateful for the backside acreage my mother gave me.

"Post it," I say.

As she complies, my phone buzzes.

Finished an interview early. You free?

100

I ease myself a few degrees around in my chair so that there's no chance Evie can see my screen.

> Kinda tied up right now. At Evie's. Your latest shopping trip caused quite a stir.

Oh?

> Those new knickers you bought me have got half the Internet up in flames.

I regret nothing.

> Seriously, it's ridiculous. We're two frogs and a drop of blood short of a full-on biblical apocalypse here.

Yeah, but you look really hot in purple, so on balance, I reckon we're coming out ahead.

I try to smother the smile that tugs at my cheeks. I'm wearing them now as it happens. Somewhere inside me, the prim, shy fan I was five months ago gasps, but I feel like I'm on an extended holiday from her right now. I hit *send*.

It kills me, watching the three dots flicker as he considers his reply. Then I lick my lips, wondering what flirtation he'll come back with.

I'm on my way.

I'd laugh out loud, but Evie would definitely want to know why, so I swallow it, and make do with typing. LOL.

> I'm not kidding. You said she lives on Clapham
> Common, right? I'll be there in 15 mins.

The swallowed laughter turns to rocks in my throat.

> Ryan, no. Just no. Do not come here.
>
> DO. NOT.
>
> Evie CANNOT SEE YOU!!!

He doesn't reply. I sit there, smiling and sweating. He can't, can he? No. Clapham Common's massive. It's not like I gave him the address. Slowly I start to feel better, and turn my attention back to the unfolding drama on my feeds.

With the receipt to boost it, #Knickers4Nick really starts to fly; it spreads organically from Twitter to Tumblr to Insta. At first a couple of *well actually* types try to complain that the size is pretty big even for a boy's bum – Nick's not exactly known for his childbearing pelvis – but we push back on that with links to the stories that he's been bulking up for his role in that new Jacob Owen film, which in turn gives us an excuse to deluge the naysayers with the gym selfies he posted on Instagram, which in turn only lifts the hashtag further aloft. People RT, adding: OMG T.H.I.S. and *Slurps* Delicious tea, and Rick 4eva!!!!!!!!!!!!

I feel a little coal of pride, just under my ribs, at how vast and *fast* my community is. It takes eight minutes for us to trend. Half an hour later, the first fic featuring the notorious knickers appears on RickResource. I read it. It's good.

"Nice work, Horse Girl," Evie murmurs.

A message window pops up over my browser.

102

Coming up the drive now. Better make sure
it's you who answers the door! ☺

"Shit!" I exclaim, lurching to my feet.

"What?" Evie looks up.

"I – uh, cramp," I explain feebly. "Must be from sitting cross-legged."

"Ouch."

"Yeah, I'd better, I'd better, uh … just walk it off."

She shrugs, and I try simultaneously to limp convincingly *and* scramble at maximum speed down the stairs to the front door. I spy him through the faux stained glass. He's got his hood up and his head down, but I'd know the roll of those shoulders anywhere. I open the door before he reaches it but the gunshot sound of the latch still draws an enquiring call from Evie.

"Someone at the door, Cat?"

"Uh … yeah," I call back, and utterly fail to say anything else.

"Well, who is it?"

"Ah'd like to talk to you about Jaaaysus," Ryan says, loud enough to be overheard. He says it in a truly egregious American accent, which is just as well, because Evie would recognize his normal speaking voice in two-fifths of a heartbeat.

"Jehovah's Witness," I call back up to her. Ryan gives me a big thumbs up.

Evie's scorn echoes down the stairs. "Tell 'em to shove that magazine somewhere only God can see it."

"Sorry!" I announce to Ryan. "We're quite happily steeped in sin here."

"Prove it," he whispers and pulls me into a positively incendiary kiss. He holds me there, right over the threshold, until I melt.

"Circumstantial evidence at best," he murmurs, when our lips finally part. "I'm going to need more convincing."

"You're very frisky this morning."

"The little coffee place on the corner opposite my hotel was closed. I need stimulation."

"This is London – you couldn't find another coffee shop?"

"It's Italian. You know where I grew up?"

"Biddinghuizen," I say automatically.

"Right. Population me, six sheep, a couple of dozen angry-drunk Dutch farmers and a crowd of rowdy metal fans for three days in August. I haven't got over the sheer joy of decent coffee, and I don't intend to. Besides, Gennaro's is my local."

"So?"

"So, I'm a creature of habit. And you're a habit I've got into."

"Wow, the lines are coming thick and fast today."

"Like a Norwegian fishing fleet," he agrees. "Have I caught anything?"

I grin at him, but then the word *caught* snags my attention, and I picture Evie coming down the stairs. "You're *mental* coming here. How did you even find this place? I know I never gave you the address."

"I'd recognize that bike anywhere. It saved my life. I walked around the common from the station until I saw it."

"All the way around the … but that's *miles*."

He smiles. Suddenly earnest. "I wanted to see you."

I just stare at him. Momentarily paralysed by those words coming out of that mouth.

"Uh, Cat?"

"Yeah."

"Since you told our religious friend to do one, don't you think Evie'll be expecting to hear the door close, y'know, sometime today?"

Blushing and flustered, I yank him across the threshold by his belt and slam the door.

"Look, Ry, it's *incredible* to see you, always. But you can't … you have to… Look, if Evie sees you…" I tail off, unable to finish a sentence. My brain is still grappling with the fact that *Ryan Richards* came all the way across town and walked around two miles of dog-turd-covered scrubland, daring recognition by Clapham's infamous battery of fancy pram pushers, taking all that hassle and all that risk …

… just to see me.

I gape at him, and he takes the opportunity of my slightly open mouth to ease his own onto it again. He tastes of mint and tobacco. I lock my arms around him, my fingers finding the grooves between the muscles under his hoodie.

There's a creak on the landing above me.

Shit!

There's no time to even pull out of the kiss. In desperation

I just push harder into him, bearing him back to the wall, under the overhanging landing.

"Horse Girl?" Evie calls from above us.

There's a door beside us. His fingers grope for it.

"Dubs?" I hear. "Cat?" She's light enough that the stairs barely whisper under her feet as she descends.

We slip through the door and it closes on us, sealing us in darkness. I feel a dreadful urge to laugh, but manage to stifle it before it ruins my life. I can't see. I can barely breathe.

"This is *insane*," I whisper.

"I wanted to see you," he whispers back.

"How's that working out, given that it's pitch dark in here?"

He chuckles deep in his throat, and pulls me in tighter. "I'll take the trade to the other senses." His mouth hovers just over my ear, like the promise of a secret. I feel his words as much as hear them.

"Cat? Have you been kidnapped by Jesus freaks?" Evie's right outside the door. She'd probably be able to hear us if our whispers weren't muffled up in her cashmere coats. Every exhalation seems to make it hotter. Ryan's breath swirls against my skin.

"There's a closet in my house we can snuggle up in all day if you're into that, *but…*"

I'm not sure I actually say the *but*. Certainly Ryan doesn't seem to hear it.

"That a promise?" He kisses my neck, just below my ear, then places another just below that, and below that, and now his lips are hot and feather-light along my collarbone.

"Cat?" Evie sounds puzzled now, annoyed. My heart is like a hummingbird in my chest. This is crazy. We have to stop. I have to tell him to stop.

But what if he never asks again?

His fingers tease between the waistband of my jeans and my stomach and then delve deeper, sliding inside my underwear. I flush as his fingers brush stubble. *If I'd known you were coming I'd have made myself less yeti-like,* I want to tell him. But now I can feel the pressure of his fingertips, circling, and I have to bury my face in his jacket to kill the moan easing its way up my throat.

"Seriously, Cat. Where the fuck have you gone? We're in the trenches here."

But Evie's voice is dulled now, distant. Everything's distant. And Ryan's fingers are moving faster and little tremors are pulsing through my thighs. It's only when my head brushes a coat rail that I realize I'm up on tiptoe, leaning into his body heat.

"Cat?"

I try to bite it back, but there are sparks in my abdomen and every muscle's tensed. I can feel it building and there's nothing I can do to stop it.

"Cat!" Evie yells, furious, just as I shudder hard against Ryan. His free hand clamps onto the back of my head, pressing my mouth into his chest as the groan escapes me. I can feel his grin.

Ow! Ow! Ow! Ow! Ow! Now I actually *do* have cramp.

My right calf feels like a bowling ball's been shoved under the skin. Ryan senses the change in me.

"Cat," he whispers, "you OK?"

Through gritted teeth I make a noise like a rusty gate opening, and then freeze. There's no sound from outside, but I can feel Evie's attention. I picture her looking at the door. Under me, Ryan's chest has stopped expanding.

Oh shit oh shit oh shit oh shit. That's it. I'm going to die here. She knows. She knows I'm here. But she's not going to open the door. She's just going to wait for me to die of cramp and fear and embarrassment. I feel sick.

Ryan twists, fractionally. I feel the familiar slab of an iPhone in his jeans. My whole right leg is now one big seizure. Not daring to breathe, I slide the phone from his pocket. The light casts a submarine glow. I dial 141, then plug Evie's number in and hit *call.*

"Burning in my veins like teenage petrol, you do things to me I just can't control."

I give the world's smallest and most pained air punch as the strains of Evie's ring tone rattle out from her bedroom. She didn't bring her phone down with her.

"Fuck's sake." I hear her mutter through the door and then her footsteps as she stamps back up the stairs.

It takes all my willpower to wait until she answers the phone. I hang up and we explode out of the closet. Sweat slathers our hair to our foreheads. We strain to gasp quietly for breath. I hobble around, trying to get circulation back into my calf. Ryan drops to one knee and starts to knead the

108

muscle until it gradually abandons its grudge against me.

He stands back up, smirking. I stand in front of him, sweat-streaked and trembling. Feeling utterly without authority, I whisper, "Please, you have to go."

Still smirking, he brings his heels together and snaps off a military salute. Then he eases the door catch, pulls his hoodie up and slips out onto the drive while I stare after him.

"What the hell happened to you?"

I start, and turn. Evie's looking down from the top of the stairs, her phone dangling from her fingers.

"Jesus Christ, Cat. You look like you've just come round from a two-week fever dream."

"Yeah, I was…" I swallow. "I was in the loo. I'm not feeling very well." Now that I say it, it's not even a lie. The pain in my leg has receded, but the nausea that came with it hasn't. It must be the adrenaline.

Evie's face creases. "Poor thing. Need a pill? I've got basically the entire generic pharmaceutical output of southern India in the bathroom after my trip to Goa last month."

"No, it's OK. I think I'm just gonna go home."

Evie smiles. "No worries, sweetie. You did *amazing* today. Knickers for Nick is trending globally. The Internet loves you. Toothpaste officially retubed. Get some rest. You've earned it."

I nod, let myself out without another word and totter towards my bike. I just about manage to make it to the bushes at the end of the driveway before I vomit.

CHAPTER NINE

Amy

The clippers buzzed like a large angry beetle being held next to my head. Clumps of hair dropped past my eyes into the sink. The baby monitor crackled on top of the bathroom cabinet.

I'd pleaded sick, and Dad had smiled indulgently as if to say, *Of course, darling, you can have as many migraines as your little heart desires right now,* and called the school. It was just me and Mum in the house, and she was asleep. It was one of those periods in the slow, hopeless, downward sine wave of the disease when she could outsleep a cat.

When I was done I stood blinking at my reflection, wisps of hair tickling my nostrils and making me sneeze. God, my head was tiny! I never realized how much I had relied on my hair to disguise my freakishly minuscule cranium.

I touched the soft bristles on the back of my scalp and

they quivered under my palm like a prey animal. It was only then I noticed I was trembling.

The cardboard box sat in front of me on the side of the sink. I yanked the tear-pull. Inside that, there was a smaller plastic box, enclosing another smaller cardboard one, enclosing a plastic pouch that had to be torn open with your teeth because the fine people at Heartstream Inc. apparently really needed you to *prove* you wanted it.

I did.

I slapped the little oval patches of material to the back of my skull. Immediately they went warm, drawing from my body's electrical field like tiny symbiotic creatures.

I opened the app on my phone.

A smiley-faced, radioactive-blue heart (Hettie, the achingly hip tech kids at Heartstream Inc. had named her) bounced onto the screen.

Hi Amy! it said. *How are you feeling today?*

That key question asked, the face vanished from the heart animation, replaced by a question mark, and it settled into an icon at the top of the screen. The background to the button – a wash of sunsets, silhouettes of people kissing, racing car cockpits with grandstands blurring past them – gave a clue to the kinds of feelings that Heartstream encouraged you to share.

"Well, Hettie," I said, my thumb hovering over the icon, "I kinda feel like killing myself."

I pressed down.

I didn't know what to expect. First the warmth in the

patches redoubled. The heat bled into my neck muscles, easing tension I'd more or less forgotten was there. I felt a wave of dizziness. The phone screen blurred in front of me.

The little red counter in the corner of the app started to tick up: 1 ... 3 ... 8.

One person following my stream, three people following ... eight people...

Without really understanding why, I started to dwell on the memory from the previous night. The awkward weight of Mum's limbs under my arms. Her clammy nightie. The sickly smell of the ointment on her.

30 people following ... 87 ... 116...

I can't help her I can't help her I can't help her.

210 people ... 387 ... 540...

She's going to die, and I can't help her.

Messages started to pop into my inbox.

♟ Oh god, this is exactly how I feel.

♟ Thank you for sharing this.

♟ This is painfully real, thank you.

I can't... I wish this would all stop, I can't handle it. I can't. I wish... I recoiled from the thought. I jabbed my thumb down on the icon, and killed the stream. I was sweating and breathing hard. I blinked at my phone screen.

1,305 people following your stream.

How long had I been streaming for? Ten seconds? Twenty? I felt light headed.

No, I just felt *light*.

I looked again at the messages. I read each one over,

and when I reached the end I went back and read them again. I ran my thumb over the icons of the users who'd sent them to me, reading their bios. There was a baker. There was a girl in Star Wars cosplay. There was a boy who said he was an artist. There were pictures linked to his profile; he worked in charcoal, just like me. A spike of something *good* pierced the armoured numbness I'd built around my emotions. A harpoon tied to a thread of contact.

For the first time in I couldn't remember how long, I felt connected to the world.

"Where are your patches?"

I ask it more to keep the conversation going than anything else. Polly's subsided into silence, and I'm terrified she'll stop drinking the tea and let it – and my hopes of escape – go cold. Thin strips of light cross her face through the closed venetian blinds. "Police will have marksmen here by now," she explained, almost apologetically, as she dropped them. She hasn't switched on the lights and I haven't either. She sits in shadow, surrounded by cling-filmed sandwich platters and packs of sausage rolls that cover every available kitchen surface, the glow from the phones she's studying glimmering off her chin. The two enormous fruit cakes my dad made for the wake sit like squat suet fortresses at her elbows. Nobody actually *likes* fruit cake, obviously, not even Dad, but when Mum died, he baked, and I didn't argue. You do whatever works.

Nothing works.

"My ... patches?" Polly seems to come back to herself.

Her hand goes to her own close-cropped hair. "Oh, of course. No. I didn't think I'd be able to do what I needed to do today, if I could feel what you feel."

My stomach cramps up. "And what is it you need to do?"

Again, that apologetic smile. She reaches for the remote and flicks on the TV mounted on the wall. Instantly the sirens from outside redouble, echoed from the speakers. I see the front of my own house framed on the screen, a weird moment, like déjà vu, with white text scrolling in a red banner underneath. My name is sandwiched between the prime minister's and the name of a town in Bangladesh that's been hit by an earthquake. I've spent so many years reading that little ribbon of chaos and misfortune and not caring, not properly, and now I'm snarled up in it.

"I'm here to make a point," she says. "While everyone's watching."

Here to make a point. I swallow hard. *In a suicide vest.* "What point?"

"That I'm real." She shrugs. "That I exist and I matter. Just like you do. That I can't be shoved away in a cupboard like a dress you got too big for and forgot about."

She beams at me suddenly, and raises her mug in a salute. "Thank you, Amy," she says.

"For what?"

"Here I am, holding you in your own house against your will, and you're being so *nice* to me. You're the first person in I don't know how long to treat me like a human being."

She drains her mug with a show of great relish. I hear her

slurp the dregs, and the tension in my chest ratchets down a single notch.

"Now *that*," she says, "was a truly extraordinary cup of tea." She stands, collects my empty mug as well, and beetles over to the sink to wash up. On the telly, my house has been replaced by the familiar bulk of Adrian Rijkaard, London's mayor. He's standing outside the giant collapsing glass testicle that is London City Hall, microphones shoved in his face.

"The incident is rapidly evolving," he says. *"At present the police believe there to be one hostage, and no casualties. They have a principal suspect for the hostage taker. They are not prepared to release the name at this time, but that suspect does have confirmed terrorist contacts."*

I shiver at the word *terrorist*. Since the mayor came in, there have been more guns, more police, more shots and fewer questions. The cops killed all six of the Tufnell Park attackers within two hours of the first blast, but some claim they put two innocent bystanders in the morgue alongside them. The official report was that those two were hostages executed by the terrorists. Like always, it depended on who you trusted. But the next day all the news sites were full of words like *decisive*, *no nonsense*, even *heroic*, and the picture on every front page was of the cop who was killed.

Around the streamer forums there were other rumours too. That terror suspects were having patches slapped to their heads and being forced to stream off end-stage cancer patients. The Met denied it, but noted a legal opinion that if they had done it, it wouldn't be torture since, technically, they wouldn't have actually been *creating* the pain.

"So we haven't ruled out terrorism," the mayor rumbles on. *"But very little is known..."*

A loud crash of breaking ceramics startles me. Standing at the sink, Polly's back has gone completely rigid. She starts to tremble, gripping the edge of the kitchen counter like it's all she can do to stay standing.

"I haven't ruled terrorism out of your *face*, you duplicitous little shit!" The force of her shriek pins me back in my chair. She whirls and flings Mum's teapot at the TV. It misses, smashing into the wall underneath the screen and dragging a dark smear of suds down the paintwork. Fragments of the Hatter's face stare up at me from the red tiles.

"Oh," she says, in a small voice. "Oh, Lord, I'm so sorry, Amy. I didn't mean to..." She drops to her knees and begins to collect the pieces of shattered pottery. "I didn't mean to; I didn't..." she mumbles over and over.

"It's OK," I find myself saying. I crouch down to help her, but she pushes me gently away. Her eyes are unfocused.

"No, pleassse, I'll do ... do ... duuuuuuh." Her movements slow. She grabs for one big chunk showing the shattered top hat and misses by six inches. "I didn'... I did."

She goes still, slumped forward heavily on her elbows, her breathing suddenly laboured and wet. Then her arms go out from under her, and she collapses on the floor.

For a split second, I stare at her, my heart locking up in horror. Is she unconscious? Is she *dead*? Then my eye lands on the Hatter's yellow bow tie.

"You've got a job to do," I mutter. *"Survive."*

But how? The silver tape glints mockingly from the window frames. I don't dare disturb it. I make a grab for my phone where it sits on the table. My hands are so slick with sweat that the touchscreen doesn't answer; my fingers leave wet smears on the glass. I wipe it off on my dress and try again, frantically scrolling to the recent calls. One unknown mobile number sits at the top of the list. I call it.

"This is DCI Singh."

"Hello? Hello? Are you there?"

"Yes, this is DCI Singh. Am I talking to the individual holding Amy Becker?"

"No! No, this is … I am Amy."

"Amy?" The voice sounds startled. *"I'm Sammi. I'm the officer in charge of this situation. Are you all right?"*

"I'm fine. I just… I need help. I managed to … I don't know. I think she's unconscious. She might be *dead*." My guts twist and I almost vomit up the word.

"Who is?"

"The woman holding me hostage. I put some of Mum's old drugs in her tea. She's out cold on the floor."

"You … that's incredible. Brilliant work, Amy. We'll come in and get you."

"NO!" My startled yelp is so loud that, for a second, I think I'll rouse Polly, but she stays motionless on the tiles.

"She's put some kind of tape around all the doors and windows. She said if anyone fiddles with it or breaks it the bomb will go off."

"OK. OK, Amy, we'll get you out of this. I need to talk to some other people right now. Stay on the line, OK?"

"OK."

Silence crackles over the phone. Distantly, I hear snatches of a muttered conversation:

"Can we jam the signal?"

"Only if we knew the frequency, and even then she might have wired it to blow if it's interrupted remotely."

A chagrined silence falls. I hang desperately on the line, listening now only to my own laboured heartbeat. And then:

"Amy?"

"Yes? Yes. I'm here."

"I'm going to hand you over to DS Atkinson; he's from the bomb squad, OK?"

A new voice, cigarette-coarsened, comes over the phone. *"Amy?"*

"Yes."

"I'm Tom, Tom Atkinson, pleased to meet you. I know this is scary, but you're going to be fine. Do you trust me on that?"

I can feel myself starting to hyperventilate. I grit my teeth, forcing my breath out slowly through them.

"Yes." It's a lie, but a useful one, and I've got used to telling those recently.

"First, we need to find the bomb; do you know where it is?"

"It's … it's on her. It's strapped to her."

"Like on a vest?"

"Yes. There's two lights, some ball bearings and … and a load of wires."

He mutters something I don't catch.

"OK, I need you to go over to her."

I crouch beside Polly's prone form. She's sprawled, face down. One leg is cocked up under her.

"I'm there."

"Can you get at the wires?"

"No, they're underneath her. She fell on her stomach."

"OK, we're going to need you to turn her over; can you do that?"

I try to put my hand out to touch her, but it's like trying to force it into a fire – it won't go. "No … I … I can't. I'm scared."

"Amy, this is really important. We can't come in if you can't get at the wires."

"OK, I… OK." I pin the phone between my cheek and my shoulder and slide my palms under Polly's stomach. For a split second I think I feel her jerk and I scream.

"I can't… I can't…" I'm crying, my tears running down my jaw to the phone, making it slick.

"You can," Tom says gruffly. *"It'll be OK."*

I drag in three, four, five deep breaths. "OK." I tense and pull upwards on Polly's stomach. She's so light, she flips over almost immediately. Her head lolls back, but she's breathing, her chest full of wires rising and falling.

"OK. OK, I've got her on her back."

"Brilliant, that's brilliant, Amy. Well done. Can you see the wires now?"

119

"Yes."

"What colour are they?"

"There's … there's two black, one green and one blue one."

"Can you see the explosive? It'll be in blocks or bottles."

"Yes, it's in little plastic bottles of clear liquid on her chest and her back."

"How big are they?"

"A … a half-litre each? Like water bottles."

"And how many are there?"

"Six."

"Holy—" Tom swallows his oath. *"OK, well, that's quite a lot. But it doesn't matter, because it's not going to go off, is it?"*

"No."

There's another muttered conference on the other end of the phone.

"Is there a small box anywhere on the vest? It should have a little nub on top, like one of those old car door locks."

"Y-yes? Yes."

"OK, good. That's the aerial. That's what picks up the signal from the circuit she's put round your house. Somewhere, hooked up to that tape, there's another one of those. In an ideal world we'd look for that one, but it's not an ideal world, is it?"

I swallow hard; my throat is dry and sticky at the same time. "Not today it's not exactly, no."

He laughs. *"Good stuff, Amy. OK, now tell me, what colour wire goes into the aerial on the vest?"*

"The green one."

"OK, *then that's the one we need to cut. I don't suppose you've got a set of wire cutters in the house?"*

"No, but I'm in the kitchen. There's a knife block about four feet away."

"Great. That'll do. Grab the sharpest one you can find."

I slide the carving knife out of the big pine block and crouch back beside Polly's slack form.

"Got it."

"OK. We want one smooth, clean cut, so try to bend the slack of the wire around the blade."

"OK." There's enough, just barely, to get a loop of acid-green flex around the blade. My hand is shaking so badly that the tip of the knife is a blur. Polly's chest rises and falls, regular as the tide.

"OK, then whenever you're ready, cut."

I blow out hard, and feel every muscle in my body tense as I—

"You probably ought to know I wired it in reverse."

I jerk backwards. The phone slips out from my cheek and skitters away over the tiles. For a moment, I think I've severed the wire, but then I realize my arm hasn't moved. Polly's hand is locked onto my forearm. Her fingers are digging under my muscle like needles. Her eyes are open, her expression rueful.

"Cutting that wire will bring the house down," she goes on, "so you really don't want to do that, unless you're looking to call it a day. Which, given the day you've had, I wouldn't blame you for."

"Amy?" Tom's voice crackles over the phone. But I can barely hear it; my gaze is locked on Polly's green, sad eyes. *"Amy, are you there?"*

She twists my wrist and the knife slips from my numb grasp onto her chest.

"I thought we were becoming friends," she says, sadly.

CHAPTER TEN

Cat

The light in the waiting room is like a drill to my eyeballs.

All around me, women try to manage their nerves with varying degrees of apparent success. Some perch right on the edge of the polythene-covered benches, drumming their hands on their thighs. Some scroll feverishly through their phones for distractions, unable to settle on anything for more than a few seconds. Others are very still, holding themselves with something like dread. Every time a high beep cuts the silence, all our eyes dart to the dot matrix display over the windows where the next patient's name has flashed up.

Roughly half of the women are accompanied by men. The men murmur soothingly to their wives and girlfriends, and squeeze their hands. My chest hurts and I turn away from them. All I can do with my own sweat-slick palms is rub them on my jeans.

Stop feeling sorry for yourself. You're the one who decided not to tell him.

Yet. I correct the thought. I haven't told Ryan *yet.* He'll be there for me, I know he will. I feel a little twinge of guilt at keeping it from him. I *will* tell him; it's just… Look, it's my uterus and my hormones, and I want to get *my* head straight before I involve his.

In the corner, two women kiss. I hadn't realized they were here together. The older one, the one with grey hairs creeping in at her temples, rocks gently in her chair. She has the face of someone who knows this is her last chance.

A chair tips over with a clatter and a girl with dyed dreadlocks scrambles for the bathroom. We all look sympathetically after her. For me, at least, that's stopped, for now.

Still, I suppose I should be grateful for the two-week breakdance party in my stomach since it was that which *finally* tipped me off. My boobs had been sore and I was knackered, but I just thought I was sick. I'd lurched into the living room, pale as a zombie, sipping the Bovril that Mum swore by for stomach flu. On TV a harried-looking blonde woman was hurtling into a toilet stall for a projectile vomit that rivalled my own spectacular pukeathon.

"What are you watching?" I asked Mum.

"I genuinely have no idea," she said, and checked the TV menu. "*Up the Duff Without a Paddle.*" She shrugged and crunched another crisp. "I remember I had *terrible* morning sickness with you. Cat? Are you OK?"

But I couldn't answer. I was frozen in place, Bovril mist

wafting over my face like beefy weather.

It just hadn't occurred to me. I was on the pill; I had been since before Ryan and I had started hooking up. OK, when I really racked my brain I couldn't remember whether I'd taken it *every single day*, and my periods had been light, for me, but they'd kept coming, so...

"I'm fine, Mum."

In fairness, it was only the next day, when the fifth stick I peed on gave me the same message as the four before it, that I really *knew* that wasn't true. I stared at the little blue cross, acid panic burning in my throat. Ryan, Mum, school, Evie – my world dissolved into a storm of questions, and no answers.

The beep from the dot matrix is like a knitting needle in my ear.

Ms Hippolyta Richards.

I peel myself off the seat, wincing at the sound my sweaty thighs make as they come away from the polythene. Some of the older women throw covert glances my way. I think I'm the youngest here, and I'm suddenly painfully aware of the empty air around my right hand.

"Ms ... Richards, is it?" The doctor has a beard that could give half of London's homeless a new wardrobe if you wove it into clothes.

"Mrs," I correct him. If you're going to do wish fulfilment on your alias, you might as well go all out.

"Hippolyta, eh," he says.

"Yeah," I reply.

"Queen of the Amazons." He grins; he's enjoying showing off. "Horse let loose!"

"'S'right."

"Parents are classicists, are they?"

"Uh ... yes. They, um ... they love all that stuff."

Not even a flicker of the eyebrows, which I put down more to the number of women who come in here with fake names than my outstanding thespian skills.

"I'm Dr Jenkins. Please just lie down there." He scrolls through a couple of pages on his screen. "How long has it been since you last bled?"

"My periods kept coming." He looks up at me. "But I took a bunch of tests, and they all said I was pregnant." Hope flares briefly. "Why, could they be wrong?"

He barks a laugh. "Don't worry, I'm sure you're pregnant. Can you roll your top up? And just unbutton your shorts and pull them down a bit so I can get below your belly button."

He tucks some tissue in around my waistband, pulls on a plastic glove and then smears a jelly that feels like a concentrated arctic snowmelt around my abdomen. A rash of goosebumps covers me.

He mirrors my wince. "I know, sorry. It is a *little* cold."

I can't help but flinch when he touches the probe to my skin. A little electric shock goes through me and I can feel every beat of my heart throbbing up into my jaw. He moves the wand this way and that, head cocked slightly to the side, like he's a burglar and my uterus is a safe he can crack. Then I realize he's watching a computer screen off to one side.

I don't know how long has passed. About 3,657,955 years judging by the number of heartbeats I'm getting through. A wave of feeling, part relief, part anticlimax, washes over me. *The tests were wrong. There's no baby. Nothing's changed. Everything's OK.*

And then I hear it.

Via a trick of technology, it sounds like it's coming from a speaker on the rack of the machine beside me, but I know where it's really coming from. Steady, but rapid, putting my own frantic pulse to shame.

A heartbeat. A second human heartbeat. Inside *me*.

I can't breathe.

"Mrs Richards?"

I don't answer.

"I'm sorry, Mrs Richards?"

I blink and look down. There's a white blur about nine inches from my face, and when I blink away the tears I didn't know I was crying, and clean the fog off my glasses, I realize it's a box of tissues. I have to wrench my hand free of the rictus grip it has on the armrest to take one.

And all the while the little heart goes *duh-dum, duh-dum, duh-dum*, fast as a butterfly's wing.

"It's as well you came when you did," the doctor says. "By the looks of things it's been about eleven weeks. We'll need to take some blood for tests."

"Why?" I look up sharply. "Is there something wrong with it?"

"Well, that's what we'll be testing for, but I don't have

any reason to believe there would be. Speaking solely in biological terms, you understand, women your age are well-oiled machines for this."

I nod, astonished by the surge of emotion welling up in my throat. Relief and gratitude and ... something else. *Where is this coming from?* I examine the feeling suspiciously, like it's counterfeit, like it's not really mine. I shouldn't be *able* to feel this way about something so small and simple, something that's barely there, that doesn't even know my name, that doesn't even have a brain yet, not really.

Duh-dum, duh-dum, duh-dum.

But it has a heart, and that's enough.

CHAPTER ELEVEN

Amy

One hand still gripping my wrist, Polly stretches like she's just had a refreshing daytime nap, and gathers up the fallen knife. I stay in my crouch, paralysed, while she unfolds over me.

"There was a bitter edge to the tea," she says, "and where I've come from, I've had to become quite good at pretending to swallow things. Honestly, Amy. You could have *killed* me."

She yanks me to my feet and nods towards the nearest of Dad's monster fruit cakes. For a moment, I don't get it, then light glimmers in just the right way and I see how wet it looks, the plate it sits on brimming with cloudy liquid.

I'm here to make a point, she'd said, after she'd flicked the TV on. She must have soaked the cake while I was distracted by the news.

"You didn't mean to hurt me, did you?" Her eyes are

wide, vulnerable. "You just wanted to get out of here, to see your father and Charlie. I understand."

I nod frantically, unable to speak because my throat has closed to what feels like a needle's eye. I can't take my eyes off the knife.

"That's only natural." She says it like she's reasoning it out, talking herself around. "So you were careful with the dose of whatever you put in that cup. You made sure it wouldn't do me any permanent damage, just put me to sleep, right?"

I don't answer. My eyes are stretched so open I can feel every stirring air current against them.

"I haven't been fair to you. I should have thought more about the stress this would put you under," she muses. "I was selfish wanting to talk to you. Perhaps this *would* go easier on you if you slept through it."

She smiles glassily at me, and sets the edge of the knife to the cake. "Hungry? You've not eaten anything since I've been here, and tea does go *marvellously* with fruit cake."

Recoiling, I lunge for a shard of the Hatter teapot. My fingers claw the air a centimetre from the sharp ceramic, but she just tuts like I'm a dog that's peed on the carpet and hauls me back, dragging me onto tiptoe. Her fingers are like iron wires around my wrist.

"No, Amy," she says. And now I can't see the knife any more, but there's an edge of something hard and horrifyingly fine at my neck. My throat feels like it's been sandblasted, but I don't dare swallow. The gentlest pressure lifts my chin until I'm staring into her eyes.

I've never understood what's meant by people having mad eyes until this moment. It's not all that cartoonish bug-eyed swivelling. It's the opposite, a stillness. Normal people blink. Normal people *care* how you're reacting to them, so their gaze flickers from your eyes to your mouth and back, reading your expression and responding in kind. Polly's eyes are like a doll's.

"None." She bites off each word. "Of. *That*."

The blood is hammering in my skull; I'm held on tiptoe by the knife. I hold her mad gaze, trying to plead without speaking.

A scream lances through my ears. Polly's head whips around to follow it and the knife falls away. I look too, because I know that voice.

It came from the TV, so loud it made the speakers crackle with feedback. Caught in extreme close-up, microphones shoved under his chin, the lines of running green mascara criss-crossing his cheeks like rivers on a map, is Charlie.

He looks different, and it takes me a handful of my racing heartbeats to put my finger on why: he's shaved his hair to an indistinct brown fuzz and his pupils are dilated to dark pools.

He's streaming.

In the bottom right corner of the screen, an unobtrusive sign announces that the TV footage is live.

Charlie's mouth gapes slightly. He looks horrified – no, he looks *terrified*.

He looks exactly how I feel.

"Charlie?" an off-screen voice asks him. *"Charlie, what's going on?"*

His lips struggle to shape the words. *"She's scared,"* he's saying. *"Oh god, she thinks she's going to die."*

His face vanishes as the screen goes blank. In the darkened glass I see Polly's face, pinched, pale, furious. She casts the remote aside in disgust.

"You're streaming right now?" she demands.

I don't answer. It's not bravado. I just can't speak.

She yanks me round to face her. "YOU'RE STREAMING RIGHT NOW?" she yells into my face. She drags Charlie's scarf away. My patches hiss faintly as they begin to cool in the open air. Polly looks thwarted and betrayed. Her hands twitch forward like she wants to pull the pads off me, but when I flinch she flinches too. It's too late and she knows it. Her once immobile gaze is flickering to the corners of the room, as if she could meet the eyes of all three million people who are streaming off me right now, feeling every jolt of my frightened heart, every drop of blood as it forces its way through my veins, every fraction of the terror and the pain she's inflicting.

She looks like she wants to plead with them. The knife clatters to the floor.

I'm here to make a point, she'd said. *While everyone's watching.*

But, judging by her panicked expression, this wasn't the point she wanted to make. For a split second I feel how I felt staring into the bathroom mirror that first night. Connected, unified, *powerful*.

"There's no time for this!" she snaps, seemingly as much at herself as at me. She grabs me and pulls so hard on my arm I almost come off my feet. I stagger down the hall after her, the pictures and mirrors and floorboards a blur of wood and silver.

"Stay in here and think about what you did!" she yells as she hurls me through a doorway. My feet go out from under me and I tumble hard to the carpet as the door slams behind me. I lie spread-eagled and panting. I stare at the ceiling. The bare bulb tells me which room I'm in.

I roll onto my elbows and try to get up, but adrenaline buckles my knees and I collapse. I crawl to the door and pull the handle down but it doesn't budge. I bang on the door, throw my shoulder against it again and again until the pain in the bruise blossoming through it sickens me.

"Let me out!" I cry. "Please! Put me somewhere else! Anywhere else!"

But whether she's suspicious or she just doesn't care, there's no answer.

I turn and slump against the door. And then, staring at the bed Mum died in, sob after gasping, terrified sob, I break down.

"PLEASE!" I howl it. The syllable's barely comprehensible, barely human. *Get a grip, Ame. Think of Charlie. Charlie who just saved your life.*

And then I *do* think of Charlie; I think of him with my

133

arms around him, holding him outside this very door while he sobbed. "You shouldn't have to see her like that," I whispered to him, as if the problem was fucking *aesthetics*.

I stay in that moment for longer than is good for me. The memory's as tempting as a scab to pick at. I really, really hope Charlie's stopped streaming off me by now.

Why am I so scared of this room? It's dumb. I know it's dumb and I'm furious at myself. For God's sake, I've already *been* in here today. But then I had a specific goal, and I could and *did* leave as soon as I had what I needed. I'm pretty sure I held my breath the whole time. My gaze lands on the window and its vicious glinting tape.

Being *trapped* in here is a different thing.

You see, this room is haunted.

Not by the literal ghost of Mum, of course. And anyway, why would I be scared of that? That would be fantastic; I'd get to talk to her, and maybe now she's lost all the weight she's ever going to lose, she'd stop badgering me with diet tips.

No, this room's haunted by the ghost of her pain; by the slow revolt of her body against her mind; by the unfair but utterly unshakeable feeling that her family were betraying her by not helping, even though there was nothing they could do; by the nurses' instructions to "make her comfortable", a laughable endeavour that was more of a sop to our angst than her anguish.

It's haunted by her knowing that she was going to *end*, far, far too young. And what could conceivably make her comfortable with that?

I let out a breath I didn't know I was holding. A sharp-sweet scent pricks my nostrils and I almost gag. I put my arm across my nose instinctively, but of course, the smell isn't in the room; it's in my head. It's the mingled tang of open sores and antiseptic, of mud-thick meal replacement drinks and incontinence pads and fear sweat. Over the past six months, the air in here has been replaced one molecule at a time with whatever chemical compound comprises raw desperation, and even though Dad bundled all the soft furnishings into bin bags and kept the windows open for three days straight, here it's stayed. It'll probably still be here when the sun consumes the earth. At least it will for me.

I try to stand, and this time I do make it onto my feet. I sway like a lantern at sea. I'm drained; the muscles in my legs and chest feel like wrung-out rags. I try the door again. It's as immovable as death. I lurch over to the bare mattress and gape at it, blinking like a drunkard staring into headlights. Partly out of morbid fascination, partly out of an instinct for self-punishment, but mostly because I'm just really fucking tired, I lie down.

I put my limbs where hers were the night I started streaming, one leg hanging over the edge of the bed frame. I stare up at the ceiling, my eyes finding the tiny hairline cracks in the paintwork, the cobwebs like an architectural five o'clock shadow. These were the last things she saw.

I close my eyes, and feel my breathing go regular.

♥

When I become aware of my body again, pins and needles are marching down my calf where the edge of the bed's cut off circulation. The light coming in through the window has dulled to a burnt street-lamp orange, the trees outside clawing long shadows across the floorboards.

I've got a really pig-ugly ache in my lower back. There's a lump that feels like an anvil in the mattress and God knows how long it's been pressed into my spine.

For Christ's sake, Amy. You were supposed to try and keep her comfortable. You couldn't even make sure her mattress wasn't lumpy?!

Except the mattress *isn't* lumpy: at least, not anywhere else.

I stretch my arms and legs like I'm making snow angels, but my limbs only encounter smooth memory foam. I roll off the centre of the bed and look. There, hard to see because of the striping on the fabric casing, is a solitary, suspiciously regular bump. It's in the exact centre of the mattress, and it's a near-perfect rectangle.

What the...?

I prod it delicately, like it's a lump in my breast rather than in Mum's old robo-bed. It moves. I push it again, harder this time, and it slides further under the surface of the mattress. I push it once more and this time it snags, a smooth corner of black glass emerging from a split in the fabric I didn't know was there.

Excitement and bafflement bubble up together in my throat as I dig my fingers into the slit and pull.

The material rips loudly. I flinch like I've let out a deafening fart in a classroom and jerk around towards the door. My heart thuds, but the handle stays untipped. Slowly, I look back down, reluctant in case what I thought I glimpsed isn't really there, but it is.

Boxy, shiny, and unmistakably solid. A mobile phone.

What the…?

I picture Mum. Crippled, shrunken, sleeping eighty per cent of every day at the end. Even when she was awake she barely had enough strength to hold her eyes open, but with her last breath she protected … this? *What* is *this, Mum? What was it for? What on earth were you—*

"Amy Becker," I tell myself aloud, cutting the thought off. "If you die in here because you were too busy pontificating on the reasons for this godsend to actually make a call, no one will be able to say you didn't deserve it."

Breath stalling in my chest, I press down on the power button. Mountains must have crumbled into dust in the time it feels like it takes for the little white apple to appear on screen, but I finally see it, and exhale.

I'm so intent on the light coming from the screen that I don't hear the door swing open behind me.

2
WHO DOES NOT KNOW THE DARK

CHAPTER TWELVE

Cat

"What the hell, Horse Girl?" Evie complains when she opens her door. "It's the middle of the damn night." She peers up at me, her expression a mix of affront and curiosity at my appearing without being summoned.

"Can I c-c-come in?" I ask. I'm shivering, though it isn't cold.

She stands aside wordlessly and leads me upstairs. Her cavernous bedroom is in the same war-room configuration it's been in for the past three months. Monitors and iPads are spread in a panoramic sweep across the desk, each open to a different site as Evie stamps out the brush fires that have popped up in Rickdom ever since the rumours about Ryan and his mystery girl started to appear.

"The bed's made," I say stupidly.

"Of course the bed's made," she says, sitting cross-legged on it. "I'm not a farm animal."

The phone clock, superimposed over my lock-screen pic of Nick lying atop Ryan after extinguishing his flaming quiff, informs me that it's 02:47, but Evie's make-up is once again in immaculate order. She replied immediately when I texted her too. It's like she's a new species, evolved to get all her sleep in microsecond instalments between notifications.

"What is it, Cat?"

I open my mouth and then shut it again. Dammit, Cat, you had this all *scripted*. But faced with this calm, beautiful inquisitor, my mind is a blank. Suddenly I'm sweating. This is insane; what am I doing? But I *have* to talk about this. I have to, or it'll burst its way out of my chest.

Evie rises from the bed, crosses the acreage of carpet between us, and stands on tiptoe to kiss my cheek. I flinch from her lips. I'm sweating so much inside my coat, I probably smell like the boys' locker room at school. She must sense my fear, my weakness. She takes my hand and guides me to sit beside her on the edge of the bed.

"Whatever it is, you can tell me," she says.

But it turns out I can't. Open shut, open shut goes my mouth, but no words come out. I'm a muppet with no actor to voice me. Instead, my fingers go to the pocket of my coat, produce a folded piece of paper and pass it over. She frowns, but she takes the paper and unfolds it.

She stares at my baby.

"Dubs!" she exclaims, mock-scandalized. "What *have* you done? Or rather, who have you done? Or rather, who's done you?" She laughs, genuinely delighted. Evie loves

a crisis, she always has. She's like a witch, only instead of the moon, the source of all her power is drama.

"Well, I'm…" She tails off, apparently too astonished to know what to say. At last she drops her hands to her sides and asks, "Who's the lucky fella?" I strain every sinew to detect any hint of sarcasm in the word *lucky*, but I can't.

"You don't know him." This part of my prepared story, at least, comes back. "He's at school."

"I know *some* of the people at your school," Evie contradicts me.

"You do?"

"Sure. You think you're the only Ricker at Granford High?" Evie's tone is innocent, but her brown eyes are like a terrier's trained on a stick before you throw it. A shiver runs through me.

"A … different school… I mean, he's still *at* school. But not my school. Parkborough." I seize on the Streatham grammar school on the assumption her Rickdom-based web will have fewer strands running through an all-boys' place.

"No," she says gently. "No, I don't know anyone there. What's his name?"

I *did* have a name prepared, I swear I did, but my mind is blanking on it. Evie's painting of Ryan dipping Nick back into a ballroom kiss is in the corner of my vision, and then all I can think of is the Dance Hall with its peeling murals of Fred Astaire and Ginger…

"Roger!" I blurt out.

Her brow wrinkles. "Oh, honey," she says. "That's unfortunate. Surname?"

I stumble on the question, and then it's too late and any answer I can think of will sound made up, so I just stare at her. She claps her hands together.

"You don't know!" she cries, with a little laugh. "Well, well, Cat. Never mind Wild White Horse, we should be calling you *Dark* Horse; you're going to have to change your handle. Have you told him? Is he a regular thing? He can't be, can he, if you don't know his whole name? What, was he just a passing house party hook-up?"

I stutter and choke, but my old familiar blush comes to my rescue, igniting in my cheeks, and she seems to take my inarticulacy as embarrassment rather than flat-out prevarication.

"Oh my, he was. Do you even have a way to get in touch with him?"

"We can communicate."

"Via smoke signals? Or carrier pigeon? Or—"

"I've got his number, Evie. Come on."

"But not his surname," she muses. "Interesting. Let me guess: he said he'd call, but never did?"

I manage a tiny nod, like I'm ashamed.

"Oh, kitty cat, don't look like *that*. It's not your fault he didn't know what he had with you. Want me to track him down for you? I imagine that Parkborough's digital records are, like most schools, about as secure as a wet paper bag, and there can't be *that* many kids there unfortunate enough to be called Roger. I could call him out for you. Find out

144

some stuff about him, remind him of his responsibilities."

My throat tightens to a pinprick, but I manage a smile. "Tempting, but before you go full Spanish Inquisition on him, I should probably give him a chance to step up first."

"You haven't told him?"

I shake my head.

"Have you told your mum?"

I don't answer.

"But you're telling me. I mean, I'm flattered, but ... *oooh*." She puts a tiny manicured paw to her lips. "Because you're trying to decide whether to keep it. And if you don't, then you don't have to tell him, or her, or anyone else."

She stands, smooths down her PJs – blue silk toucans tonight – and takes one of my hands in both of hers. "I'm so glad you came to me with this," she says. "Really, I am. I'm honoured."

Then she does something I've never seen her do before, not with me, not with anyone. She settles herself cross-legged on the carpet at my feet, and looks up at me.

"I know," she says. "I am serious now, Cat. I know right now the decision feels impossible: it's too big, too permanent, just too *much*. Will I get sick? What will Mum say? How will the kids at school react to my bump? How will I *pay* for it? And on and on..."

I stare down at her in astonishment; she smiles a little sadly.

"Believe it or not, I've been where you are myself a couple of times, years ago. I made the choices I made, and I don't regret them. But that doesn't mean that you need to choose what I did."

My blood is seething in my veins and there's a rock of panic lodged in my diaphragm. I bury my head in my hands, which means also burying it in hers. Evie's tiny, careful fingers find the pressure points on my skull and begin to massage the tension out of them.

"It's just … it's like someone's stuck my brain in a blender. How would I even *do* this?"

"The practicalities are important," she concedes. "And they will be tricky, no doubt. But honestly, dubs? I don't think that they are what will make the difference between the right call and the wrong one here. That's down to how you feel. Not how you think anyone else will feel: how *you* feel."

A hopeless laugh escapes me. "I can't even tell that, right now."

"Well, then, let's try and find out," she says. "Close your eyes." I obey, and I feel the mattress squish down as she kneels on the bed behind me. She resumes her massage of my brow and my temples. "Breathe in," she tells me gently, "and breathe out. Slowly. There's no rush here tonight, and no judgement. In," she repeats, "and out. In and out."

Gradually I feel the swelling of my lungs inside my chest slow to match the rhythm of her voice. I feel calmer, in the wrung-out way you do after a good cry.

"OK, now imagine yourself going to the doctor and saying you don't want to have the baby. There's an operation, but you're in and out in a day. After that you're pretty much back to life as you have it right now. The only difference is you've had this experience and remember it. How do you feel?"

I try to think about it. My hand steals to my abdomen, as though I could feel that second tiny heartbeat inside me, echoing mine. For some reason, I picture myself pulling out a plug from a wall socket, and the second heartbeat stops. My stomach flips over.

It's not real! I bark fiercely at myself. *It's just your hormones lying to you. It's not alive, not conscious, not yet. It's not like it can love you back; it…*

But then it's too late, because I've already thought the word, and it's the only word there is: *love.* Alive or not, conscious or not, rational or not, I love the tiny being growing inside me.

"Sick," I say. "I feel sick."

Evie's voice is suddenly alarmed. "If you're going to puke, do it in the bathroom; these are thousand thread-count sheets."

I laugh, and surprise myself at having to snort back tears. "Not like that; that's subsided, thank God. I mean, I just – I don't want to. But then when I try to think about actually having a *baby*, it's all so big and scary."

"I know. And no one can make this choice except you, but I'm seven years older than you and you're like my little sister, so let me give you some big sisterly advice, OK?"

I nod.

"It's OK that you're scared. In fact, it's mandatory that you're scared. If you aren't shitting yourself at the prospect of bringing another human being into the world and having it be utterly dependent on you for everything in its tiny, helpless life, then frankly, honey, you aren't tall enough to get on this ride, OK?"

"OK."

"But the fact that it's scary doesn't mean you shouldn't do it. It's scary because it's hard, and because it's change. But hard and change don't mean wrong. They just mean hard and change."

As she speaks, a little warm pool of certainty is growing in my solar plexus. "OK," I say again quietly.

"I don't know what the right thing for you to do is, dubs. But I can tell you this: I'm here for whatever you need. Always. If you choose not to have it, I'm here to talk you through it. If you keep it – you need money, you got it; you need child-care while you're at school and your mum's at work, well, I can…" For the first time she falters as she looks around her plush surroundings. "Well, I guess I can laminate everything in here until it's proof against the various fluids that babies emit, and learn to change nappies and stuff."

I feel such a warm rush of gratitude then that I cling to her.

"Thank you, thank you, E, you're a hero."

"Of course, Horse Girl." Evie squeezes my hand. "How could I do anything else? You're my ride or die. I tell you, when all this shit about Ryan and his secret girlfriend hit, I was a *mess*." She laughs. "Couldn't eat, couldn't sleep, couldn't put on make-up because I was so angry my hand was shaking."

If she feels me tense, she must take it for a tightening of the embrace, and she responds in kind.

"Almost no one else I know IRL would understand that, but you did. I called, you came. You were there for me. I'm here for you always." She squeezes me harder, and her arms are like steel.

"Always," she promises.

I do my level best to open my front door quietly, but the key in the lock still sounds like a gunshot in the quiet street. I wince, but it doesn't matter anyway, because when it swings open I see light spilling from the kitchen, and find Mum sitting at the table with a cup of that weird potpourri stuff she drinks steaming in front of her and a bottle of her latest insomnia prescription casting a long shadow over the wood in the downlight.

For a long moment, we just stare at each other. As always, I crack first.

"Trouble sleeping?" I ask, trying to sound casual.

"Indeed," she says, quite calmly. "I often have that, as you know. Of course, having a daughter with a penchant for sneaking out at two in the morning doesn't help."

She holds up the envelope with my scrawled note on that I stuck to the fridge:

> Just nipped out to Evie's. Please don't panic or call the police or anything. I'll be home soon.
> Cx

"Care to explain?"

I start, and then freeze. I realize I'm not ready. I'd expected to have all day tomorrow to get it in order and now it tries to rush up out of me at once in a tangle and it gets stuck in my throat.

Not that it winds up mattering, though, because before I've even got my mouth halfway open, Mum says, "You're pregnant."

I start violently, the shock shaking my voice free. "How … how did you…?"

"The question ought to be: how did I *not* know until now?" She shakes her head in quiet astonishment. "Sneaking around in the night. Weeks of projectile vomiting, odd appetites. Nervously announcing you're just off to the loo when you've never felt the need to keep me informed about that before. I assume you were peeing on a stick? No, a series of sticks; you wouldn't trust just one."

I flush but stay silent.

"Honestly, Catherine, you're a terrible liar, for which I've always been grateful." She barks a short, bitter laugh. "I'm going to have to get a refund on my maternal instincts – these are seriously defective."

She stands, rounds the table, and sweeps me up into a hug.

"You … you aren't angry?" I ask incredulously.

"Oh, Christ, love. I'm *furious*," she laughs. "At myself as much as anything. Trust me, tomorrow you and I will have an excruciating conversation about the precise mechanics of when and how this happened, and don't be alarmed if the house spontaneously combusts from my pure incandescent rage."

She strokes my hair. "But just because I'm angry, it doesn't mean I haven't been in your place. It doesn't mean I don't remember the fear. It doesn't mean that I haven't fantasized about what it would have been like to have a mother who was still alive when I found out I was pregnant. I've spent so much time when I should have been sleeping, staring at the ceiling, dreaming up every detail of how I wish she would have acted." Something warm spots onto the top of my head and I realize she's crying, although her voice gives no sign of it.

"I guess I'll just have to live up to that now." She takes a deep breath, as though drawing strength from the universe for that incredible feat. "Have you told the boy, whoever he is?"

"Not yet."

"No telling how he'll react, then. Although if he's as much of a prick as your father was, I might find a more constructive use for my fury than involuntary arson." She snorts, then stands back from me and wipes her own tears from my cheeks. *"Not yet,"* she says. "That means we're keeping it, then."

We. I never thought a single syllable could mean so much to me. I nod.

"Well," she says. "I could give you a whole screed about how hard it is to bring up a child on your own, and I was older than you are now when I had you, mind. I could try to scare you into reconsidering, but there'd be no point, because then you'd only ask me."

I don't follow. "Ask you what?"

"Whether any of that means I wish I hadn't kept you, and of course it doesn't. You're the best thing in my life, always have been." She smiles at me. "Even though you fray my nerves to tatters half the time. I can only hope my grandchild does the same to you." The smile fades. The bags under her eyes are bruise-blue in the unforgiving kitchen light. "It *will* be hard, though, Cat. No kidding."

"Hard doesn't mean wrong," I say softly, echoing Evie.

"No." She pulls me back into the hug. "No, it doesn't."

It's only later when, throwing away some orange peel, I find a long white stick with two blue lines on it in the kitchen bin, where I *definitely* didn't leave it. Mouth still full of orange segment, I perch on the kitchen counter and stare at it.

I wonder how long she's known, how long she's been waiting for me to tell her. I picture her up at night, ready to storm into my little room and demand an explanation, a culprit even, not knowing his face was plastered on the wall before her, but then holding herself back, bracing herself, preparing her little speech.

It doesn't mean that I haven't fantasized about what it would have been like to have a mother who was still alive when I found out I was pregnant... I guess I'll just have to live up to that now.

The little blue lines blur as my eyes fill with tears.

CHAPTER THIRTEEN

Amy

"What are you doing?"

I *just* manage to stifle the urge to clap my hands over the phone on the bed, which would pretty much guarantee giving it away. I look back over my shoulder. Polly stands in the doorway; my body will screen the handset from her as long as she doesn't come any closer. I pray she can't see the tension that's entered my back. She's ditched the down jacket, and has her sleeves rolled up under her bomb vest. Sweat's running down her forehead like damp down a cellar wall. She's panting, the evil little green light rising and falling with her breath.

"Nothing as hard as what you've been doing by the looks of things." I try to keep my voice light. "You look like you just ran a marathon uphill in a lead coat."

"Close enough." She beckons. "I need your help."

She turns without waiting for me to follow, and I finally

153

manage to exhale. I grab the phone, but then hesitate, frantically patting the sides of my funeral dress. Finally I hitch up the hem and tuck the phone into my underwear, where it digs *very* uncomfortably into my soft bits.

"If I get out of this," I mutter to myself, "I'm never again buying a single piece of clothing that doesn't have pockets. I don't give a shit if it's just a scarf. Dresses? I want pockets. Shorts? Pockets. New bra, madam? Only if I can smuggle half a kilo of cocaine and a corgi puppy in a zip-up compartment in one cup, thanks."

"Amy!" Polly calls back up the hall. Trying to walk like I don't have four inches of cold glass and metal shoved down my pants, I follow.

Before she got sick, Mum was always the last to bed. At the end of every evening, she would move through the house, stacking bowls and switching off lights, straightening piles of paper. "Making right", she called it. We used to joke that the only reason she never had another kid was that if there were more than two of us she wouldn't be able to decide whether to get us to stand in order of age or height. Still, even though neither Charlie nor I would ever admit it, we found the ritual comforting; it felt as essential as the setting of the sun. When she got too ill, I tried to take over, but despite my best efforts, little by little, entropy had its way.

No wonder Polly's sweating – she's just given entropy a *huge* helping hand.

The living room looks like a hurricane hit it. Papers lie

in drifts on the coffee table: tax letters, bank statements, invoices from Mum's old digital security business, all sagging over the edge like an incipient avalanche. Dad's box files sit upended on the floor. The old wooden bureau's doors flap open. The painting of Chicago's skyline has been yanked from its frame, the canvas slashed. Both Mum's and Dad's laptops sit open on the sofa cushions, and she doesn't seem to have had any problems with the passwords. She's even ripped the cushion covers and pulled out half the stuffing. Feathers are strewn over the carpet, like it's the site of some hideous poultry massacre.

"What did you do?" I ought to be angry at the destruction she's visited on my house, but instead it feels weirdly ... *satisfying*, like the violence was just sitting there, latent in my universe, and I'm almost jealous that she was the one who got to make it manifest.

She barely seems to hear me. "Nothing," she mutters. "Nothing. I've looked and I've looked and I've looked, but there's *nothing!*" The last word rises to a strangled shout. She stands in the middle of the devastation, but it's like she can't even see it. One hand kneads the fuzzy hair on the back of her head, the other holds Mum's phone. She scrolls feverishly, her eyes flicking back and forth.

"*Ach!*" She throws the handset down in disgust and it bounces off the carpet. I swallow, uncomfortably aware of its secret cousin chilling my privates.

"There's no time," she mutters, shooting a look at the blinded windows like she's waiting for something to come

155

crashing through them. "No time, no time, but it *must* be here, it *must*. She kept records of *everything*; she never threw *anything* away."

I look up at her sharply. "How do you know that?"

"What?"

"How do you know she never threw anything away?"

She snorts and points to where she's tipped the contents of the bureau drawer in a brightly coloured sprawl all over the floor. "It seems like a fair conclusion to draw from the fact that she kept forty years of old birthday cards." She licks her lips and her eyes flick around her.

"They're get-well cards," I say quietly.

"What?"

"Most of them are get-well cards."

She ignores me. With her cropped, streamlined head she looks like a cornered snake. "It must be here," she says again. "It *must*."

"What must?"

Her eyes land on me, and I can see white all the way around the iris. I take a step back from that gaze, and as I do, I feel the treacherous slide of metal against the skin in my nether regions. My stomach flips over as the elastic in my knickers gives just that bit too much and my illicit package slips half out. I drop into a semi-squat, just managing to catch the offending device on my thigh, aware all the time of Polly's jaundiced gaze on me.

"What was that?" she asks.

In a blast of panicked invention, I clutch my hands to

my lower abdomen, just managing to pin the top edge of the phone to myself through my dress.

"I've been locked in there for hours: I'm bursting."

Polly starts like I've slapped her. "Oh, good Lord, so you have!" She claps a hand to her forehead. "I'm so sorry! You must think I'm some kind of *kidnapper*!"

The irony of this statement – massive enough to stun a raging hippopotamus though it is – leaves her untouched. "Of course, of course you must go. Go!"

Her voice rises to a shout, and for a split second I'm tempted to relax my bladder and piss myself in front of her to see what she'd do – I wonder if she'd understand what kind of kidnapper she is *then* – but now she's got her arm around me, physically ushering me towards the downstairs loo, and I'm crabbing my way along the hallway, clutching the phone through my dress, a cartoon of incontinence, and feeling a genuine spasm in my bowel every time she threatens to brush up against the damn thing.

I bustle into the loo, slam the door, shoot the bolt and set my forehead against the wood. Trembling, I slip the phone from its hiding place. I listen out for her footsteps retreating back up the hallway, but they don't come. Fuck, is she still there? Ear pressed to the door just inches from my own, listening out for my *pee*?

I scramble to the toilet, throw the seat down as loudly as I can, bunch up my dress and pull down my underwear. I strain and think of the endless cups of tea people make you drink when you're bereaved. I think of waterfalls, and singing in the rain, but just when I need it, my bladder lets me down. *Come on, bladder,* I think desperately, *you and me, we've been places; landmark toilets on four continents,* but nope, it's a desert in there. I cast around. My eye lands on the tap – but no, idiot, that sounds nothing *like* the same. I need a tinkle, tinkle, tinkle, tinkle … the mouthwash!

There's a bottle of the bright blue liquid sat on the edge of the sink. Mum brushed her teeth downstairs for the last few weeks, and we must have left it here. I unscrew the cap and, thumb over the neck, I let a drizzle, then another, then a steady stream into the bowl between my legs. There's a creak from the door, and I imagine Polly easing back from the wood, satisfied.

I still don't hear her walking away, though. No matter how quietly I whisper, I don't dare risk a voice call. No 999 for me. I lift the phone, and—

Who on earth are they?

I haven't had a chance to look at the handset since it booted up. A cloud of blocky apps obscures the wallpaper, but when I sweep them aside, I see two pretty young girls in braids and braces, grinning right into the camera. They're definitely sisters, maybe even twins. I've never seen them before.

A stock photo, maybe? Perhaps it was just the wallpaper the thing came with and Mum had never bothered to change it; but generic wallpaper's normally sunsets or tropical frogs or some similarly bland picturesque shit, isn't it? Not actual, *real* people.

Banging on the door makes me jump. My mouthwash-slicked fingers slide over the phone and, for a heart-stopping moment, I almost drop it between my thighs into the toilet bowl.

"What are you doing in there?" Polly yells through the wood.

"What do you want? A lecture in biology?"

"I haven't heard anything in a while."

"I'm just waiting for the last few ... drops," I snap back. "After the last time you *locked me up*, I don't know when my next toilet break is coming, so I'm making the fucking most of it!"

That seems to shut her up, for the moment at least.

I eye the bolt on the toilet door. It's no thicker than a pencil, the screws holding it in already halfway out of the wall (another tiny chaos Mum would never have tolerated). Polly could easily have it open if she wanted. I don't have long.

My thumb hovers over the text icon, but in a momentary spasm of uselessness, I realize I don't know either of Dad or Charlie's numbers by heart. I stab the email app instead.

The inbox loads, and I just gawp. The screen is full of names I've never seen before.

Suzanne Jamieson

Zaha Patel

Nick Groomsman

I scroll down, glancing from the names to the subject lines:

▼ **Re: Bed Availability in G Ward**

▼ **Dosage limits for alprazolam in advanced cases**

I feel a little pang in my heart. Is that why Mum kept her secret phone? Was she maintaining a private dialogue with her doctors? Maybe she thought we were sugar-coating her diagnosis, and wanted it from them straight.

I think of her moving through the house each night, setting it in place for the coming day. How badly she needed order in her world; how much the chaos in her cells must have terrified her. This was as close as she could get to control.

I open the top email in her inbox. *Dear Ben,* it begins. I blink. Did I just happen to land on a misaddressed email first time out?

I tab back out and go to the next one. Dear Ben,

And the next one. Ben.

Hi Ben!

Dear Dr Smith.

Dear Ben...

I exit the email app and breathe out, staring at the two smiling girls. I was wrong. Mum didn't keep this phone to talk to her doctors. It wasn't *her* phone at all.

Mum nicked some doctor's phone?

My mind races. Is there some kind of app only doctors have, maybe? Something to do with prescriptions? Was she sneaking her own meds? But it's not like there were any drugs they refused to prescribe her; and anyway, where did she *get* the damned thing?

More banging on the door, and I start, sweat stippling my forehead.

"Are you all right in there, Amy?" Polly sounds genuinely concerned.

"Hang on!" I scramble, and yank the flush. "Just washing my hands."

I move to go back into the email app – I'll work this out later; for now, I need to get a message to Dad – but my fingers are trembling and I hit the wrong icon: not email, but the friendly green maps one that's right next to it. Swearing under my breath, I go to close out of it, but then I freeze. The little blue dot showing the location of the phone has appeared on screen, but the map it's overlaid on doesn't show our street. It doesn't even show London.

According to this phone's GPS, it's in a big house at a crossroads surrounded by fields in the middle of *Surrey*. Which is weird because, looking out of the narrow bathroom window, I can see a street sign with an SE22 postcode.

I stand frozen for several seconds, the slamming of my pulse in my ears drowning out the taps as I fight to make sense of it. Polly could be hammering the door down right now and I don't think I'd hear her.

I think back to the invoices strewn across the living room. Invoices for the digital security Mum sold, protection against the million and one dirty tricks someone on the Internet can use to sneak into your online life. I was wrong about her for the second time in as many minutes. This phone isn't stolen.

It's a *clone*.

The handset's here with me in East Dulwich, but the operating system it's reading from is loaded onto its twin in the leafy Home Counties.

I exhale. I'm shaking so hard, the map in front of me blurs. A voice swims up out of my memory.

She never threw anything *away*.

The tone Polly said that in – it wasn't a surmise based on the contents of our living room drawers – she said it like it was a long-recognized fact. She didn't guess it; she *knew* it.

She knew Mum.

Mum never threw anything away she thought might be useful one day, but she never *kept* anything without a purpose either. There are lots of reasons you might keep a secret phone; there are probably a few you'd keep a stolen one; but there's only one reason you'd keep a *cloned* one ...

... to spy on the owner of the original.

I shoot another glance at the bathroom window. It's too small to climb out of, but she's diligently sealed it with bomb tape anyway. Thorough, methodical, just like Mum.

I don't know what the connection is between my mother and the woman in a bomb vest waiting not so patiently for me to finish evacuating my bladder, but I'm starting to think that maybe, just *maybe* – despite her streamer's haircut – I'm not it.

There's a loose tile where the floor was cut to install the toilet. It's the work of a moment to turn off the phone – I don't know when I'll get a chance to charge it – jam it in the gap and replace the tile.

"OK." I set my shoulders, staring myself down in the mirror. "I'm coming out."

CHAPTER FOURTEEN

Cat

The dancers loom over me in their weathered finery. I gaze up at them on the pitted walls. On each of their corroded faces, I picture an expression that Ryan might wear: shocked, delighted, furious, betrayed.

Trembling, I rub my thumb over my phone. His reply still shows on the lock screen.

What's the rush? OK, I'll be there as soon as I can.

I'm not sure why I chose the Dance Hall. Maybe because, even now, it's the place I've felt closest to him, and I hope he feels the same. Right now, I feel like I need all the help I can get.

"I dreamed last night I rode a white horse, rode a white horse to the ocean," I sing softly, my breath ghosting out into the lamp light. *"And the white-crested waves, they crashed in the caves, but there was never a sound of you. So I rode to New York, but amid all the talk and the traffic and noise and*

commotion, the yellow cab drivers and far-war survivors they hadn't heard tell of you…"

I go on, my voice getting stronger and stronger with each verse. I vaguely wonder what passing strangers on the street outside would make of the mysterious pop ballad B-side coming out of the condemned building, but it feels better than the silence, so I keep singing.

"I rode my white horse to a secret city, the streets were paved with staaaars…"

"… but wherever I ride, I know I'll decide to stay wherever you are."

He's standing by the entrance, one hand still pushing the hoarding aside as his voice dies in the air. He smiles that perfect, curious smile and at once I'm ashamed I ever doubted him. Of course he's here; of course he'll stay with me. Ryan loves me.

I quirk an eyebrow at him. "You just happened to arrive on that line?"

"Well, you know, fifty per cent of everything is" – he pauses dramatically for long enough to cross the rubble-strewn floor and kiss me – "timing."

I laugh. "Which means you've been waiting out there since the third verse, waiting for your cue." *Listening to me sing,* I think, but don't say. I feel a hot pinprick in each cheek at the thought, but it's not unpleasant.

"Middle of the second, but not because I wanted to make a dramatic entrance. I just like listening to you. Besides, in this place, it felt appropriate."

"Why in this place?"

"Look down."

I do. At first all I see is dust, small stones and mouse droppings, but then I notice the way the street lamp glow, peeping in through the manifold holes in the roof, speckles the floor with points of light.

The streets were paved with stars...

"'White Horses' is about this place?" I ask, agog. "*This* is your secret city?"

He beams at me, and suddenly I feel so close to him, knowing that this place, so precious to us both, is the foundation of my favourite song.

"What's the emergency?" he asks, breathing on his hands and rubbing them. I guess it's cold, but I can't feel it. You could sear steak on my forehead right now – I suppose that's the baby. That's every second thought in my head now – *I suppose it's the baby.* Knees hurt: *baby*, a bit dizzy: *baby*, funny gurgle in my abdomen: *baby.* I listen to my body like a little girl listens to an old house she's been told is haunted, attributing every creak and shudder to the mysterious presence growing inside me.

"If this is a pretext for a late-night hook-up," he says as he wraps his arms around my waist, "then don't get me wrong, I applaud the thought, but we've got a morning TV slot tomorrow, and the bags under my eyes look like a pair of fat dudes in hammocks as it is, so..."

"I know," I stammer, "I'm ... I ... I'm sorry, I just..." My pulse is hammering hard, and that makes me think of the

166

baby's even faster heartbeat; and for a split second, against all reason, I think he'll hear it, that my secret will give itself away before I can get the words out.

"Hey, hey, what's wrong?" He tilts my chin up and gently presses his lips to mine until I stop shaking.

"I'm so hot it's a wonder I haven't set you on fire," I mutter.

He laughs. "Can I get a judge's ruling on that? Ding! Unanimously agreed. And extra points for the confidence." He pulls himself in closer. "That's a turn-on."

"No, I mean *physically* hot."

"So do I."

"I mean, like, *thermodynamically*. I suppose it's the baby—"

We both freeze, me with my mouth still shaping the word so it trails out *babeeeeh*, into the empty air.

I'm the first to recover the power of speech ... ish. "I didn't mean to ... that wasn't... It just came out... I..."

I had a super complex triple-backflip dive planned into this conversation, and instead I just belly-flopped because I misjudged the length of the board. Oh well, I'm in it now. He's still gaping at me like he's been put on pause, so I grab his hand and lurch awkwardly into the silence.

"I ... I am. I'm pregnant. It's been almost three months but I only found out yesterday. And yes, I'm scared and a little freaked out, but I'm also happy." I breathe out long and slowly.

He opens his mouth, but before he can speak, I say, "And I'm keeping it."

He blinks. His mouth is still open. He shuts it again.

"Ryan?"

"Yeah?"

"You know you didn't say any actual words just then, right?"

"Yeah." He blinks again and shakes his head like he's just waking up. "Yeah, sorry. I, uh, three *months*? How is that even possible?"

"Well, when, um, a mummy bear and a daddy bear—"

"I *mean*, how did you not know?"

I shrug. "It's not like I've ever done this before. I had a bunch of things that are symptoms of pregnancy but they're also symptoms of, like, six hundred and fifty-seven other things I found on WebMD."

"I just figured you'd *know*, like in your gut."

"I don't have some earth-magic mystic insight into the contents of my uterus, Ry. I find out what's going on in my body the same way you do – a bunch of vague and confusing signals, a dollop of wishful thinking and an eventual trip to the doctor."

"But you're sure."

"I've had a scan. I saw both feet. Yes, I'm sure."

He winces. "I mean … you're sure about keeping it."

A knot ties itself in my gut. "Yes," I say. I'm trembling, but I make my voice firm.

"'Cause you're—" And thank God, thank God, *thank God*, he catches himself. "I mean, *we're* pretty young."

I tighten my grip on his hand. "I'm old enough to know what I want."

He swallows hard. In his eyes I can see him going through the same process I did, flipping down possible futures like faces on a game of Guess Who. I watch him anxiously, hoping he'll like the one that's left. He seems to study me back, as though trying to gauge my thoughts. His eyes dart from my face to my stomach to my hands and back again. He looks around at his secret city, closes his eyes, and breathes out. He looks at me for a long time. I smile at him, trying not to let my desperation show.

"Well," he says, "I think it's great."

"You … do?"

"Yeah! I mean, you know I've always wanted to be a dad, right?"

I actually didn't know that. Before I came, I pored over his last year of interviews like they were the entrails of a chicken, trying to divine some sense of how he might react. He was asked, of course, about his plans for a family, for a future, but all we got was a vague "Right now I'm focused on the music" robo-response.

"I mean," he goes on, "it's a lot to take in, of course, but…" He gives me the smile I know from seventeen music videos, five album covers and one point nine bajillion magazine spreads. "We're going to have a baby."

Abandoning all pretence at coolness or control, I fly at him and hang off his neck, kissing his cheeks and his forehead and then finding his lips and melting into them.

When, at last, I come up for air, I ask, "How should we tell people?"

169

He looks at me sharply. "You want to go public now?"

"Don't you?"

He hesitates. "Yeah, yeah, of course I do, but … it'll be carnage. The full-on Cirque du Pap, every inch of your life, every minute of your day. I want to spare you that if I can."

"And can you?"

He sucks in air through his teeth and thinks about it. "No."

OK, that's blunt. He must see my expression, because he rushes to reassure me.

"But we can *ease* it, together, maybe. If we're careful. Besides, you were always as keen as I was to keep this quiet."

Only because I didn't want my head decorating the spikes on Evie's fancy wrought-iron bedstead, I think, and my stomach hollows out a little at the thought of her face. My brain races away, composing the tweets and notes and updates, imagining the digital munitions that I have no doubt are heading my way. Still, avoiding that is just one of the options I don't have any more.

I guess that's the baby.

"I don't think quiet is an option, Ry. I've only seen it on TV so far, but from what I understand childbirth is noisy. And messy."

He makes a face. "We've got time before that."

"Six months," I say. "Three at the most until I start to look like I swallowed a VW Beetle, which might prompt a question or two from my more inquisitive friends."

"OK." He starts to pace, the rubble on the old music

hall floor cracking under his heels. "OK. Leave it with me, OK? We've got … people who do this kind of thing for a living."

"Have your babies?"

"Tell the press about them."

"Your babies? You've got enough love children out there that it's an *industry*?" I'm teasing him, still glowing with his affirmation *we're going to have a baby*. But he doesn't laugh.

"I *mean*, these people help us with sensitive news, so we can control the story when one of us makes a…" He tails off, not wanting to say *mistake*. But I know that's what he was going to say, and even though I know it's the truth (and it's not like it was deliberate on my part either) it still feels like a little punch in the stomach.

He sees my reaction and comes back to me, cupping my head in his hands. "I love you, OK? Trust me. Do you trust me?"

I look deep into eyes that, just six months ago, I never would have believed would look back into mine.

"Of course I do."

"It makes a huge difference, how this kind of thing breaks. And our guys, they're the best at making sure it happens the right way. So please, *please, Cat*, don't tell anyone. Leave it up to me."

His eyes are so wide and earnest and worried for me that I can't help but nod.

"Soon, though, right? As secrets go, this is a big one to keep, and it's getting bigger by the day."

"I'll call them about it this week," he promises, and kisses me, as though sealing my silence with his lips.

My phone buzzes in my coat pocket. I dig it out and look at it over his shoulder. It's from Evie. I slide the message open and suddenly feel like the inside of my stomach has iced over. This time I don't think it's the baby.

The message is one word – Explain – and a link. The URL says it's to *The Sun*'s website. Fear parches my throat, but there's nothing for it. I thumb the link.

IS THIS THE VOICE OF RYAN'S SECRET SQUEEZE?

Below it is an embed of Ryan's disastrous parkour video; it links back to YouTube, which is weird, because I'm sure he originally posted it to his Instagram.

"Ry?"

"Yes, babes?"

"You know when you posted that video of you doing parkour to your Instagram?"

"Yeah?" He's barely listening. He's squatting on the rubble, knocking a pair of small stones together, like a bored toddler pretending he's making two dolls fight.

"When you wiped off the audio, did you edit it out of the clip on your phone before you posted it?"

He frowns. "What? No, I never bother with that; I just toggle the sound off on Insta."

Wordlessly, I pass my phone down to him. I've centred

the screen on the relevant passage.

> Now, an anonymous Instagram employee
> calling themselves only "A Fan" claims to
> have posted the video with the original
> sound restored.

A crackling echo tells me that Ryan's hit *play*. I hear Ryan's running footsteps, his grunts of effort as he springs from wall to wall down the stairwell, his yelp of surprise as he misses his handhold, and then…

"RYAN!"

My voice, made tinny by the phone speaker, but unmistakably mine, screaming his name. A name Evie's heard me scream a thousand times before.

> Explain.

It feels like the world's tipping, and I have to sit down. I hunch over amid the dust and the mouse crap. Ryan squats anxiously in front of me. It takes me four goes to find my voice.

"You might," I say hoarsely, "have to call your people a bit sooner than you thought."

CHAPTER FIFTEEN

Amy

"What's it like?" Charlie asked. His face was turned up towards me, the vulnerability of it only emphasized by his closed eyes.

"You could try it, and find out," I offered, gently stroking the mascara brush down his lashes.

"And sacrifice all this?" He put his hand to his hair. It was his time for wearing it long like the singer of that gothy band whose riffs shook the walls when I was trying to do my homework.

"You could get an undercut."

"Unlikely. Besides, I don't need to try it; you can explain it to me."

"It's tough to describe."

"I believe in you."

"It's … I guess the way I'd put it is, it's safe."

"Compared with what?" Charlie sounded amused. "Or

do you mean you've been streaming off a bunch of base jumpers rather than risking the real thing?"

"No, I mean it's safe because it's intimate, but there's no chance of rejection. You don't have to worry that whoever you follow is being two-faced, or trying to spare your feelings. It's getting out of yourself, seeing the world through their eyes; it's knowing the person you're streaming off is being completely open and honest with you. It's ... *trust*, I guess. I sometimes have difficulty with that."

He laughed.

"What?"

"Keep an eye on the sea," he said. "If we see a bunch of tidal waves it'll be because the moon got shunted out of its orbit by the weight of that understatement."

"Oi!" I cuffed the air over his head.

"Come on, Ame. I could tell you the sky was blue and you'd pull out a Dulux chart to check."

"Well." I set aside the mascara and grabbed the eyeshadow. "You could use a little more scepticism yourself, kiddo. Then maybe you wouldn't have let me make you up like a drunken clown."

His eyes snapped open and he threw up his hands to guard his face from the brush.

"Kidding! I'm kidding. You're going to look exactly like the goth prince your mopey shoegazing maiden desires."

He looked uncertain for a moment, then settled back in the chair, closed his eyes again, and his smile returned. I marvelled. He really did trust the whole world, which was astonishing given that the world was busy kicking him in every soft place it could fit its steel-toe capped boot.

"Who's the last person you did it with?" he asked.

"I'm not sure that's a question I'm comfortable with my kid brother asking me."

He slapped my arm. "You know what I mean. The last person you streamed off. Some rich kid? Some model?"

"Why? Because, fug that I am, I desperately want to know how it feels to be beautiful?" I asked huffily.

"Summon up all the fake offence you like; it's not going to change the question."

I sighed. "A girl I found on a forum. Her dad died about two years ago."

"Jesus," he muttered. "I would have thought you'd go for someone who worked at a petting zoo or something."

"Why? If I want to look at cute animals, I can do that myself. The Internet is plentifully supplied."

He didn't voice the obvious reply: that if I waited a few months, I'd be able to feel bereavement for myself too. Instead, he asked the question *I* would've asked. The only question that mattered.

"Is it always like this?" The need in his voice was a cramp in my heart muscle. "Does it get any better?"

Just for an instant, I considered lying to him, putting all that trust to good use.

"Not for her it hasn't yet, no," I admitted. "She warned me as much before we linked up."

"Then, why?"

I weighed the question for a while before answering. "To know this is normal. To know I'm not weak for being this scared."

He sighed, his breath warm against the inside of my wrist. "I hate what they say about you, you know."

That morning's consignment of abuse flashed briefly up from my memory: there'd been a minor storm when a bunch of dickhead dads complained I was turning their sons into cucks (*cuck* is a fantastically useful word online; it flags anyone who uses it as instantly ignorable).

After that, a handful of concern-trolling anons had shriekingly accused me of ending society as we know it, and linked me to an article about four boys who'd wound up in hospital after hacking their safety settings and streaming for thirty-six hours straight without any sleep or food except Doritos. Apparently they'd only followed what we call "bad news bear" accounts – reporter embeds from war zones, frothing conspiracy theorists, and a couple of the more intense emo accounts, including mine. Heartstream's official take was that the safety limits were there for a reason, and blaming them was like blaming hand gel for an alcoholic drinking it. I wasn't so sure, and reading the report made an anxious little hole form in my gut. Still, for every story like that one, there were a hundred DMs from followers telling me they didn't feel alone any more, so what was I supposed to do?

Mum, Dad, even Heartstream Inc., begged me not to engage. "It's not your problem," they told me. To which

I could only gape at them. How could I make them understand? What on earth was the point of all this, all this communication, all this connection, all this *feeling*, if, sometimes at least, I didn't make it my problem?

"Into every life a little rain must fall," Mum had said, the day of her diagnosis, "and sometimes more than a little." And now the Internet can pipe every drop into your front room. I guess some people need the irrigation; others, if they're not careful, might drown.

"I asked you not to read my mentions, kiddo," I told Charlie.

"I know, but it makes me so *angry*. You're the strongest person I know."

It was bizarre, how I could spend hours a day hooked into the most intimate emotions of strangers, but a splash of in-person earnestness from my little bro was enough to light a forest fire behind my cheeks.

"All done," I said hurriedly. "Open your eyes."

He blinked and stared into the mirror I held up.

"Like it?"

He squealed in what I hoped was delight. "I look like a zombie! A totally miserable zombie!"

"Who's just dropped their brain-flavoured ice-cream cone, no less!"

"It's perfect!" He hugged me. I squeezed him back. The chains attached to his PVC trousers jingled.

"I'm not the only one getting shit for being myself in public right now," I said anxiously. "You know those dumb pricks in your year will lay into you for walking around school like this. I'll have your back, but when I'm in lessons…" I left it hanging.

"I know, but they're always going to find something to give me shit for. Might as well look awesome when they do."

He swallowed, but under the white make-up I saw his little jaw set. I squeezed his shoulder. "Know what, Chucklemonster? I reckon the strongest person you know might be a little closer to home."

I ease the bathroom door open. Polly folds her arms.

"You OK?" she asks.

"Tiny bladder," I say. "Shrinks even more when I'm scared."

She looks awkward. For a woman whose entire MO at this point has been threatening me, she really doesn't seem to like being reminded of it. "All better?"

I nod.

"Good."

She leads me back into the devastated living room. She kicks up clouds of cushion feathers like a small child wading into a snowdrift.

"Polly…"

She stiffens at the name, and I realize it's the first time I've used it.

"Yes, Amy?"

"How did you know my mum?"

She licks her lips. "We met through mutual friends.

179

I once thought she had the answer to a problem I had. But it turned out I didn't know her as well as I thought. I came here to try to get to know her better."

I cock an eyebrow. "You just missed her."

"Oh, I don't know about that." She chews a hollow out of one cheek and perches herself on an arm of the savaged sofa. "They used to say the eyes were the window to the soul, did you know that? Of course, we can hardly gaze into your dear mother's now, but fortunately" – she bends and regathers Mum's phone from where she threw it on the floor – "it's the *phone*, not the eyes, that's the window to the soul these days."

I just stare at her.

"Come on, think about it: an opening into an immortal, indelible trace of yourself, left in the ether – what fits the description better than this?"

"Your phone can tell you things about a person they can't remember," I concede. "Things they never knew, or at least never admitted to themselves."

She affirms this with a shake of the handset. "And now, with the advent of Heartstream, it's all got even more sepulchral. You of all people know that."

I don't answer, but it's true; anyone who manages to erase my Internet footprint after I die will probably have a valid claim to being an exorcist.

"The thing is, Amy," – and she fixes me suddenly with her doll-like eyes – "I've looked and I've looked and I've looked, not just through her phone, but her laptop, her papers, even her bloody cushion stuffing, for your Mum's soul, and you know what? *She didn't have one!*"

I want to bolt. Tape or no tape, bomb or no bomb, it's almost more than I can bear to stand there and hold her gaze.

"That's why you came here, isn't it?" I ask. "Not to meet me, but to find something of Mum's?"

And as fast as it came the anger in her stare is gone, like a match blown out. She purses her lips, tilts her head in allowance. "Meeting you is a *big* side benefit, but I confess if that was all I'd wanted, I wouldn't have bothered with the waistcoat." She plucks at the bomb vest.

"So why *did* you need to wear that?" I ask, when I've managed to stifle my urge to dive behind the sofa. "Because I'm not going to lie, if you want to be my friend like you keep saying you do, that is a weird way to get me to like you."

A smile flickers over her lips. "I told you, I needed time, time inside your house, which isn't a thing a girl in your position, quite sensibly, is inclined to give a mad-looking stranger. I knew what I'm looking for would be too well hidden to find if I turned up pretending to be a meter reader or some such. So I went all in, as it were."

"And what *are* you looking for?"

"I wish I could tell you," she says. "I really do, but there's simply no way you'd believe me. And that would ruin everything between us."

More than holding me at gunpoint and bomb-point and smashing up my house and telling me to my face that my

181

just-dead mother didn't have a soul? I want to ask, but, judging from the earnest expression on Polly's face, yes, it really would ruin things between us more than that.

"Try me, I might surprise—"

I cut off in mid-sentence. I've more or less tuned out the rumble of vehicles and the hubbub of voices from the street outside, but all at once it seems to grow louder. Somewhere overhead, a helicopter's blades hack the air.

"Back away from the building!" The voice is so loud it shakes the glass in the blinded windows. Its emotion is sapped by the electronics of the loudhailer, but I can still make out the desperation in it. *"For your own safety, please disperse."*

Polly wheels and plunges for the bay window. She parts the venetian blinds and I see her face go pale. She fumbles for the back pocket of her jeans, pulls out my phone and thrusts it towards me.

"Call them!" she demands. "Tell them to get back!"

Tell who to get back?

Taking the phone into my hand feels like having a missing organ returned to me. I press my thumb to the home button, and the lock screen vanishes. The Heartstream icon catches my eye – *holy shit…*

570,544 notifications.

I open the app. There are too many – far, far too many – to read, but that's OK, because they all seem to be a variation on the same theme. One message sits at the very top, shared over forty thousand times, along with my address.

We're coming for you, Ame.

I lower the phone. Polly doesn't try to stop me as I approach the window. I put my finger and thumb to the blinds beside hers, prise them apart and press my eye to the gap, and actually, physically gasp.

There's an *army* of them.

Shaved heads, crow T-shirts, rank upon rank, crammed in on the other side of the street, pushing and jostling like a living wave behind the police cordon. There were hundreds of them at the funeral; there must be *thousands* of them here now. All here for me. All here to protect *me*.

I feel a rush of love for them.

My patches go warm, even crackle faintly, working under the load of transmitting the intensity of my emotion. An instant later a cheer goes up across the street. Out of the corner of my eye I see Polly blanch.

A blur of movement drags my attention to the right, down the road. Neon police tape flashes under street lights, flapping ragged, torn by the press of bodies surging forward. The cops try to push them back, but they came here for a hostage situation, not crowd control. They're not wearing riot gear, just high-vis anoraks, and there are far, far too few of them.

"Disperse! For your own safety, get back!"

But nobody's listening to loudhailer man. Beside me, Polly's face is pinched in fear. Her hand twitches towards the box at the collar of her bomb vest, but then goes back down again.

"There are so many," she murmurs. She sounds horrified. "So many."

The plastic bottles of explosive seem to press themselves out of the vest at me. Six of them; I remember the shock in the bomb disposal officer's voice when I gave him that number. *Enough explosive to level Big Ben,* Polly had said. Across the street, the crowd pushes closer. Forty, now maybe only thirty metres away. Now twenty-five, now twenty…

Closer. Closer. All those people who've come for me. Who are streaming off *me*. Far too late, I duck my head back to my phone, trying to type out a message to them to *get back*, but my fingers are too slick with sweat and the screen doesn't answer.

A shout, louder than the others, carries through the glass, and my head jerks up. A policeman stumbles; my stomach lurches as his neon-yellow vest is obscured by trampling feet. With a roar of triumph, the crowd surges forward.

Polly puts her hands to her vest.

CHAPTER SIXTEEN

Cat

It happened as fast as a change in the tide. One moment the path to our front door was clear, the next, the narrow box of our front garden was packed with men in T-shirts and hoodies with massive cameras hanging around their necks. The boldest, a balding white guy whose eyes had a faint yellow cast, like they'd been poached in leftover cooking fat, walked right up to the front door and just leaned on the bell for about five minutes until I eventually scrambled downstairs and snatched the batteries out of the ringer. The shrill insistence of the buzzer was like a drill breaking into my life.

Now they just mill around outside, staring at their phones, smoking, littering our path with cigarette butts like they're at a house party that's spilled out into the street. They've only been here for about fifteen minutes, but there's an aura of bored professionalism around every one of them that says they're prepared to wait for as long as it takes.

I shift my weight from foot to foot, still not used to the change in balance caused by my ever-expanding womb. Every other second, I take a step towards the door, ready to yank it open and scream at them to get away, to beat them back like they're a cloud of flies buzzing over the corpse of my privacy. Every other second, I hesitate, terrified of exposing myself.

Instead, I haul myself back up the stairs and, easing the curtain away from the window, I snap a picture of the paps on my phone. I text it to Evie. Is this you??? I ask.

I haven't heard from her since her one-word demand for an explanation, the night the video broke with my voice on it. I never replied to her, obviously. What could I say? And she didn't ask again.

Of course, if Evie wanted to dox me, she could have done it that night. Why wait four months? Teenage Petrolhead was always an instant gratification kind of girl. "I thought revenge was a dish best served cold?" I asked her once, when she was laying into some Ricker turned sceptic who'd betrayed us. She looked at me, amused. "Don't worry, there'll be leftovers."

I stare at my phone until the screen goes dark, but no reply comes. Maybe it wasn't her. What was it she said? *You're not the only Ricker at Granford High.* Maybe one of the other girls heard the tape and put two and two together.

My thumb hovers over the RickResource icon, but I don't press down. If I *have* been doxed, I'm not sure I can face what I'll find there. Instead I open my messages and text the photo of the paps to Ryan. Looks like we're both famous now, I write, adding a worried emoji face. You're the expert, what do I do?

To my borderline astonishment, his reply swoops in immediately, and its brusqueness makes me cold.

Do nothing. Say nothing. Stay indoors.

Jesus, Ry, I text back.

Don't let them see you.

That's it. The exchange might be as brief as a series of drill sergeant barks, but it's the most I've had out of him in a fortnight. I flick back up the message chain. Rereading it is like probing a sore tooth with my tongue.

For one thing, the ratio just *looks* bad. Three sky-blue boxes for every grey one, the little seam of anxiety in them growing more and more obvious with each.

Hiya, it's been about a week. Just wondering if you'd had a chance to talk to your guys yet.

Hey, Ry, hope all good in Tokyo. Just checking in. Bump's definitely bumping now. Wondered if we were any closer to a plan?

'Allo, me again. I know you're crazy busy with the tour and all, but time's ticking on and junior's making me

look more and more like a minivan
with each passing day. The girls
at school all want to know who the
father is, and it would be a real relief
to know when I can tell them...

I wince at the winsomeness of *the girls at school all want to know who the father is.* I made it sound like we were all flocking together eagerly gossiping like something out of *Grease.* In reality it's more like a maths lesson with Mrs Chen asking, "As x tends towards zero, what tends towards infinity?" and Lauren Cole answering: "Is it the number of men who've been in Cat's pants, miss?" With everyone laughing, and Mrs Chen just sternly eyeing my bump and not saying anything, like I deserved it.

A little spider of anger crawls up into my throat. I cannot *wait* to rub all of their spiteful faces in the fact that the number of men is *one*, and he's been *Elle*'s sexiest man alive for two years running.

Ryan's replies always come when I most need them, when my feet feel ready to fall off just from the short walk home from school, or when I'm lurching around in the morning like a concussed foal because it took me three quarters of the night to find a comfortable position to sleep in. I treasure them, and reread them, again and again, crouching over my phone screen in the dark of my bedroom like its light is a candle flame, a source of warmth as well as light.

Every message from him reassures me. His media guy was off sick, but he's back now. We're almost there, just fixing the final details. Something's come up and they need to rethink, but it'll be fine. The time difference is making it tricky while they're in Asia, but he'll call him to finalize as soon as he's back. Every message ends the same way.

I love you. I can't wait to meet our baby.

Our baby. I wonder if he knows how every time I read those words, it feels like a sip of a hot drink on a freezing night.

Of course, my belly is expanding so fast it's like it has plans to conquer Western Europe, so he's likely to get his wish soon enough.

It's not that fast, a nagging voice in me keeps pointing out. *It's been four months, and he still hasn't gone public with it.*

He will, I keep pushing back. He has to, because soon either word or the baby will get out, and if it's the latter then the news will follow anyhow.

A hubbub outside drags my attention off the phone screen.

"Mrs Canczuk! Mrs Canczuk! Laurie!"

"Who the hell are all of you?"

I peek through the curtain. Mum's struggling up the path, trying to manoeuvre the bulging Tesco bags around the paps. They're not making it easy for her.

"Mrs Canczuk, is your daughter dating Ryan Richards?"

"Get away from my front door, you pack of hyenas!"

"Is it true they've been meeting in secret for months?"

"I'll tell you what's true: if you don't get off my property and leave my daughter the hell alone, you'll find that camera in a very surprising place; and no, I don't care what turd rag you work for."

The pap she's talking to, by coincidence the man with greasy-spoon eyes who leaned on the doorbell, makes no effort to get out of her way. He's sneering. Mum sighs. She puts the shopping down, careful not to disturb the eggs sitting on top of the right-hand bag. Then she straightens up and slowly, deliberately, ties her hair back, before taking a step so that she's less than a foot from Mr Eyeball Grease.

"I know what you're thinking," she says, loud enough for me and all the paps in the little front garden to hear. "I'm a big tough man, and it's kind of adorable that this little woman is threatening me. What's more, I've faced down the meanest professional security the rich and famous can hire – what could I possibly have to fear from a middle-aged insurance saleswoman from Dorking?"

Mr Eyeball Grease is still grinning, but there's a glimmer on his pate that might be sweat. I don't blame him, because that sweet, reasonable tone Mum is using is a sign that the gates of hell are hanging off their hinges.

"But," Mum goes on, "there are a few things you haven't considered." She counts them off on her fingers. "One: at least *half* of the training those professional crushers you're so proud of going head to head with get is actually in how *not to hurt you too badly*. It's their job, after all, and they're going to do a lot of enforcing; they don't want to be getting sued all the time.

"Two." The greasy eyeballs flick nervously towards Mum's hand as a second finger extends. "While I might only go once a week on Tuesdays, I have been doing Krav Maga for long enough to get my black belt. No training in how not to hurt people unfortunately, just in how to dislocate joints and break bones. You don't want to *know* what they teach us to do with genitals.

"Three." The final finger extends and then the hand falls like a guillotine blade. Mum closes the remaining distance fast. Eyeball Grease visibly flinches. "It's not my boss I'm protecting; it's my daughter," she hisses at him. "Which means if you try to test me on this, *I will fucking own you.*"

Eyeball Grease isn't smiling any more. He tries to back away from Mum and tips backwards into our rose bush. He scrambles up, his face webbed with scratches. She watches him impassively as he edges his way around her.

I exhale slowly, feeling my heartbeat gradually calm. My window's open a crack at the bottom, so I hear him quite clearly when he mutters, "Whatever. Your little slut's time is coming, whatever you do."

Mum's expression doesn't change, but she moves like a snake. She seizes the pap's wrist and spins it into a lock against his back, forcing him to his knees with a sound like a kicked pig. With her free hand she snatches up his heavy camera by the lens and raises it like she's going to bring it down on his head.

The air fills with the buzzing clicks of shutters snapping. Mum stands frozen with every lens levelled on her like a gun barrel firing over and over again. She looks confused now, and frightened, and I can see that photo going up all over the Internet and no no no no NO!

Before I know it I'm at the front door, wrestling with the latch, dragging it open, screaming "LEAVE HER ALONE!" at the very top of my lungs.

There's a single second of shocked silence, and then the click storm of cameras returns, redoubled, like a rainstorm repelled by a gust of wind before flying back with full force, and this time they're all aimed at me. Mum's forgotten. Even Eyeball Grease has somehow retrieved his camera and is frantically snapping.

"Cat!" they yell. "Cat Cat Cat Cat Cat Cat Cat!" I'm drenched in my own name.

"Cat, is it true you're dating Ryan Richards?"

I just gaze back at them, dumbstruck. Mum runs to me, trying to herd me back inside, but I'm rooted to the spot.

One of them, a girl in a headscarf, barely older than me, walks right up to me and takes a photo of my bump right under Mum's arm.

"Cat! How far along are you?"

"Cat! Is Ryan the father?"

Don't answer, I think. *Don't answer. He said not to speak to them.* But all of the nerves and frustration and the months and months of waiting and hiding break in me like a wave.

"Why don't you ask him?" I say.

CHAPTER SEVENTEEN

Amy

It happens in the space of two ragged breaths.

Suddenly unrestrained, the mass of bodies boils out over the road. One figure, a muscly boy in a crow T-shirt, outpaces the rest. His eyes gleam in the street lights. He crouches without breaking step, gathers something from the road: a chunk of broken asphalt. He's making straight for this window, for me. I can taste my own fear in my throat as my voice rises uselessly to meet him.

"Stop!"

I blink and another figure has separated itself from the crowd. Shaved head down, arms pumping. I can't see his face, but I don't need to. I did up the cufflinks on the white shirt he's wearing this morning.

Charlie.

I've never seen him move so fast. He looks up and his face is dark with effort. He's arrowing towards the boy at the front of the crowd. I can feel his desperation just by looking at him. I see his lips shape the words as he bellows.

"DON'T TOUCH THE WINDOW!"

The *thud-thud-thud* of the helicopter chops time into pieces. Shaved-headed streamers charge the house, their white T-shirts like the crest of a wave. The trampled policeman's back on his feet, his face bloody. He looks like a horror film extra. He's waving his arms, yelling, but not at the muscly boy, not at my brother either, but at another policeman, the one in the flak jacket rising to his feet on the bonnet of his patrol car with a look of panic on his face, lifting a rifle to his shoulder.

Ten metres, nine, eight, the muscly boy jumps the low wall; he's so close now I can hear his boots on the gravel through the glass. There's no thought at all on his face. Charlie's just behind, one hand outstretched almost close enough to snare the boy's crow T-shirt.

"STOP!" I scream, but whether it's to my follower, my brother or the man with the gun, in that moment, I can't tell.

Three metres, two metres. I'm looking the boy dead in the eye. In the window, the ghost of my own reflection surrounds him. His arm coils back, the chunk of road clenched in his fist.

The shot sounds like the world breaking in half.

The glass in front of me dissolves into a blizzard. Both Charlie and the boy in black fall. I jump between them and Polly, instinctively trying to make myself as big as I can, trying hopelessly to shield my brother from the blast I know is coming.

The floor slams into my body like a train, shoving the air out of me. Prickles run over my face, then heat. Not the piercing heat of fire, but the gentle warm throb of blood. Shaking, I push myself to my knees. Fragments of glass glitter on the carpet in front of me like tiny rubies. Judging by the searing sensation in my cheek, some are embedded in my face.

No blast, I think, frantically. *There was no blast.*

An arm curls around my throat and locks in place. My head is wrestled back hard, and I see the window. The middle of it – all but a few fragments of glass – is gone; the cold night wind rushes in and stings my slashed cheek, but the *frame,* and the precious, vicious silver tape that seals it, is undisturbed. Polly hauls on my neck and I feel the unexploded bottles on her vest an instant before the cold circle of her gun barrel presses into my head.

Charlie, I think frantically. *Where's Charlie?*

I try to struggle, but her skinny arm might as well be an iron bar. The patches on the back of my head are burning hot under the load of my fear. She takes the gun from my head, points it over my shoulder and fires. It's like someone slamming a knitting needle into my ear.

"*GET BACK!*" She yells it, but I can barely hear her. Her order is redundant. The tight-packed mass of bodies has broken. Figures in crow T-shirts scramble in all directions, mouths working like they're screaming, wrestling and

195

tangling and pushing each other, panicked by the shots, their terror amplified by my own.

The shots. Charlie. Where's Charlie?

I try to say the words but all I hear is a static whine, like a TV that's just been switched off. My heart trips in my chest. My eye falls on the shattered window. The few bits of glass still clinging to the frame are clear at the top, but at the bottom they're red, like bloodied fangs.

"CHARLIE!" I shriek it loud enough this time that I *can* hear it, loud enough to tear my throat. I slam my head backwards and feel a crunch as something meaty and cartilaginous gives way. Polly's arm goes slack and I spring forward towards the window, the flower bed beneath it coming into view.

The boy in black, the one who broke the cordon, lies tangled in the flowers. His eyes are open, pupils dilated. His chest rises and falls in time with my own; his face is a mask of *my* terror. I read the shape his lips make.

Charlie.

But Charlie doesn't answer either of us. Charlie doesn't move. He's sprawled face down across the boy in black's chest, red smeared all over his forehead, matting into his fringe, soaking into the other boy's T-shirt.

Hot breath hits the back of my neck. Polly's arm locks around me and drags me back. I go limply. I want to struggle but my legs and arms just won't answer. *Turns out I'm not the strongest person you know after all, kiddo.* A pair of black-clad men in flak jackets jump the wall, rifles aimed in our direction. Their gun barrels weave like snakes looking for a strike, but there's no shot, except through me, and that's one chance these stupid bastards won't take.

My patches are searing hot. I can hear them humming. They vibrate against my skull as the charge in them builds.

The marksmen stop at the window, but we keep retreating, and they get smaller. One keeps his gun levelled at us while his mate stoops, grunts and lifts. Charlie appears, sagging, hoisted by his armpits. I glimpse the bloody mess of his face for a fraction of an instant before the living-room door slams.

Polly casts me aside like a rag doll and I fall like one, my injured cheek smacking into the hall floorboards. I try to get back up but there's nothing in my legs. Nothing in my arms. She's pressing silver tape to the door jamb. The pain from my patches is blazing. *They're overloading,* I think. I can smell smoke, but I can't even lift my hand to them.

"Charlie," I whisper. Still face down on the floor, I find the only muscles I can move are those in my jaw. "Charlie…"

Black spots fill my vision; a whine fills my ears. The world vanishes.

CHAPTER EIGHTEEN

Cat

Why don't you ask him?

Even now, my voice, carrying over the storm of firing shutters, haunts me. The question spins round and around my head:

Why don't you ask him? Why don't you ask him? Why don't you ask him? Why don't you ask him?

"Why don't you ask him?" I whisper it to my phone, to all the music journos and fatuous beautiful TV anchors who post new interviews with the boys to their YouTube channels every other day in the run-up to the Everlasting's new album, because none of them do ask. I watch video after video, listen to clip after clip, pore over transcripts and in-depth embedded features with the boys, *my boys*. There are lots of questions for Ryan about the music, his new hairstyle, who won the bet between him and Nick for the most viral video and whether breaking his arm was worth it (*totally* worth it, says Ryan), even a couple about whether "Rick" is real, but no one mentions a girlfriend, let alone a baby. It's like they've all signed some kind of secret contract not to ask about it, in exchange for this flood of access.

We have people who handle this kind of thing, he'd told me, back in the Dance Hall what feels like a century ago.

I slump over the phone. I'm sitting at the corner table of the Starbucks opposite the Tube station. Mum didn't want me to go out – after Papgate she likes to keep me close – but it's been weeks, and I couldn't stay cooped up in the house any longer. The paper cup at my elbow on the faux-pine tabletop has the word *Hippo* scrawled on it in magic marker. I tried to give my name as *Hippolyta* to the barista, just in case my real name pricked up any unfriendly ears, but she just stared at me.

"How do you spell that?" she asked.

"H–I–P–P… You know what? Just put *Hippo*," I told her. She eyed me sceptically. "'Ippo?" she said. "You sure?"

I opened my coat and gestured to the geological immensity that my midsection has become. I smiled. "Don't you think it fits?" She laughed, and congratulated me.

I take a sip and make a face; the coffee's long since gone cold. Feels like a waste, but it's not like I could have drunk the whole thing anyway. You could bail out the North Sea in three scoops using this cup. Given the way junior's leaning on my bladder, I'd be having to pee on every other lamp post like a dog if I put away even a quarter of it, and knowing my luck someone would film me, and wouldn't *that* be a gift to the fandom?

Oh yes, because while respectable journalists might not want to mention the baby, the inhabitants of RickResource have been nowhere near as restrained.

My thumb hovers over the app button on my phone. *Don't do it,* I tell myself. *There's nothing good there.* But it's like having an infected spot: sometimes squeezing is just too tempting. So I squeeze, and watch the pus come flooding out.

> 👤 Ahahahahaha delusional cow
>
> 👤 Do you think she's actually crazy or just lying for attention? #Rick4Eva
>
> 👤 She goes to my school and every guy here has had their 💣 💣 💣 💣 💣 in her, so there's no way she can possibly even know who the father is

Half of the people discussing it have bright purple drawing-pin ribbons on their avatars, because there's a theory going around that in the pap shots of me standing in my front doorway my bump is a balloon shoved up my top, and they want to pop it.

The only small mercy is that Evie has so far refrained from weighing in. In fact, all of the Teenage Petrolhead accounts, across all platforms, have been dark since the news broke. This must really have shaken up her sense of order; I guess she doesn't know what to say.

There's one video I can't stop watching. I click on my

YouTube app now and it's right at the top, helpfully suggesting itself. It's a breakdown of Ryan's parkour vid. I watch in slow motion as he runs and leaps, catlike, onto the concrete banister. I watch the frame of the video lurch after him as he drops into the stairwell. I hear myself, slurred into drunken slow motion, calling his name as he falls, while the narrator, a girl who sounds *far* too self-assured and convincing, relates her theory that I'm screaming his name because I'm a deranged, obsessive stalker, and Ryan was *running away* from me, and I *chased* him into that stairwell, and so *I'm* the one who broke his arm.

"Someone should teach her what it's like to be followed," the voice concludes.

My head throbs and the screen swims into a blurry fruit salad of coloured lights. I take off my glasses and pinch the bridge of my nose until the pain goes away. I've been getting headaches like this more and more. I guess I've been looking at screens too long, but there's nothing else to do cooped up at home.

My thoughts are a welter. Me, Ryan, Evie, Mum, the baby. It's hard to keep them straight under the sheer *weight* of all the tweets and Tumblr posts and videos going around and around my head. GetRickorDieTryin', Sat3amforEvelyn; these are my *friends*, *all* of my friends. I've spent years listening to them, believing them, and that's a tough habit to break. Now and then, I catch myself thinking, *What if they're right? What if I* am *hallucinating?* What if I had sex with some random and am somehow suppressing it? After all, isn't that more likely than me happening to run into my favourite pop star in my favourite place and him falling in love with me?

A memory swims up, a GCSE RE lesson last year, before Ryan, before any of this. Mr Garfield told us about this guy, David Hume, who had a theory about miracles. The problem with someone telling you they've witnessed a miracle, he said, was that in order for you to believe them, the idea of them being wrong, lying or crazy had to be more miraculous than the miracle itself. And in those terms, that night outside the Dance Hall on Streatham High Road feels more and more miraculous every day.

Rain hammers the windows of the cafe. Outside, blurry figures hurry back and forth in the gloom. The Starbucks starts to fill up with people shaking out umbrellas and wet hair and laughing about the sudden downpour.

I look around, feeling a sudden, sharp pain in my chest. There are too many people now, hogging the space, the light, the air. They're all on their phones, thumbs stroking the screens like lovers. Sure, they all look like they're just checking Insta, but there are at least six, seven, no, *nine* of them holding their cameras at an angle which would put me in frame. Under the cafe fluorescents, the little black lenses glint like fish eyes.

I have to move. I stand up unsteadily and stumble out of the door, instantly soaked by the rain. The clouds have brought twilight at mid-afternoon, everything's grey and murky. I shove my hands in my pockets, bend my head, and start to walk home, but I've not even reached Mitcham corner when I hesitate. There's a shadow at the corner of my vision. I pull out my cloth and wipe my rain-smeared glasses clear to see a girl in a dark jacket and hijab, sheltering under the awning by the entrance to the market, phone out. Did I see her in the Starbucks? Did she leave at the same time as me? What is she doing standing out in the rain – waiting for an Uber?

Without another thought I take a right, and then lurch into the first left. There's still that shadow in the corner of my eye. A woman, in a dark jacket with a hood up and her head down. Did the girl by the market before really have a hijab or was it just a hood? Everyone looks the same in the rain. I'm not on the route home any more; I can't risk leading them there. I'm taking random turns. Housing terraces pass me in a blur, the cross-lattice of their bricks like cage bars. *You're panicking,* I tell myself. *You're being stupid; you're not Jason bloody Bourne.* But I can't stop. My reflection in the wet pavement shambles like an ungainly monster. The sweat inside my coat is like a second rain, and I wrestle my hood down so I can breathe.

Eventually, I pause. I feel like the jackhammering in my chest will kill me if I don't. My jaw aches. I think I'm going to be sick. Isn't that a symptom of a heart attack in women? Or maybe it's just the baby. I look around. I'm on a stretch of waste ground between the back of a housing terrace and the looming concrete edifice of an estate. A mound of grass shows all the signs of being a public toilet for dogs and drunks; the street light in the middle of it has come on in the gloom. I look around, blowing water off my top lip as I huff after my breath. I'm alone.

"Of course you're alone," I mutter to myself. "It's not like anyone's going to follow you in *this*, even if they were inclined, which they're not. You're not that interesting; get a goddamn grip, Cat."

"Oi! Hippo!"

I wheel around. The rain parts like the curtain of a waterfall as a dark shape comes storming up out of it from the end of the alley, far, far too fast to be running. A dark shape on a bicycle, head down, pedalling frantically, wheels throwing off spray. It's holding a long thin shape, hooked at one end. A hockey stick.

"This is for breaking Ryan's arm!" The hockey stick swings, right at my upper arm. I sprawl out of the way, just, but fall awkwardly on the sodden grass; something nasty smears across my right cheek. The figure on the bike hoots victoriously and I see a camera flash and then they're gone.

"Catherine?" Mum looks downright horrified as I stand in front of her dripping on the welcome mat. "What on earth happened? You're soaked. You're … what's that in your *hair*?"

I fight to smile at her. "I just… I just got caught by the rain on the way back from Starbucks, that's all."

She frowns at me. "It stopped raining twenty minutes ago; the walk back from the high street is only five. You must

204

have taken a hell of a long way round."

"Well, you know. Needed a leg stretch. It's important to stay as mobile as you can in the final weeks; that's what the doc said, remember?"

"I do remember. Just as I remember you pleading your bump when asking me to get up to pass you the crisps last night, so forgive me if I view your new-found enthusiasm for exercise in a downpour with a *little* scepticism." She catches my expression and her face softens. "What happened, Cat? Tell me, so I can help."

I waddle towards her, and she wraps me in a hug, ignoring my sodden clothes and the stink of whatever's in my hair.

"You believe me, don't you, Mum?" I ask quietly. "You're on my side?"

"Always," she says firmly. But she can feel me shaking, and I know that won't help her sleep tonight.

Upstairs in my room, showered and towelled off, my eye falls on the poster of Ryan over the bed, and I feel my fear ebb to fury. How *dare* he? How dare he not be here for this! I drag my phone from the sodden heap of my tracksuit trousers where they lie abandoned by the door and message him.

> No more time, no more excuses. One of your fans just tried to hit me with a hockey stick. We go public, this week, or I'm getting a paternity test and a lawyer.

As soon as I send it, I'm quailing at the tone, wanting to apologize, to hedge, but it's too late. The three dots appear almost immediately.

OK, I'll get my guys to draft a press release.

A release? I feel my heart plunge. Didn't he say they'd already done that weeks ago, that they were just looking for the right time in the press cycle around the new album or something?

No, no press releases. A video,
live-streamed. You and me.
Here or there, I don't care.
You put your hand on my belly
and you say that it's yours.

Three dots again. I hold my breath.

Don't you trust me?

I want to write of course I do. I want to apologize for my presumption and for hurting his feelings. Instead, I just repeat.

A video.

OK, he replies. I'm sorry. I love you.

As I read those words, a warm glow suffuses me, pushing out the last of the chill from the rain. Finally, I begin to feel calm. This week. Soon this'll all be over. Everyone will see, everyone will believe me.

I love you too, I text back.

Something's missing from the conversation, but it's only later that night, awake, my sea lion-like bulk wedged in with pillows while I stare at the wall, that I realize what it is. I told him a fan of his assaulted me with a hockey stick, and he didn't once ask if I was OK.

CHAPTER NINETEEN

Amy

I heard the trouble before I saw it: a change in the quality of the laughter. Laughter's like air, or water; it's vital to life, but you feel it instantly when it turns cold.

I might have said as much to Christina, to explain why I had to leave at this inopportune moment, but that was made tricky by the fact my tongue was in her mouth. All I managed to get out was a spitty "Goddago!" before extracting my hands from under the back of her top and haring down the school corridor, my trainers squeaking on the lino. The laughter was coming from a couple of doors down. Charlie's classroom.

I arrived at the wired glass porthole in the door just in time to see my little brother stagger over a not-so-accidentally stretched-out leg. I was about to explode into the room like a vengeful crop-haired tornado and bite the faces off the little dickheads surrounding him, when Charlie looked up.

His eyes met mine. I caught an infinitesimal shake of the head. I rocked back on my heels.

Watch, he mouthed.

With a supreme effort, I wrestled my rising bloodlust under control, opened the door as quietly as I could, and slipped into the classroom of Upper 4B.

"Where's your tiara, princess?" a gorilla of a kid – I think it was Martin Gollings – sneered.

Charlie straightened slowly, keeping his back to Gollings for six long seconds. Then, theatrically, he checked his make-up with his phone camera.

"Marty, honey." He let out a long sigh. "This is a non-realist late century throwback goth look." He spun on his heel. "I wouldn't dream of wearing a tiara with anything other than a full-on glam rock ensemble, and even then, it's a bit … *de trop*, don't you think?" He drawled the term, relishing the look of confused irritation that crossed Gollings's face. "It's French," Charlie supplied with a glassy helpfulness. "For *a bit much*. Not a term that's likely to be applied to *your* fashion sense any time soon, I know. But we can try."

A handful of uncertain titters broke the air, and I couldn't tell if they were directed at Charlie or Gollings. The expressions of the kids laughing said maybe even they didn't know. The expression on Charlie's face said he didn't *care*.

My little brother actually *skipped* over Gollings's accomplice's outstretched leg, until he was mere inches from the lumbering behemoth's face.

"You *could* – with a bit of work – be almost handsome,

you know," he said brightly, stroking one finger down Gollings's cheek. More titters as Gollings recoiled. "I'd be happy to give you advice, I'm a charitable soul. First idea – that gormless expression is *soooo* last ice age. I'd ditch it if I were you."

The laughter got louder, and this time the pink-faced boys guffawing were looking at Gollings. Yep, the wind was definitely changing.

Gollings's jaw worked, but no words came out. Charlie eyed him sympathetically. "No, I said *get rid* of the gormless expression, not *intensify* it. Never mind. We'll work on it. Baby steps!"

And then, standing on tiptoe because Gollings was a full head and a half taller than him, Charlie kissed him on the cheek before resolutely turning his back on him.

Laughter exploded, filling the room. Gollings's face was purple, like an overripe raspberry. I saw the tension enter his ludicrous-for-a-fourteen-year-old muscles, and I started to move, to get between him and Charlie's exposed back, but then a wiry kid with a fancy quiff standing next to Gollings gave him a warning touch on the chest, and with a visible effort, the massive child restrained himself.

Charlie raised one hand and then sank in a thespian bow, as though U4b were his adoring audience. The laughs got louder. A couple of kids even applauded.

On his way past, he leaned in and whispered, "There's only one way to respond to people who give you shit for being yourself: be yourself ten times harder." He flashed

210

me an exhilarated grin. He was breathing hard and I figured this must be the first time this routine had worked for him. Pride surged up from my chest, tugging upwards at the corner of my mouth. I'd have hugged him if it wouldn't have cramped his style.

Instead, I wandered over with him to the lockers at the back of the classroom and leaned against them smugly while he spun the combination lock on his and yanked it open.

I was side-on to him, so he was in profile when I saw the smile freeze on his face.

The air in the room had changed again, this time turning clotted, ugly. More uncertain laughs, but these seemed more in shock than mirth. Gollings leered. The kid with the quiff was looking intently at Charlie.

Charlie's jaw worked. "Wh…" he began. "How…" The smile that had been frozen melted away; his black lacquered nails rattled out a tattoo on the metal of his locker door.

"What's the matter, princess?" Gollings asked. The wiry kid with the quiff was smiling now, a small satisfied smirk. "Run out of fancy shit to say?"

I'm ashamed to say it took until the first tear dragged a black lightning bolt down Charlie's whitewashed cheek for me to run the three paces to him, then I stopped cold. It was like a kick in the guts.

Charlie's locker was full of tumours.

Tumours cut from cigarette packets. Tumours printed off from the Internet. Swollen and red and bleeding, set into sunken ribcages and bursting from papery skin. They

211

covered every inch of surface space.

Pride of place in the middle of the backplate of the locker was given to a page torn from a medical textbook. A photograph of a woman from the waist up, naked, yellowing, with huge lesions whipping across her stomach. She was dead.

I felt rage blossom inside me; my hammering pulse blotted out the rising "ooooooh" from the crowd. I turned, but Charlie got there first.

He flew at the kid with the quiff, fingers hooked, nails like black claws, but Gollings was far too quick. With no visible effort, he planted a hand on Charlie's chest and shoved him sprawling into a desk. Charlie crumpled to the floor, burst into tears, scrambled back to his feet and fled the room. I sprinted after him, throwing a pointless elbow in the direction of Quiff, who just ducked it.

I caught up with him in the boys' loos. A wobbly-looking fifth-former at a urinal tried to voice an objection to my presence, but I just snapped *"What?"* at him and he fled.

Charlie was washing his face, his ruined make-up staining the water as it swirled in the sink. I hovered uncertainly at his shoulder. I wanted to hug him, but I couldn't see an opening.

"Those kids are pricks," I said. "Fuck 'em."

He didn't answer. His whole body was shaking. I put a hand on his shoulder. "Charlie?"

He mumbled something, but it was drowned out by the taps.

"What was that, Charlie?"

"I said DON'T TOUCH ME!" He screamed it in my face as he recoiled from my hand. "I had them," he choked. "For the first time, they were with me … and then … that."

"I know. I'm sorry. They're stupid arseholes. Like you said, they'll always find some way to give you shit."

"They didn't find this," he snapped back. The make-up I'd done for him was gone, his eyes wild and red and raw. "*You* gave it to them."

I come to on cold tiles, the kitchen spotlights glaring down at me like tiny suns. The skin behind my ears and on the back of my neck is hot and sore where my patches burned it. My head feels like a tiny martial arts expert is repeatedly and determinedly kicking it from the inside.

Feedback, I think groggily. *I must have passed out from the feedback.* I've never experienced it before, but I've heard of it – every streamer with a big audience has.

The technology Heartstream's based on, intra-limbic transduction, is inherently two-way. Both parties to the stream draw from the other. But that creates a problem – feedback. You feel them feeling you feeling what they're feeling and so on. If you're streaming to more than a few people, it quickly spirals, overwhelming the brain.

To combat this, the Heartstream exchange has built-in safety protocols that dampen down the flow in one direction. These dampeners kill about ninety per cent of the feedback but you still get a bit of emotional backwash from everyone streaming off you. It's minuscule, so minuscule that no one

I've ever met has been able to detect it, but – theoretically at least – it's proportional to the strength of the signal you're sending, and they all add up, so if you have enough followers and you stream a really, *really, really* intense emotion...

The effect is bigger with close friends and family members, and you've got to be careful: the dampeners are built into the software, not the patches themselves, so if you're bypassing the app to create a private loop you need to remember to set them up manually. Last year there was a story going around about a pair of twins who forgot and were in a coma for six weeks. Right now, the way my head feels, I believe it.

Using the cabinet behind me as an impromptu crutch, I drag myself to my feet. Polly's sitting at the table, her head propped on balled fists. She's singing to herself, like a mantra or a lullaby, so soft I can't make out the words. I'd say she has a nice voice, if she hadn't broken into my house, threatened me with a bomb and got my little brother shot.

"Charlie." My throat's all torn with screaming, and it comes out in a croak. I taste blood in the back of my mouth. "Is he—"

"No," she says, cutting me off, which is just as well, as I'm not sure I could have brought myself to finish that sentence. "At least, I don't think so. I..."

She tails off and clicks on the TV. It's showing football. She makes a throaty *tch* sound and rewinds it. As a consequence, the first news I see of Charlie is a surrealist nightmare of him being unloaded in reverse out of an ambulance by paramedics who walk solemnly backwards.

I stare at the remote. *If only I had one of those that worked on real life.* Rewind or fast fucking forward, though, the blood seeping through the bandages wrapped across his eyes is very visible, and very red.

"I ... I think some of the glass from the window must have got in his eyes." Polly's voice is desolate. "They can do wonderful things these days; I'm sure..."

Thankfully she stops before she can say *I'm sure he'll be fine.* Otherwise I'm fairly certain my response would have sprayed both of our internal organs over the walls in a fine red mist.

They can do wonderful things these days; I'm sure she'll be fine. I've heard that mantra from well-meaning people so many times over the last year I've all but ground my teeth to dust.

I picture that locker full of tumours. I force myself to hold it in mind. *Well, Amy, you can't say you weren't warned. It's all very well claiming you're prepared to sacrifice your privacy, but it's never just* your *privacy you're sacrificing, is it?*

Oh well, they were only his eyes; he wasn't using them for anything.

I picture the paintings in Charlie's room. Hot acid sweeps into my throat. I feel a sudden, mindless impulse to gouge my *own* eyes out. I stifle it, but still, my thumbs twitch a couple of inches into the air.

Don't be an arse, Becker! I snap at myself, lowering my hands. *Charlie has no more use for a blind sister than he does for a wet fart. Stop making this about you. What he needs right now is someone to love and take care of him.*

Which brings us back, as ever, to every captive's first order of business:

Escape.

I feel the familiar numbness steal over me. It's so often been my refuge in these last few months and I eagerly climb inside it once again. Feelings: *pause*. Practicality: *play*. Make the best of it, even if the best of it is still so awful you want to dig your fingers under your skin and pull it off in scraps. Do the work.

Do.

The.

Work.

Polly's talking. Her eyes plead with me, but it takes me a moment to tune in to what she's saying.

"... so, so sorry," she says desolately. "I never meant for this to happen. You do believe that, don't you?"

I let the question hang. It's not even an act of deliberate cruelty; I just can't summon the will to make her feel better. Eventually I put my hand on my lower abdomen.

"Sorry, I'm not feeling too well. Can I go to the loo again?"

As soon as the door's locked with Polly safely on the other side, I scrape Mum's illicit clone of Dr Ben Smith's phone out from behind the loose tile. Whatever the reason for Polly's eruption into my life and her mysterious obsession with my mother, there must be a clue here somewhere.

I stab the mail app open and type *Becker* into the search bar. No results. I try again with Mum's first and then maiden name, but nothing comes up then either. I type in *Polly*, but that also yields no reward.

I chew my lip, throw a nervous glance at the door and consider trying to make a *plopping* sound with my mouth, but decide against it. I start to scroll down through Dr Ben Smith's emails, painfully conscious that there are – according to the counter in the corner – more than fifty-six thousand of them. Dr Smith is apparently another of the never-throw-anything-away brigade – and I don't have a prayer of making it through even a fraction of them before Little Miss Bomb Vest boots the door down and demands to inspect a stool sample.

I read the first couple, then I start to skim, not really sure what I'm looking for, but with a growing nausea because I'm sure I don't have time to find it. Dr Smith's emails are a mess of file requests, shopping lists and notes to himself stuffed with medical terms I don't understand. I flick faster and faster, barely even reading any more, frustration, anxiety and finally fear taking bigger and bigger bites out of my innards. Tears blur the screen. There has to be a clue here, something *somewhere*, but—

Hang on.

I jam my thumb onto the glass, but not fast enough to keep the words that snagged my eye from flying off the screen. I scroll back frantically, half certain I've imagined it.

But no, there, in the *From* column, sandwiched between

emails from Riley, Susan, and Bharath, Vikram, is a message from one Hatter, Mad.

My mind flickers back to the fragments of the shattered teapot, the Hatter in pieces, face down in drugged English breakfast blend.

Could be a coincidence, I warn myself as I stab the email with my thumb. *It's not like she was the world's only Alice in Wonderland fan.*

The email is titled *Our Agreement*, and is brief, almost to the point of poetry.

"Adherence advised. I advocate absence of activity."

Puzzled but intrigued, I filter for other messages from the mysterious Mr Hatter. I find only one and stare in frank incredulity at the date.

The first and only other email was received the better part of two *decades* ago.

Baffled, I gawp at the phone for a few seconds, feeling the bite of the loo seat set off pins and needles in my thighs. Two messages, and two messages only, sent years and years apart: what the fuck kind of relationship does that point to?

I open the earlier message. If anything, it's even more brusque than its belated follow-up; there are no words at all, just a mobile number I don't recognize and a JPEG attachment. I press the little paper-clip icon. The circle fills and an image pops up.

"Huh."

I don't know what I was expecting, but it wasn't *that*.

I'm no expert – I consider myself an enthusiastic amateur if anything, very much part-time – but nevertheless I'm fairly sure that the object currently filling the screen is a man's erect penis.

It's a white guy's, of moderate size (I think; again, I'm no expert – I don't have charts or anything) protruding straight at the camera from a nest of wiry brown-grey hair. There's a blur of out-of-focus scrotum at the bottom of the shot, and a purplish, kidney-shaped birthmark on a hip right at the top.

I sit back against the chilly porcelain loo tank.

"Mum, what were you doing?" I whisper, but a knot of dread is tying itself in my guts, because I think I already know.

The alias, the anonymous phone number. A menacing nude photo. You can't be even a *semi*-famous girl on the Internet and not know what all that adds up to.

I eye the kidney-shaped birthmark, the temperature seeming to drop further every second. The threat implicit in that image is very specific. Mr – or shall we say *Ms* – Hatter isn't going to just stick this up on some blog somewhere. The kind of greasy skidmark who publishes stolen nudes online for all to see doesn't warn you like this; they just go ahead and post for kicks and clicks. It can't be a revenge porn thing, either – the photo doesn't include the face, so the subject could always just deny it's him. No, this image has been carefully selected so that only someone already intimate with the man in it could identify him from it. Mad Hatter has a very particular audience in mind – a husband or a wife, the mother of Dr Smith's grinning be-braced twin daughters, perhaps – who might be prompted to ask awkward questions about who he's been showing his junk to.

Our agreement. Adherence advised. I advocate absence of activity.

Mum's voice swims back into my head: *And is your relationship administrative, amorous or purely adversarial?*

There are 8.5 billion people on our dear planet Earth, so the odds are pretty good that *someone* else is that alliteration-happy, but a Lewis Carroll obsessive who just happens to be emailing a man whose cloned mobile was hidden in my mother's deathbed? A woman who just *happened* to have the professional expertise needed to crack his cloud accounts like an egg, and rummage in them for incriminating material?

As much as I might want to believe it, I don't think it's a coincidence any more.

Our agreement. Adherence advised. Those four words are a threat.

I hope I'm wrong, but the only sense I can make of this is that Mad Hatter was Mum, and she was blackmailing this guy.

Something in me rebels. A wave of self-disgust crashes against the inside of my skull and I almost throw the phone down. My mind holds up the image of Mum, withered and watery-eyed, moaning with pain every time I tried to touch her. *Haven't you failed her enough? How can you even* think *this?*

I exhale hard. Emotions: *pause*. Practicality: *play*. If I'm wrong, no one will be more relieved than me, but I have to follow this where it leads.

Let's just say Mum *was* trying to coerce the unfortunate Dr Smith. Coerce him into doing what?

I advocate absence of activity.

Or *not* doing what?

A thumping on the door jerks me out of it.

"Amy?" Polly calls. "Are you all right in there?"

"Fine, just a bit ... blocked up."

A long pause.

"Oh... Anything I can do to help?"

"Like what? Come in here with a crowbar?"

No response. I can almost feel the heat of her blush through the wood of the door. Hopefully her embarrassment has bought me a few minutes.

On a shot to nothing, I try googling *Dr Ben Smith* but get the inevitable eleventy-jillion results and close the browser.

For Christ's sake, Mum, couldn't you have found a doctor with a weirder name to put the squeeze on? Professor Facsimile Hornswoggle, for example? Cardinal Dresden Butterfield?

Of course, there basically *aren't* any real people with properly unique names: culture plus the natural human inclination to mimic plus the aforementioned 8.5 billion folks guarantee that, if anyone actually went by that kind of name, it would have to be a pseudonym...

... just like Hatter, Mad.

The loo seat clunks as I shift position. A little lighter

flame of excitement kindles at the base of my throat. Mum used a fake name, sure, but what if that didn't work? Dr Ben Smith was presumably smart enough to get into medical school, and he had *years* to investigate. What if he managed to uncover the identity of whoever was sending him threatening pictures of his own dick?

I remember exactly when Mum died, not just the day, but the minute. I watched it happen, I'm sure of it. I was just walking back into that wretched room with the pretty folio edition of *Alice's Adventures in Wonderland* under my arm. Charlie and I had given it to her for Christmas years ago, and when she'd asked me to bring it to her, I'd almost cried. I opened the door, and my eyes met hers just as her face, already sagging and skull-like, took on its final pallor. I remember slamming the door and holding Charlie back while our mingled tears soaked my collar – another choice I denied him.

And then, eleven minutes after his wracking sobs had quietened enough for me to slacken my grip on him, I pulled my phone from my pocket, opened Heartstream, and made it public.

10:27 a.m. on 25 June.

Had Dr Ben Smith been eagerly following my feed, knowing he'd finally be out from under the thumb of his tormentor? And, if so, what did he do when he found out he was?

I go to the *Sent* folder in his email account and filter the date for 25 June. There's only one email sent out that morning, at 10:51. I open it.

To: Ingram, Jennifer E.
From: Smith, Benjamin P.
Jen – bit urgent I'm afraid, hon – could you bring me
a patient file? Catherine Canczuk. You're a star.

B

Anticipation pinching the back of my throat, I stick *Catherine Canczuk* into Google. The results are the usual hotchpotch of Facebook and LinkedIn profiles. There's a professional ice hockey player for the Calgary Cormorants, and an academic whose thesis *Choo-Choo Pain: Torture and Punishment in the Universe of Thomas the Tank Engine* is available in full online.

My eye, however, is drawn to the row of image search results displayed at the top of the screen. The second from the left is a girl about my age: glasses, ginger, curvy, smiling shyly behind a hastily raised hand. She's almost unrecognizable.

Almost, but not quite.

You can see it in the nose, and the shape of the jaw, although the amount of weight she's lost in the years since the photo was taken nearly disguises it. Above all, though, it's the green-grey eyes that give her away.

I exhale hard and my breath fogs the screen. I wipe it clear and stare into the screen, and Polly – half a lifetime younger, but Polly nevertheless – stares back.

The picture is from an ancient Tumblr account called Hippolyta the Hypocrite. I hit the link and start to read.

CHAPTER TWENTY

Cat

👤 Dear **@WildWhiteHorse**. Stop lying. Just. Stop.

👤 What a shock. The delusional **@WildWhiteHorse** is
a fat, sad white girl.

👤 There is no **@WildWhiteHorse**. Management made
her up.
> "**@RickLover545** This must be breaking
> **@RealNickLamb**'s heart. Hope you're fucking
> satisfied **@WildWhiteHorse**, you bitch."

👤 His contract forbids it. They'd sue him into oblivion.
> "**@CyberSally** "Why doesn't
> **@RyanRichardsOfficial** speak out and debunk
> this baby crap?"

👤 Come on, guys, we can totally get this to number 1:
"**@Rainin_Lou**: Sings *I don't want a lot for Christmas, there is just one thing I need, **@WildWhiteHorse** cut open, just so I can watch her bleed*"

👤 Dear **@WildWhiteHorse**. Stop talking. Just. Stop.

👤 I'M SCREAMING.
"**@Cybersal**: I know a nurse at the clinic where @WildWhiteHorse went to get her 'pregnancy' checked out. Guess what fake name she used? HIPPOLYTA RICHARDS."

👤 Dear **@WildWhiteHorse**. Why do you hate Ryan and Nick so much? Why don't you want them to be happy?

👤 Dear **@WildWhiteHorse**. Why do you hate gay people so much?

👤 Ding-Dong the Witch is Dead #BabyFake
"**@RickYouUpAndDown**: Result! [Search text = "WildWhiteHorse" User not found.]"

👤 Hey! Guess who found her FB and private Twitter? **@CatCanczuk**
Facebook.com/Catherine.Canczuk.1598

👤 Dear Mrs Canczuk, you don't know me, but I just wanted to know how you feel about raising a lying, homophobic slut for a daughter.

👤 😂😂😂
    "**@CatCanczuk**: Please, just leave me alone. Leave my mum alone. Please. I can't sleep. Please."

👤 Dear **@CatCanczuk**, we've got eyes on you.
    "**@BabyFakeandBake**: So, here's a photo of **@CatCanczuk** a heroic Ricker took while she was changing at school for gym. She's tubby, sure. But pregnant?!?! [WhiteHorse.jpg]"

👤 Needles ready!
    "**@CatCanczukReallyNeedsToFuckingDieNow**: OK, so now we know what school she goes to. Who's up for paying her a little visit?"

👤 Fic Title: Merry Christmas Rickdom! Category: Comedy. Summary: **@CatCanczuk** gets kicked in the head until her delusional brains ooze out of her ears.

👤 Dear **@CatCanczuk**, why don't you and your white trash fake baby just die in a fire?

👤 Dear **@CatCanczuk**...

👤 Dear **@CatCanczuk**...

👤 Dear **@CatCanczuk**...

👤 **Dear @CatCanczuk**, stop breathing.
Just.
Stop.

CHAPTER TWENTY-ONE

Amy

She isn't waiting for me when I unlock the door. I pad out into the hallway, and then I see her, framed in the doorway to the kitchen. She's slumped in her chair like a boxer between rounds, staring into space.

My mouth is suddenly dry and I struggle to swallow before I speak. "Catherine?" I say tentatively. "Catherine Canczuk?"

For a moment she doesn't react at all, and I wonder if I've got this all wrong. Then she shakes herself, blinks and straightens. Her whole demeanour changes as she turns to look at me, as though "Polly" is a dream she's waking up from.

"My friends called me Cat," she says.

Are we friends? I wonder, eyeing the flickering green reflection of the bomb light in the hollow of her throat. And then I remember her saying, a mere handful of hours and blood and screams ago, *Because I'm your friend, Amy*, and it occurs to me that *she* thinks we are, and I need to work with that, if I'm ever going to get out of here.

"Cat, then," I say, coming into the kitchen and perching on the edge of the table. "Where's your kid, Cat? Wouldn't you rather be hanging out with them than holed up in here?"

If she's shocked by my sudden wealth of information, she doesn't show it. It occurs to me that, for all the unpredictable outbursts of childlike delight and fury, there's an inner core of this woman that's locked down like a submarine at full dive.

"I lost the baby," she says distantly. "The stress. The doc said I couldn't handle it."

Did you lose someone? I remember the expression of distant pain when I asked her that.

"Oh, I'm … I'm sorry."

"Don't be. It was hardly your fault, was it?" The pleasant, vague smile returns.

"What happened?"

"Since you're suddenly so well informed, why don't you tell me?" An edge enters her voice, but I don't take the bait. I just wait. When she exhales, and starts to speak again, I'm not surprised. People need to talk about painful things; lonely people doubly so.

"The dad was famous; I'm guessing you know that?"

I give a curt nod, but don't speak; I'm not going to interrupt her if I can avoid it.

"He had a lot of fans, including, at one time, me."

229

A rueful smile. "When word got out he'd knocked me up, those fans didn't take too kindly to it, including pretty much all of my friends."

She turns my phone over and over in her hands, then holds it up.

"Window to the soul, right? Well, what did mine show me when I looked into it? A bitch. A liar, deluded or plain faking it, who couldn't handle being just another teenage pregnant fuck-up and didn't have the guts for an abortion."

She drops the phone onto the table with a clack.

"My friends wouldn't talk *to* me, but that didn't mean they wouldn't talk *about* me. All of a sudden, they had the juiciest gossip. Maybe you've seen some of it? Apparently, I'd had sex with every boy in our school, so there was no way I could know who the father was. Another said they'd seen the contract I'd signed with management to pretend to be Ryan's lover, and another swore blind they'd caught me shoving a balloon up my jumper. For a while, everyone on RickResource stuck a needle emoji on their posts, because that was what they would jab into my belly if they saw me."

I just stare at her, waiting.

"There were threats too, obviously. I was going to be strangled, stabbed, burned, beaten to death because I was getting in the way of the greatest love story the world had ever known between Nick and Ryan, who had obviously never heard of me, and wouldn't touch a vagina in a month of Sundays. How exactly I was getting in the way of that romance if neither of the protagonists had any interest in the contents of my knickers was unclear, but apparently I deserved to die for it." Her face twists into a wry smile, but then it flickers and fades. "They even threatened my mum.

"I reported the threats to the police, but nothing was ever going to persuade them to take a bunch of girls on the Internet seriously. They said if it bothered me so much I should just stay off social media."

I snort. That, at least, hadn't changed. "Digital solitary confinement," I volunteer. "That's a hell of an alternative to them doing their fucking jobs."

She laughs. "Exactly. It was everywhere. My Facebook, Twitter, Tumblr, even fucking Instagram. I couldn't block people fast enough, and the sheer effort of trying was *exhausting*."

She sighs. "It's weird. Even though I knew they were wrong, I couldn't stop myself from listening to them. I started to feel guilty, like I *was* lying, like I *was* just attention-seeking. A few times, I wondered if I really was delusional, and had hallucinated the whole thing. After all, looked at in the cold light of day, it *did* seem improbable."

"It's hard to get out of the habit of believing someone," I say. This is something else I've learned: trust isn't rational; it's emotional. It's like religion, if you had the evidence to prove you ought to trust a person then you wouldn't need to.

She nods, puts a grateful hand on mine, and I let her.

"It went on for days, then weeks, then months. It just didn't let up. A community of antis cropped up, people who believed me. At first I was grateful, but then I realized they were just adding fuel to the fire, keeping it burning.

"I was going mad. So was Mum. She was always a bit of an insomniac – my dad had sneaked off in the middle of the night and she didn't like to sleep in case something else important disappeared when her eyes were closed. She had to take pills to knock herself out. Ryan promised a press release, but it kept not appearing. There was always some detail to be worked out, some last-minute hitch, the lawyers were begging him to wait. Weeks bled into months with no word. We barely saw each other for weeks on end. He kept making excuses. But then a girl actually tracked me down in person, came after me with a hockey stick. I shouldn't have been surprised. When I was in the fandom we could track Ryan or Nick to one specific chair in an airport lounge. Sooner or later they were going to turn those skills on me. Still, that was when I knew we couldn't wait any more.

"It was a Thursday night. At 7:30 Ryan was going to come round – he resisted at first, but I begged and wheedled and he eventually relented. At 8 p.m. we'd do a webcast together. We'd sit on my living-room sofa, and he'd put his hand on my Zeppelin-sized belly and say *this is my child*. I posted about it on all my accounts, just to make sure *everyone* was watching."

She breathes out, and seems to deflate; her eyes turn to the clock on the wall.

"At 7:40, when he still hadn't turned up, I started to worry. At 7:55 I was shaking and crying, Mum trying to comfort me but not knowing how. At 8:05 p.m. I had the live-stream chat window open, watching people call me a psycho and a whore and a liar in real time, and I knew: *This is it. If I let this pass, now, it's proven: I'm a psycho liar whore for ever.*"

She's recited all this in the same calm, detached voice, like she's reading a weather forecast on the radio. Now she stands, and smooths out the front of her slacks.

"So I took my phone" – she lifts my handset from the table – "and I set it up like this." She props it against the fruit bowl. "Because Mum refused to hold it. She thought it was a bad idea. I knelt – actually *knelt* – in front of it like this." She drops to her knees on the kitchen tiles. "It was the only way I could get my face into shot properly. And I logged onto the stream, and I said I was sorry I was late, and that Ryan wasn't there, but I was sure he would be soon, and in the meantime at least they could see that I really *was* pregnant, that the photos I'd posted of my bump weren't faked or of someone else."

Still staring into the dark mobile phone, she lifts the hem of her shirt where it sticks out under the bomb vest, displaying a flash of concave belly and a long appendix scar.

"Ten minutes went by, then twenty, and by then I knew that Ryan wasn't coming and I ought to shut off the stream, but I couldn't stop myself from reading the comments. They Photoshopped me onto *everything*: dogs, fish, turds, corpses,

Pinocchio, Trump. It went on until exactly 8:47; I know because I was looking at the clock in the corner of the screen."

I try to imagine it. The humiliation that must have burned in her. That sense of everything dissolving, with no way out, no plan, no way to make it better.

"What happened at 8:47?"

She turns to me; her smile is as wide and glassy as a frozen lake.

"The police kicked down the door. Some *scamp* had called them and said there were terrorists making bombs at our address. Eighty thousand people got to watch as they burst in with guns and shields and ground our faces into the carpet. It was as if I'd done it onstage at Wembley. It gave them all the meme material they'd ever need."

I swallowed. *Swatting* they used to call it. In America, where it originated in the live gaming community, it had got people shot.

"I'm sorry," I say again, and mean it.

"Oh, don't be. The coppers were quite charming when they realized their mistake, and very apologetic. We gave them a cup of tea and a digestive. They promised us they'd investigate the false tip-off, although we all knew there wasn't much they could do. It could even have been a *good* thing, if I'd been paying attention."

"What do you mean?"

"I'd accidentally left an unopened gas bill on the side. It was in camera shot. Whoever called the cops had zoomed in on it and nabbed my address." She swallows hard. "If I'd had my wits about me, I would have figured out that it wasn't just the papers – the whole damn Internet now knew where I lived, which could have prepared me for what happened next.

"Unfortunately, at the time I had other things on my mind."

CHAPTER TWENTY-TWO

Cat

"Where are you?" I yell it at the peeling walls, anger and fear and humiliation swimming high like vomit in my throat. I can feel the bruise blossom on my cheek from where the black-clad anti-terror copper slammed my face into the floor.

I can't stand still. I stomp around the condemned Dance Hall, slipping and sliding on the rubble, dragged off balance by my bump. This place, whose desolation seemed so beautiful only a few months ago, is now just cold and dusty and covered in rat shit and I can't breathe and I want to go home.

I want to, but I can't. Not until I've seen him.

Dashing the tears out of my eyes I scroll back through the texts for the eighth time.

Where the hell were you?

I'm so sorry. I got held up, call with the lawyers.

I was humiliated. I sounded
delusional. They thought
I was a lunatic.

You went THROUGH with it? Without me?

I want to see you, now.

It's 2 in the morning. Can we do tomorrow?

The Dance Hall. Be inside in
30 mins or else first thing in the
morning I'm calling the tabloids
and showing them these texts.

Cat, please, just calm down.

30. Mins.

He didn't reply. I check the clock on my phone. It's nearly four. He's not coming. I feel the liquid lurch of the baby squirming into a new position. *He's not coming.* I try to press the panic rising in my chest back down again, but it's like trying to push back floodwater with your hands. *He's not coming; he's never coming. I'm alone.*

I grit my teeth and shake my head. No, no, he's been misled. He's been convinced to lie low by the lawyers and by management. For all I know they've taken his phone and are pretending to *be* him, stringing me along. Ry's the closest thing the band have to a frontman; he's the livelihood of so many people – who knows what they might do to protect that? I have to go to him. I have to *show* him his child. Make him see.

I tug my phone out of my pocket again. My hands are freezing; there's no blood in my fingers. *Must be the baby,* I think grimly as I stab the screen, logging into RickResource as an anon. Can we do tomorrow? his text asked. He's definitely in London at least. He'll be in a hotel; they only rent an apartment when they're all here together. Which hotel, though? He never told me that.

I hit the ornithology hashtag Rickers use for sightings of the two lovebirds, filter for Ryan, and sort by date, most recent first. There's one from about forty minutes ago in Brazil and another from midnight in Glasgow, but I ignore them. Rickers are always making up or imagining sightings for kudos. The next handful are from last night in LA, but I figure them for wishful thinking, since that's where Nick is right now, filming his first film role, and Rollerboy55 and Rickismy3verything would really, really like to think Ryan was there with him. I scroll on. I'm looking for clustering.

It takes me about three minutes to find it. There are more than seventy claimed sightings of Ryan in London, spanning the last week and a half. Of those, the critical mass, thirty-five or so, were in and around Mayfair.

My heart leaps briefly – *Mayfair, that makes sense; there are a boatload of luxury hotels around there!* – and then takes a nosedive again – *Mayfair, bollocks, there are a boatload of luxury hotels around there* – at the prospect of somehow sieving the right five-star bolthole from the pack.

But then Ryan's voice floats up out of my memory, his grinning mouth inches from my own as we clutched each other on Evie's front doorstep. My heart hammering so hard against the inside of my ribs I was sure he must feel it.

You're very frisky this morning.

The little coffee place on the corner opposite my hotel was closed.

This is London – you couldn't find another coffee shop?

It's Italian.

He did tell me the name, but however hard I strain, I can't remember it. I'll have to do it the hard way. I pull up Google Maps, and start to work. By the time I'm done my eyes ache from lack of sleep and staring at the screen in the dark and my throat's burning from the dust, but I know that of the forty or so five-star hotels listed in and around Mayfair, only two have coffee shops with Italian names on the corner opposite them. Prego sits opposite Claridge's, but, according to Wiki, Claridge's has more than two hundred rooms, which is an awful lot of eyeballs for a celeb looking to keep a low profile. That leaves the Grammercy, a tiny twelve-room boutique tucked away on a mews behind Berkeley Square, with Gennaro's, a "friendly family-owned cafe and eatery", a stone's throw across the street.

Of course, it was more than eight months ago that Ryan mentioned that place, but then again, as he said at the time, *I'm a creature of habit.*

I hesitate with my hand on the brass door handle of the Grammercy, go over the plan one more time in my head, and immediately wish I hadn't. It seems insane. I'll be spotted; I'll be caught, arrested; I'll be on the news and then Rickdom will *really* go to town on my aching pregnant backside.

But what's my alternative? Do nothing? Go home and wait for the next overzealous Ricker with a hockey stick? Or a baseball bat? Or a flask of acid? A knife? I suck in a deep breath, trying to use the pressure of the air inside my chest to still the urge to tremble, and push into the lobby.

Thank all that's holy there's an untended trolley full of luggage right by the door. There's only one girl on reception and she's got her head down, staring at her phone. Before she can look up, I yank the most unmanageably huge suitcase I can off the top of it. I turn my phone off – a mistimed notification would blow this whole thing – and then I waddle towards the black marble desk, leaning into the awkwardness my bump gives me, visibly struggling with the case, which isn't hard because it feels like it belongs to an Olympic weightlifter who packed his entire gym in it. Phone stuck to my ear, I bawl so loud my mum could probably hear me back in Tooting if she hadn't taken her pills.

"Jeff, *Jeff*, listen to me. I know it's late, but how do you think *I* feel? Three and a half hours sitting on the tarmac at JFK, and then there was turbulence, with your son tap-dancing on the inside of my uterus for half the flight, and then the taxi driver just *would not shut up*. And I haven't charged my phone and I swear to God, you're going to have to stand between me and that minibar with a cricket bat… No, no, but wait, Jeff, my phone's almost dead. I'm just downstairs in the lobby now; can you come and get me? What do you mean you're in the *bath* – it's gone 4 a.m.! Is the jet lag that bad? Fiiiiiine, I'll just come up. Oh shit, my phone's dying. Jeff, which room are you—"

All of which patter brings me red-faced and puffing to the desk, staring into the pitying eyes of the reception girl. I flash the dark screen of my phone at her.

"Bloody thing, no battery life any more. Bit like me at the moment."

"Tough night?" she asks with professional sympathy.

"You literally would not believe it. Don't get pregnant at thirty-five, sweetheart; the bank account may be willing, but the flesh is weak."

"You are *not* thirty-five," she gasps, as I'd hope she would. Get them to think of you as *older*, Evie once told me; people have it in their heads that older women don't cause trouble, God knows why.

I laugh. "I *love* you," I say, extravagantly.

"No, seriously. I don't believe it," she says. "You don't look a day over twenty-three. What moisturizer do you use?"

"*All* of them. I literally bathe in them. Speaking of which, my useless husband has picked the most inconvenient time in history to get his rubber duck out, and after the night I've had, I really don't want to wait for him to work out which dripping foot goes down which trouser leg, otherwise I'll still be down here when Jeff junior's born. Can you let me know the room and I'll head straight up? Briggs is the name," I tell her. "Jeff Briggs."

Jeff was Ryan's best friend when they were kids; now he does his security – *my babysitter* Ryan calls him – and so always sleeps near by. I picture him, hulking like a good-natured iceberg at the edge of the stage at Everlasting gigs. Asking for the room number of a bodyguard no one's ever heard of is – I hope – less liable to arouse suspicion than demanding the room number of a pop star with a more famous name than Big Ben.

The girl on reception is struggling with it. I can see it in the anxious creases around her eyes. I look like that when I'm about to apologize for something – which is to say, because I'm me, most of the time. Once she says no, I'm done for, though, so I cut her off with a deafening groan, bending my back and shoving my bump out in front of me like a battering ram.

"*Jesus*, my back hurts. Do you know you basically can't lie down on your back at this stage of a pregnancy? Or your front, of course, but you can't bear to be on your feet or even sitting up for long either. You basically have to curl up on your side and wedge yourself in with pillows like an egg in a carton. Which I suppose is appropriate enough when you think about it. I suppose I *could* lie down here and wait for him, but if I do, do you think you could bring some pillows for me to prop myself against?"

That does it. I see the decision before she speaks it. I have officially rendered myself harmless.

"Room ten," she says. "First floor, on your right. Shall I show you?"

"That would be very kind..." I tail off, frowning. "Actually, on second thoughts, maybe not. Last time I hadn't seen Jeff in a month and I turned up at his hotel room he opened the door naked. There was a family of Korean tourists struggling with their key to the room next door at the time – it was *punishingly* embarrassing."

She blushes and joins in my laughter. "I'll have your case brought up to you then."

"Best leave it a decent interval," I murmur conspiratorially. "If he *is* in the mood, well ... I've not seen *him* for a month either."

We exchange knowing smiles and, heart threatening to break my ribs with how hard it's battering them, I turn to the lifts.

"Get out here, Ryan!" I holler, hammering on the door to room eight, on the basis that it's the one that looks like it's got the adjoining door to Jeff's. It's just as well there are only twelve rooms in this hotel, because every guest in them is going to be awake soon if he doesn't open the door. "The mother of your child would like a quiet fucking word with you!"

In the corner of my eye, I see the handle to room ten tip, and the familiar shape of Jeff appears, blinking into the hallway light. Jeff's got a kindly face, which I'm sure comes in handy in his job, and for the times when it doesn't, well, there's always the fact that he's the size and rough shape of one of those massive double fridge-freezers.

"Hey, miss, come away from there. Back up now, back..."

He hesitates when he sees the bruise on my cheek and then my bump, but he's good at his job, and manages to catch my wrists without coming close to my abdomen.

"It's *his*!" I scream it into his face, like I'm screaming into the 400 x 400 pixel face of every mocking, sniping coward who laughed while the police ground my face into my living-room carpet. "It *is*. It's *his*!"

Through the muddle of tears in my eyes I see the lift doors open. The reception girl's there with my stolen suitcase. She freezes in shock when she sees me. I sound insane, the very archetype of a delusional fangirl, I know I do, but all the rage and humiliation is bursting in me and I'm hacking out massive sobs from my chest and there's nothing I can do to stop it.

"It's his! It's his, it's his, it's his!"

"Come away, miss," Jeff says, his tone as patient and immovable as a granite cliff. "Or I'll have to call the police, and nobody wants—"

"Jeff." A familiar voice cuts him off. "Let her go."

I turn, pulling off my glasses and dashing tears angrily from my eyes. Ryan's standing in the now-open doorway of the room across the hall. He eyes me sullenly, tying the belt on his regulation fancy-hotel white dressing gown.

"You didn't come," I say, my voice broken.

He just looks at me. When he opens his mouth to speak, I scream at him. "YOU DIDN'T COME!"

"Look," he says. "I know you're upset, and I understand, but please—"

"NO SHIT I'm upset. Do you know what they *did* to me?"

"I didn't know they were going to *swat* you," he pleads. "I just thought they'd…"

He tails off, but it's too late. I stare at him, and he stares at me.

"Oh my God, you *do* know what they did to me," I breathe. "*How* do you know, Ryan? You acted like you didn't realize I'd gone ahead with the stream, but you did, didn't you? How? Were you watching?"

He doesn't meet my eye.

"Were you watching as they tore me apart?"

I almost launch myself at him, but Jeff's there, one girder-sized arm blocking my progress. Something, a question in his bulldog-like eyes, stops him from touching me again, though.

"Ryan, do you know this girl?"

It's when Ryan hesitates that I know the worst is true. Management hasn't talked him into anything. Management doesn't even know about me. He was never going to tell the world about our baby. He hasn't even told his best friend.

It's like a stone crashing through me, demolishing everything. He doesn't want our child. He never did.

"Yeah," I snarl. "He does. And I'll prove it." I pull my dead phone out and thumb the power button. "I've got message after message, a whole string of them showing exactly who I am to him."

But the moment my phone boots up, a barrage of electronic bleats erupts from it, like the squawks of a flock of startled seagulls. *Seventeen missed calls?* I think, *What the…* I only turned the damn thing off ten minutes ago. I check them and they're all from… *Evie?* There are half a dozen texts as well, all identical. *Call me. Now.*

I'm still staring at the last of these, when my phone starts to vibrate in my hand. It's her.

"Cat! Thank God."

"Listen, E, if you want to gloat about last night, this isn't the—"

"No! Listen, Cat!" She's yelling down the phone; there's a droning sound rising and falling on her end of the line and she's shouting to be heard over it. *"I don't know where you are, but you have to get back, right now. I saw it on the news."* And it's only then that I catch the note of panic in her voice, and the commotion in the background behind her snaps into focus – shouting, and engines, and something crackling – and suddenly I recognize the droning sound: sirens.

"Cat, it's your house; it's…"

But I don't hear the rest because I'm already trying to run, skipping and stumbling and waddling as best as I can towards the lift, Evie's panic-stricken voice buzzing indistinctly like a trapped wasp from the handset as it pumps up and down in my hand. I only turn back once I'm in the lift, gasping, already winded, and I watch the doors close on Ryan, the man I hoped – thought – would become my family. His guilty, fearful expression lingers behind my eye-blinks as I lurch out into the freezing night, flailing to flag down a cab to take me back to my *real* family.

The London night has too many sirens in it. They swell and then fade in my ears and each one quickens my pulse. *Is that it? Is that my house? Or that? Or that? Or that?*

As it is, I see the emergency at our little terraced maisonette before I hear it, as we swing around past the Tube station onto the Broadway. The light from the fire glimmers a dusty orange against the clouds.

"Evie!" I shriek, stumbling out of the taxi. "What, wh…" I tail off weakly and fall into her arms, staring over her shoulder at my home. Every window is a blast furnace, a black mouth gouting flame that surges into the night sky. It seems impossible that the sagging plumes from the hoses of the fire engines could ever make a dent in the blaze.

"M-m-m." My lips are numb, my teeth chattering, my tongue clumsy and lumpen in my mouth. "M-M-M-Mum, w-w-where's M-M-Mum?"

Evie stiffens in my arms. I pull away.

"M-M-M-Mum," I insist, even though I can barely form the word. "Where's M-M-Mum?"

She just looks at me helplessly. She shakes her head. "I don't know. The neighbours said the fire alarm went off."

I shake my head dumbly, like a dog who can't get a ringing out of its ears.

"M-M-Mum?" I stumble here and there between knots of gawpers and neighbours in their dressing gowns, ashen-faced, waiting for the fire to lick over the boundary to their houses. I pull on shoulders, tug on sleeves, look into every scared, sympathetic face, all glimmering with the flames, but none of them are hers.

"Hey, are you OK, sweetheart?" A coarse, male voice. I spin unsteadily. Battered high-vis-trimmed overalls, a beard and a hard hat. A fireman. "Is this your house?"

I nod, dumbly.

"Were you inside?"

I shake my head.

"But your mum was inside?"

"Y-yes, I think so."

"She didn't have mobility issues or anything? Not in a wheelchair, bed-bound, nothing like that?"

I shake my head again, but then freeze as the implication of his questions hits home. "Y-Y-You haven't g-g-got her out?"

"We haven't been inside yet. Need to get the blaze under control first. But I'm sure she would have got herself out. It was the neighbours who phoned the fire in, that's why there was a delay in getting here, but they say the alarm was loud enough to wake the dead."

It was the neighbours who phoned the fire in.

My legs go out from under me, but the fireman catches me under my arms and lowers me gently to the kerb.

"She … she took pills." I stare up at him, and an unnameable, impossible panic fills me up. "To sleep. I don't know if she would have woken up."

His face goes grey and he hustles off to talk to the men manning the hoses. I slump forward on the kerb, feeling my baby's heartbeat trip inside me, like it's sensed my fear. I can hear the roar of flames and shouted orders, something that might be Evie's voice calling my name, getting closer like she's rushing towards me, but the one thing filling my mind is the fireman's last question, muttered half to himself as he turned away.

"And there was no one else in the house to wake her?"

CHAPTER TWENTY-THREE

Amy

For the first time since she came in here, she's crying. It's stupid, but for a split second, the way the kitchen lights glimmer off the water in her eyes makes me think I can see the reflection of the fire.

"It was all some stupid prank. They found scraps of paper and carbonized organic material when they finally picked over the wreck. Their best theory? Some Ricker with an axe to grind had shoved a burning envelope with a dog turd in it through our letter box; the fire caught on the carpet and then the wallpaper, and then really accelerated when it hit the insulation. The smoke alarm went off, of course, but we were on the end of the terrace and the Singhs next door were away. All whoever it was wanted was for me to stamp shit into my carpet, but there was no one there to do that, because I..."

Then she sniffs, wipes her tears away with the back of her wrist and the moment's gone.

"Now," she says, her composure reasserted. "If you're done with your little interrogation, perhaps you wouldn't mind telling me how you knew my name."

I don't know why I do it. Perhaps it's pity, or fellow feeling. After all, I know what it's like to lose a mother. Perhaps it's deeper than that: she's given me a secret, and I owe her one in return, and after a year of hanging all my secrets out in public for everyone to see, I finally have one to trade.

It's a handful of footsteps back into the hall to the little downstairs loo. She follows me like a curious puppy. I pull the cloned phone out from under the loose tile, blow the flakes of enamel off it, and hold it out to her.

She hesitates, then lunges at it, like a starving woman with a loaf of bread. Her legs fold under her and she sits on the floor, muttering to herself as she scrolls.

"She stole ... no, she *cloned* his phone. Clever, clever." She shakes her head as though in admiration for my mother's ingenuity. Her thumbs flicker as she interrogates the device. "You little bastard, Smith. You spineless shitting coward... You..."

Her face is cut between the glow from the phone screen and the flicker of the green light on the bomb vest in the hollow of her throat; her eyes flicker rapidly as she scans the handset. I find myself pressing back against the cold bowl of the toilet, away from the intensity in her gaze. A helicopter chops the air overhead, dulled by the walls of the house.

Then, abruptly, she slows. Her jaw locks; she chokes out

a little sound, halfway between a laugh and a sob. She drops the phone in her lap.

"I knew it. I knew it was her."

The way she says *her* leaves no room for doubt.

"Mum was Mad Hatter," I say.

"Of course she was." She exhales heavily. "Not that she left any conclusive evidence to that effect, by the looks of things. I don't suppose *you'd* be prepared to testify, by any chance?"

"She … she was my mother."

One half of her face twists into a smile, but the expression never gets north of her cheekbone.

"Shame." She plucks at the bomb vest. "I don't think my credibility will be up to much as a witness, even if I do change my clothes and dress the part."

She stabs a few letters into the phone, then flicks her wrist, and it skitters over the tiles to my feet.

"There," she says. "Want to know what your mother did to me? What she was *really* like? Read that."

With some trepidation, I pick up the handset. She's put *Catherine Canczuk* into the email's search bar. *87 results,* the OS proudly proclaims. I glance at one of them.

From: Halaholo, Karen
To: Smith, Benjamin P.
Sent: 31/03/2024
Ben,
Hope you're feeling better. Had to write a prescription
for this patient, Catherine Canczuk, while you were out.

252

Occurred to me she's been here rather a long while. Isn't it time she was up for review?

And the reply:

Karen,
She's under review; snafu with the file, leave it with me.
Thanks for the heads-up.
B.

Karen, it seems, did leave it with our dear Dr Smith, since she never asked about it again. I scroll down.

From: Fitzgerald, Michael
To: Smith, Benjamin P.
Sent: 01/12/2024
Hi Ben,
During a consultation this morning, one of my patients
(Alexander Chariotis – see attached) claimed he'd
been talking to a Catherine Canczuk, who I believe is
one of yours? Apparently she's going around saying
she's been held here against her will for years?
I checked her file, and turns out she's a self-referral
from three weeks ago! Anyway, just thought I'd mention
it to you.

Mike,
Cheers. CC's a special case: acute psychotic episodes.

Appreciate the note; will ask the nurses to make extra sure
she's keeping up with her meds.
Best,
Ben

A self-referral from three weeks ago? But the email from Karen
was sent *eight months* before the one from Mike Fitzgerald.

Then I remember the dick pic, and the almost sing-song
threat from Hatter, Mad.

*Our agreement. Adherence advised. I advocate absence of
activity.*

"He doctored the file. He kept changing it so your review
date never came up." I must mutter it loud enough for Polly
to hear, because she snorts.

"Oh, almost certainly. But it was about the only thing he
doctored the whole time I was in there. Christ knows how that
man came by a medical licence. Maybe he forged that, too."

"But … but…" I find myself wanting to protest. It's too
appalling. My brain wants to refute it, find some reason it
couldn't happen. But as I flick through the eighty-seven hits
for Catherine Canczuk's name, I see the same story over and
over again: people highlighting the case of the woman now
smiling sadly opposite me in her explosive waistcoat, and
Dr Benjamin P. Smith smoothly fobbing them off, blaming
clerical mistakes and IT errors for any anomalies, and then
kicking her deeper into the bureaucratic weeds.

For seventeen *years*.

"Where did they keep you?"

Polly peers at the narrow window. The dirty grey of pre-dawn is leaking through the cobwebs.

"See for yourself," she proposes. "Our Ben was always an early riser. I'm sure he'll be at work by now."

I close out of the emails and open the maps app. Sure enough the happy little blue dot is glowing at a large building in Primrose Hill, which Google's label helpfully informs me is the acute inpatient wing of the Granby Hall Psychiatric Clinic.

"But he ... he *couldn't*." I say it because I want it to be true, not because I believe it.

"Why not?" Polly asks. "He was my doctor. He wrote my file. My file said I was psychotic. If your file says you're psychotic, why would anyone listen to you?"

She sucks her teeth, as though considering. "Really, no matter what clever systems you try to put in place, it all, always, comes down to who you trust. I must say, there were lots of times when even I was tempted to trust *him*. Even though I knew what he was doing to me; after all, he had a white coat and a stethoscope..." She made a face. "Actually, a golf jumper and nicotine teeth, but metaphorically you take my point. He was the expert and he said I was crazy; who was I to argue?"

"But ... others, in the hospital, they must have..."

"They did. You can see they did. But they only needed fobbing off for so long. Busy people, assuming the best about their colleague. Once you've been in for a while, they only need to review you every six months; that's plenty of time for them to forget about you if they don't have a reason to remember."

It's like a bunch of needle-sharp icicles are being fed, one by one, into my spine.

"Mum stole a naked picture of a psychiatrist and used it to blackmail him into trapping you in a mental hospital."

"So it appears."

"Why?"

For the first time since I've met her, Polly's smile turns *nasty*. "Well, I suppose because she was a very determined woman, wasn't she?"

That's not what I asked, and she knows it. She scoots forward on her bum until her face is a few inches from mine. Her breath still smells of tea.

"Do you think he was right? Do you think I'm crazy?"

It's all I can do to hold her unblinking gaze.

"Do *you*?" I counter.

She barks a delighted laugh. "Ha! Now you sound exactly like he did! Ever consider a career as a shrink, Amy? Never give an answer when a question will do."

"But *do* you?" I press, because the little green light is now close enough that, if I cross my eyes, I can see it reflecting off the end of my nose, and it suddenly matters very much to me what the woman holding the trigger believes about her own mental state.

"Interesting question. I suppose, statistically, I must be. Funny thing about mental wards, they're a bit like prisons – if you don't belong when you get there, the place has a way of making you *fit in*. Same with the ward: locked up, given plastic food and weird drugs, and the only people you get to talk to are either diagnosed themselves or doctors who probably ought to be. I tell you the worst part, though – it's the consultations. They make you pick over your thoughts again and again until the most banal ones seem spectacularly psycho. You know how if you stare at a word for long enough, it starts to look weird, like you've misspelled it? It's like that, but with your whole brain."

She takes a long breath. "I'm just saying, the place changes you, you know?"

I think of the chirpy, bespectacled redhead in the photo I found on the Tumblr site, that the woman in front of me was somehow hewn from. What on earth could have driven Mum to put her through that?

"Yes," I say. "I see." I hesitate, then ask, "How *did* you get in there then?"

"I'm sorry?"

"Mum was blackmailing your doc to keep you in, but how did you get in there in the first place?"

"Ah." Polly's smile turns a little sickly. "Well, that's another story."

CHAPTER TWENTY-FOUR

Cat

"Dubs? Horse Girl? Cat? *Cat!*"

I blink. The flames vanish and the world comes swimming back. The first thing I become aware of is the cold around my belly and aching back, and I remember that the pyjamas I'm wearing were borrowed from a woman half my size, even before I became house, home and supply depot for a whole other human being.

The second thing I become aware of is the sickening way my left foot dangles over nothingness.

"Come away from there."

I obey on instinct rather than will. I stagger back into Evie's arms and she gives a little grunt of effort as she lowers me gently to the floor, but she's stronger than she looks. In front of us, the attic window creaks as it flaps open in the wind, the rooftops of south London spread out before us like little insect carapaces, gleaming under the moon.

"What were you doing?" Evie breathes in my ear.

"I was just... I was just..." But with a little lurch I realize *I don't know.* I haven't slept more than a few minutes at a time since the fire, and my eyes throb and everything is skewed and nauseous with it. Evie's house has four storeys, and the attic looks south-west; if you get your bearings by the clock tower of the old church on Mitcham corner you can ... could ... see the little three-stack chimney of my house from there.

I couldn't sleep, so I crept past her room and up the last set of stairs, sagging winded on the banister at the top. Some tiny, mad part of my brain I couldn't silence kept needling me, asking *What if, through that window, things are different? What if you can still see it from there?*

But I looked and, of course, I saw nothing, not even the blackened slag. The ruin of the chimney had collapsed below the roofline of the other houses.

Panic and despair welled up in me. I suddenly remembered being tiny, maybe four or five, and losing Mum in the bustle of a supermarket, and running up and down the aisles of cereal and vegetables and frozen meat frantically searching for her and not finding her and battling against the growing conviction she was gone, gone, and I was never getting her back, and tears springing up hot in my throat because it was my fault, because she *told* me to keep hold of her hand.

This felt exactly like that, only edged in a leaden despair, because I knew it would never end, because there was no bored girl with a supermarket PA system who could call her to the customer information desk from where she'd gone now. And then I was back watching the burning house, and then...

And then I sort of lost touch with myself.

"I was ... I was just," I say again. I'm trying to say *I was just trying to see where the house was*, but then I remember my foot hanging out over nowhere, like I was testing the water in a swimming pool. And just like that I burst into tears.

"Hey, *hey*." Gentle fingers take my chin and turn me. A blurry cloud of dark and pale becomes Evie as she takes my glasses, cleans them on the sleeve of her silk pyjama top and sets them back on my nose. She looks at me, anxious but re-solved. "It's OK," she says. "I understand. "We'll get help."

It's not how I imagined it. There's no ambulance, just a quiet cab ride through night-time streets, with Evie gripping my hand. I don't have the strength to pull away, so I just stare angrily at the rain-streaked windowpane. Random bursts of tears keep overwhelming me, to the point where I have to ditch my glasses and put contacts in, because other-wise I can't see. When we get there, there are no sterile fluorescent bulbs and hospital lino, just smooth light wood floors for the wheelchairs to rumble softly over, and gentle recessed lighting, like a Nordic show kitchen. No figures in white coats, just a man in a diamond-patterned V-neck jumper with a name tag who greets Evie with a hug, like she's an old friend. I try to listen to their conversation but my head's swimming and I only catch fragments.

"Delicate situation, as you can see..."

"That's the problem. We're not quite sure who the legal guardian is at the moment..."

"... make an exception, for now, for you..."

"Thank you, Ben."

There are forms, lots and lots of forms. I try to read them, but I can't make myself. I can't face the words on them. They're too frightening. But the thought of my foot hanging out of that window's even worse, so in the end I just sign them anyway. To the right of my scrawl is an empty white box marked *Parent or guardian's signature (if patient under 18)* and I have to bite my cheek until I taste blood to keep from crying again.

The room they lead me to doesn't have padded walls. There's a single bed with a taupe duvet cover and an armchair in the same colour, a TV mounted on a wall bracket, a vase of yellow flowers and a window with what the businesslike, meaty-palmed nurse tells me is a "lovely view of the garden in daytime". The vase for the flowers is plastic, though, not glass; the window is cross-hatched with anti-shatter wire, and I can't see any way to open it. Looking around, I note with a queasy gratitude that there are no sharp corners or edges in the whole place. Everything is subtly rounded and cushioned, like it's been baby-proofed.

"Well, if you need anything, you've only to push that button," the nurse is saying. I give a dazed nod and sit on the edge of the bed. She smiles, and exits, closing the door behind her. I hear two clicks: one from the latch as it catches, a second that must be a lock.

I stare up into the TV and my reflection stares back. I don't know how long I sit like that – it could be minutes; it could be hours – but I'm still there when the contractions start.

"Holy *JESUS!*"

Turns out the malign goddess who created period pain has kept her masterwork back to spring on me in this moment. When the spasm finally subsides, I sag, gasping, and then yelp, because I've accidentally compressed my abdomen. I lurch for the little white button.

"Yes, love?" What feels like an eternity later, the nurse pokes her head around the door.

"I think" – the words ride a tidal surge of panic up my throat – "I think I'm going into labour."

"OK." She doesn't seem even slightly concerned. "Would you like me to run you a bath?"

"A *bath?* Shouldn't I go to a hospital?"

"This is a hospital, love."

"I mean a proper hospital, mouthwash-coloured gowns, beeping machines and obste… *Obste— Aaaah!*" The last word is cut off in a strangled yelp because another spasm is mangling my womb.

"There's no rush for that, love. How often are you having contractions?"

"I… I don't know. Too often?"

She perches on the end of my bed, looks at her fob watch and waits, patient and silent as a garden gnome, until another wave of pain blitzes through me.

262

"Not nearly often enough; that was at least twelve minutes after the last one. You'll need to be having three every ten minutes, consistently, before they'll have you upstairs. Now, let's see to that bath; it'll help. I promise."

She vanishes into the tiny bathroom and I hear the gurgle of taps over my onrushing thoughts. *Three every ten minutes?* It's unimaginable.

"I'm Joy," she says cheerily when she emerges. She extends a hand, I think initially for me to shake, but then I see the two white pills nestled there.

"Morphine?" I ask hopefully.

Her brow wrinkles. "Paracetamol. Jesus, honey, what are you trying to do to that little kid in there?"

Taking paracetamol for these contractions feels a little like trying to take on the concentrated might of the US Navy with strong language and a water pistol but I neck them anyway; and it might be a placebo effect, but the next time the agony carousel swings my way it does feel *slightly* milder.

"Bath's ready," Joy announces cheerily after the spasm dies away. She ambles over, takes hold of the hem of my sweater and starts to pull it up over my head.

"I can ... I can undress myself," I protest, self-consciously yanking the top back down.

Joy makes a *tch* sound in the back of her throat. "You can if you want, love, but shy's not really going to be an option in a few hours, so if I were you I'd get some practice in accepting help."

263

So I let her undress me, and guide me naked and Zeppelin-like to the bath. The warm water is *blissful*. I never knew it was possible to crave a bath the way you can crave toast when you're really starving, but turns out it is.

But the spasms come and go and come again, faster and harder and more often. All the muscles in my back start to lock up in sympathy with the ones in my womb and Joy kneads and pummels them with an expertise that says those axe-head palms of hers weren't acquired by accident.

Soon, though, all the warm water and massive hands and mild analgesic drugs in the world aren't enough to stem the pain. It's long since ceased to feel localized to my womb. Now when a contraction comes the pain spreads to every corner of me. It fills me up, taking the shape of me like water. I'm adrift on it, groaning and sweating and leaking spit from between my teeth. And all the while, Joy watches on, dispassionately, now and then checking her watch like she's waiting for a cake to bake and it would ruin it to open the oven door too early. Eventually she pulls a phone from her pocket and makes a call.

"Ted? Yeah, I think she's getting close. Shall I put her on?"

She hands me the phone, and it takes all of my concentration to make my fingers work enough to clutch it.

"'Lo," I manage to say.

"Hello, is that Catherine?" a jolly voice answers. "My name's Theodore, Theodore Olofade, call me Ted. I'll be your obstetric surgeon this evening. Joy tells me your contractions are coming along nicely, so it'll be time for us to see you soon. If you could rank the pain for me on a scale from one to ten, that would be very helpful."

"*Gnngh,*" I grunt.

"*Very* good, thanks, Catherine. If you could pass me back to Joy, that would be wonderful."

Apparently *Gnngh* was the magic word, because as soon as Joy puts the phone down she's easing me to my feet, towelling me off, tying a massively oversized dressing gown around me, and holding my elbow as I limp slowly towards the lift.

"The ... lift?" I mumble. "Not ... hospital?"

"I told you, this is a hospital."

"Proper – oh *Christ* – hospital."

She sighs. "You're not the first of our patients to go through this while you're with us. It's much easier for us to have it happen on site where we can manage things properly, so we had a little ward installed upstairs. Just the one bed, but all the gizmos, and of course we've got Ted on call. We put him on notice as soon as you arrived."

Where we can manage things. I remember the click as they locked me in and it flits through my mind that maybe they had some brand-new mother run out on them once, but then another star of agony goes nova in my uterus and that thought goes away. There's a liquid splatter sound and my legs suddenly feel wet and warm. I look down.

"I, uh," I mumble.

"I know, honey. Don't worry; just keep moving. You're

265

doing brilliantly. We'll get that cleaned up."

Ted's wearing the first white coat I've seen in this place and it's kind of pathetic how reassuring I find that. He's a middle-aged man with a welcoming smile and grey eyebrows so bushy and mobile I'm fairly sure they're sentient. The big mechanical bed has an ominous pair of stirrups hanging over it.

"Should I get into bed?"

"Why, are you sleepy?"

"I mean, to have the baby."

"Oh, I shouldn't think we're there yet. I'll need to check your dilation now, but other than that, the bed's mostly for sleeping in."

"*I. Cannot. Possibly. Sleep,*" I hiss at him, completely incensed that this man would even suggest that was a possibility.

He shrugs. "You say that now, but after twenty-four hours of pushing, you'd be surprised how tired you can get. Sleep's very important; you need to preserve your strength." He says it like he's urging me to take my vitamins, or floss. "But if it's a problem we can give you an epidural. No father, I take it?"

"He's…" A wave of helpless fury chokes me. "No."

"Never mind, they're really only good for back rubs at this point, and we can put Joy here on massage duty. Can you hop up onto the bed, and put your feet into the stirrups for me?"

Do I look like I can hop anywhere in my present condition, Dr Mammothbrows? I can, however, thanks mostly

266

to Joy's superhuman strength, be nudged and gentled and manoeuvred and—

"OWWWWWWWWWWWWWW!"

"Yes, bending your legs into the stirrups will put some pressure on your abdomen; it might cause some discomfort, but we'll get you out of them as soon as we can. I just need to … ah. OK, seven point three centimetres, coming along nicely but a way to go yet."

"Oh … joy."

"Yes, love?"

"Not you. Help me up, please."

"Yes, love."

The pain comes in waves, cresting and ebbing and cresting again. I'm being turned inside out, and am gripped with sudden awful panics and sweats. I scream and groan and scream and vomit and scream again, and Joy's there, she's always there, cleaning up my spit, rubbing my back and telling me I'm doing well, so, so well.

Time becomes greasy and slow. My contacts burn my eyes and I have to take them out and the world becomes a cloud of coloured smudges. Somehow, I find myself back in the stirrups screaming my head off and Dr Ted's saying, "OK, it's time to push now. Let's get you to your feet; let gravity lend a hand."

I crouch beside the bed and claw at the sheets and strain and groan and growl and mangle myself. I have never been this … *animal*. Some deeply buried instinct takes over and I *push* with muscles I've never felt like I had any control over before. I bear *down* and *out*. At some point I feel a lightness behind my spine and there's a familiar smell that it takes me long seconds to identify as my own shit, and I am vaguely aware that I ought to be embarrassed but I am so far past embarrassment right now and no one comments and Joy clears up and *I. Don't. Stop. Pushing.*

My breath comes in high, frantic gasps. I will never have enough air. *Push.*

"We're crowning," Dr Ted says from somewhere by my knees and a million miles away. "OK, Catherine, one final push."

I scream, long and high and loud. I feel like I'm being torn open.

And just like that, the pain's gone.

"Got her," Dr Ted says, behind me.

There's a coughing gurgle, and then the electrifying sound of a baby crying.

No, not *a* baby. *My* baby.

I try to stand, to turn, but a wave of dizziness knocks my feet from under me and it takes Joy, brick-like dependable Joy, to catch me and guide me back to bed.

"Her?" I breathe. A warm, crying, squirming bundle is placed on my stomach, and my heart catches and I look down, but everything's still blurry.

"I can't..."

But just as I'm saying *see*, I feel hands over my temples and the world slides into focus. "Evie went and got your glasses for us," Joy's saying.

And there you are.

You're so tiny. So small and warm and *human* and alive and you were a part of me and now you're not any more except you still are and you always will be and my head can't manage to get itself around you, but my heart can. It latches on to you and it will never let you go.

Dr Ted's fussing around you, clearing out your nose and your ears, checking your pulse. He makes a little noise in the back of his throat, and immediately I'm at DEFCON 1.

"What? *What?* Is she OK?"

"What? Oh, nothing. She's perfect."

Too right she is, doc.

You squirm and scrabble and make little mewling noises. Your tiny hands grasp and clutch. Joy wraps you in a towel, puts a little cap on your head and helps you into my arms and I cradle you next to my breast and you lick and nuzzle and latch on.

"We'll leave you two to it for a bit."

Perfect. There is no other word for the next few hours. You doze and snuffle and feed and cry and doze again, and Joy and Dr Ted bustle in and out and take your temperature and reassure me that you're fine and pull in a little plastic bassinet for you to sleep in so I can sleep too, but I don't want to, because I love you – oh God, I love you so much. There's an invisible cord binding your heart to my heart, and it will never, ever be cut.

But then *he* comes.

I hear a little cough, oh so diffident, and reluctantly

I look up from you. It's the doctor who first brought me in here, the one with the diamond-patterned V-neck. He has a binder and a solemn expression. Evie's just behind him, smiling sadly at me.

"Catherine, I'm Ben. I don't know if you remember me. It's good to see you so well. I'm afraid we need to talk."

"Afraid?"

He pulls two pieces of paper from the binder and hands them to me. They're the forms I signed when I came in. The parent signature box is still blank and I swallow against a sudden choking sensation. He's marked two printed statements with little hand-drawn stars:

* In the last twenty-four hours I have attempted to take my own life.
* I believe I am a danger to myself and/or others and voluntarily commit myself...

"Under the circumstances" – he speaks woodenly, like he's reading from a script – "we have to look to the safety and welfare of the child before anything else."

A claw clutches at my guts. "No."

"It's just for the immediate—"

"NO!" I scream it at him and you wake up and start crying. Evie sweeps you up and rocks you gently until you quiet. Ben "looking to your safety and welfare before anything else" Smith doesn't bat an eye.

"Catherine, I understand this is difficult to hear, but you

have, by your own admission and with at least one witness, sought to end your own life in the past twenty-four hours. Caring for a newborn is exceptionally demanding. We *have* to ask if you are capable of it in your current state. And if you won't recognize that, then that only makes us ask the question even more urgently, so..."

Evie mutters under her breath, *"Cretin."* She pushes him aside. "Listen, Cat, how long have I known you?"

"Three years? Since the Knockout tour; feels like for ever."

"Right, and do you trust me?"

I don't answer; my eyes flash from you to her and back again. I don't think I can trust *anyone* that far.

"Cat," she says gently. "Look at where you are; this is a psychiatric hospital. And that is, by your own *brave* recognition" – she squeezes my arm – "exactly where you need to be right now, so you can get well and be the best mum you can. But I can't tell you how long you'll need to be here, nor can Ben, nor – with the best will in the world – can you. And this is no place for a baby, for *your* baby. You understand that, right?"

My baby. I look over to you for reassurance. Swallow, and nod.

"Normally, under these circumstances," she goes on, "the father would look after the baby while you got well. But that's not really an option here, is it?"

Another swallow, and a headshake.

"Thankfully we have another option. I can look after her,

271

just for now, just until you get well. I'm my own boss, so I can take time off work; I'll bring her to visit every day and as soon as you get out, she'll be back in your arms. That's the best solution, but because we're not related, I need your consent, your signature."

Her tone is gentle, her eyes full of concern and, yes, even love. And I'm exhausted. But all of that butts up inside me against the iron-hard fact that she's planning to take you away from me.

"And if I don't give it?"

Ben Smith clears his throat. "Then I and two colleagues would need to assess your case and make a recommendation to a judge about whether you are able to care for your daughter. I understand your mother was an only child, like you yourself. Her parents have both passed away, and with her recent..." He tails off under my gaze, swallows hard and then continues. "There'd be no guarantee that it would be anyone you knew, or indeed that it would be reversible if your stay here became prolonged."

I stare at the forms in my hand.

   * In the last twenty-four hours I have attempted to take my own life.

My heart is screaming denial, snapping and hissing like a cornered animal, but I grit my teeth and swallow, and look at you and tell myself this is for you; this is for the best.

Because, damn them, they're right.

They bring me forms, and I sign them, and my hand is shaking so hard the signature's barely recognizable as mine, but they don't seem to mind.

Evie squeezes my shoulder. "Brave girl, Cat," she whispers. "This is what being a mother is."

They bustle off to arrange a car seat and leave me alone with you. You look up at me, and you must sense the part of me that's breaking because you start to cry again, and this time no amount of rocking or cooing or cradling will soothe you. You cry and you cry and I feel your voice like a piano wire over my nerves and I think, *This is proof you're better off with them.*

I try to distract you. I give you your hat and your blanket to hold, but you just throw them down, and my glasses case catches my eye, the little red cleaning cloth poking out of the corner. In desperation I grab that and give it to you, and for no reason I can think of, your cries ease.

The cloth is still clutched in your tiny fist when Evie comes back for you. I watch you as she carries you out, and the shadow of the door crosses your face. That little square of red is the last thing I see.

CHAPTER TWENTY-FIVE

Amy

I stare at the woman before me: cross-legged on the cold bathroom tiles, her hair hacked off with no deference to style, the only goal to have it shorter. I study the face so twisted and battered by suffering that she's almost unrecognizable from the girl I saw on the Tumblr account, the girl she was only seventeen years before.

Her voice was dead the whole time she was speaking. I know that tone; I know that if I streamed off her right now, I'd suffocate on the numbness she's wrapped like fibreglass around her heart. I wonder if she even knows she's crying.

But I don't stop to watch the tears spot our precious upholstery. My feet are already in motion under me, my body moving faster than my sluggish brain can follow. I'm pounding up the stairs, clawing the banister past me for extra speed, swinging right, into Mum and Dad's room. The dust sheet from Mum's wedding bolero is still on the floor where

Polly discarded it. My feet get tangled in it and I fall. My jaw smacks against the floor, and I bite my tongue and taste metal in my mouth. I spit, and the carpet's sprayed red.

Panting, I drag myself to my feet by the edge of Mum's dressing table. My reflection appears in triplicate in the three mirrors arrayed on the back. My eyes are wild, my skin flushed, the shadows under my eyes like the silhouettes of standing stones at sunset. I look deranged, and at last I see a glimmer of resemblance.

It can't be, a part of me is screaming. *It can't be it can't be it can't be no no no no NO! It can't be.*

Like she said, it all comes down to who you trust: Catherine Canczuk, who came in here with a bomb strapped to her chest? Who half the known Internet proclaimed to be a liar, a fraud, criminally insane? Is that who you'd choose?

Sure, she *seemed* vacant and numb downstairs, like she barely knew what she was saying. But maybe she *did* know. Maybe the whole story was constructed on purpose? Maybe it was all a scheme to get me to believe?

Believe what? At least say it; say it to yourself.

But I can't.

Memories rise, like tiny bubbles in the saucepan of my mind, getting bigger and faster and more numerous with every passing second. The way Mum couldn't find my birth certificate when I lost my passport and needed to get it renewed. The way everyone says Charlie looks just like Dad did at his age, but no one has ever said that about me.

I can hear creaking on the steps behind me.

275

This makes sense of everything. The phone. The emails. Mad Hatter. Everything.

But that could be deliberate. Polly knows as much about all this as I do. She could have cut her tale to fit the evidence like a key to a pre-existing lock.

Behind me, I hear the latch click as the doorknob starts to turn.

Why would she do that? Why would she lie?

She found me online. She became obsessed. There are plenty of crazy people in the world and the Internet brings them all to your doorstep.

OK, fine, then why did Mum blackmail the doctor to keep her locked up then?

I don't know she did. I'm bargaining now, desperate. *I've only got Polly's word for that.*

Then why the Mad Hatter emails? Why the hidden phone?

Because ... because she planted them! Polly, Cat, whatever her name is. She had all the time in the world while we were at the funeral. She locked me in that room. She must have meant me to find it. Yes, that's it!

That other voice inside me falls silent.

See? I think in relief. *It always comes down to who you trust.*

Except, very occasionally, it doesn't.

My gaze roves over the top of the dressing table. Hands trembling, I pluck aside the tangled clots of jewellery, the dusty face-down photographs.

And then I see it. My heart's going like a trip hammer,

pumping blood through my wounded tongue and into my mouth. I reach for it, clutching it as tight as I ever did. The little scrap of red cloth that served as a comfort blanket as a baby, the one Mum was so desperate to wean me off, but that I wouldn't let go.

The one I never told anyone about, not ever, not on Heartstream, not anywhere. The one that's just the right size and softness to clean a pair of glasses with.

In the mirror I can see her hovering in the doorway, flustered and uncertain.

"Did you know what you were saying?" I croak. "That whole time downstairs when you were talking, did you know you were saying *you*? You *looked up at me*; *this is for* you. *Oh God, I love* you *so much*?"

She just stares at me. I reach into my mouth and dab my tongue. The blood I smear between my finger and thumb is almost exactly the same colour as the cloth. I look into the mirror and meet the eyes of the woman who gave it to me.

3
LOVE ALL,
TRUST A FEW

CHAPTER TWENTY-SIX

Cat

My body gave up on you before I did.

Two days after she took you, my milk came in properly. My breasts ached with the weight of the milk and my back ached with the weight of my breasts and my heart ached with … well, my heart ached with everything.

Joy came with a pump a couple of times a day and let me squeeze out just a trickle. "Just enough to make you comfortable, hon," she said, like that was anywhere close to possible. "When your body realizes there's no call for it, the milk will go away."

"But there *is* a call for it," I said. I looked up anxiously at her kind, round, competent face. "Evie'll bring her back. She said she'd bring her back for visits. I'm her mother. I need to be able to feed her when she's here!"

Joy's expression was full of sympathy. "OK, lovely," she said gently, but she still only let me express a tiny bit into the little plastic bottle, and then took the pump away no matter how I begged.

In the days that followed, I swore blind to her that I needed more, that my breasts still hurt, that – I thought I was being crafty; she'd have to take this seriously, surely! – I might be getting an infection in them. And Joy patiently examined them for redness and swelling and gave me a pair of cold gel packs to put into my bra. "OK, lovely," she'd say mildly. But she still took the pump away.

At first, I squeezed more out myself, bent over the sink in my little bathroom, uttering little wheezes of pain as my fingers gripped the skin. But then day after day went by, and she didn't bring you. They returned the clothes I'd been wearing before the birth. They were freshly laundered and pressed, but my mobile wasn't with them, and the old black phone beside my bed stayed silent. When I tried to call Evie from it to ask where my family was, all I got was a girl from reception who informed me in a bright, clear voice that outward calls from residents in the first month of their stay were against the clinic's treatment guidelines.

And I sat, and I stared out of the window at the garden, and I ate when Joy brought food and expressed when Joy brought the pump, and fought to remember your face as you looked up at me, and flicked through the magazines they brought me without seeing them, and every now and then broke down into choking, gasping fits of tears, my chest crushed by the absence in my arms.

After a week or so, Ben started to visit. He insisted I call him Ben rather than Dr Smith. He wore the same diamond-patterned V-neck sweater he'd had on the night he'd signed me in – like he'd just wandered in off a golf course – but there were deep dark crescents under his eyes.

"Not been sleeping, Ben?" I asked. He blinked and took off his glasses and cleaned them with a handkerchief he pulled out of his pocket, and that gesture reminded me of the little red cloth I'd given you and suddenly I wanted to cry or kill him or maybe both.

"Why do you ask?" he said eventually. "Have you not been sleeping?"

"My baby's been stolen, so no, I've not been getting all forty of my winks in. What's your excuse?"

When he replied, the coldness in his voice was like a shield. "It sounds like you're fixated on this idea of 'your baby'."

I just stared at him. "Astonishing," I said, at last well and truly flabbergasted.

"How so?"

"That is the single stupidest statement I have heard in my entire life. Of course I'm fixated on my baby: she's *my baby*."

Again the glasses came off, again the cleaning. I wondered if it was a nervous tic for him.

"It's very important for your healing that you start to let go of the idea of 'your baby'. I understand it's difficult, but we're here to help you."

"It's very important for your healing that you start to let

go of the idea of 'your breathing'." I mimic the antiseptic mildness of his tone scornfully. "I understand it's difficult, but we're here to help you."

"Catherine—"

"Seriously, doc. What are you talking about? She's my baby. Evie said she'd bring her back to visit. You were there. Why hasn't she come? She hasn't even called – why hasn't she called?"

Another sigh. "No, she hasn't called. Catherine, you've had a terrible trauma. The loss of your home, your mother, that would devastate anyone. And with your father also missing… In cases like yours it's not uncommon for a patient to create the idea of another relative, so they can feel that the family unit that has supported them is not wholly destroyed—"

"You're trying to tell me my baby is a hallucination?"

"I'm trying to—"

"Fuck you."

I delved into my bra for the cotton wool pad pressed against my nipple and threw it at him. It had been in there for a couple of hours and was well sodden so it made a satisfying squelchy sound as it hit his cheek.

"So I guess my boobs are hallucinating milk?"

He peeled the pad from his skin. He looked deathly pale. Almost like he was more appalled by the words coming out of his mouth than I was.

"Catherine, I know it's difficult now. It won't come right away, but eventually we will get you to the point where you can accept the truth. That it was an extremely difficult, premature birth, that the best obstetrician in London did his utmost, but in the end, nothing could be done."

As he spoke, I felt my throat closing. I shook my head, trying to speak, but there were no words in my mouth.

"The baby was lost in childbirth. It's not fair and it's not just, but it's what happened. We'll get you to the point where you can accept that, that's my promise to you."

And – I'm ashamed to admit – just for a tiny fraction of a second, a tiny sliver of time, I wondered if he was telling the truth. Then the image of you looking up at me flashed through my mind, your eyes roving over my face like you were fixing every pore and eyelash in your mind for all time. I'm your mother; that same commitment is the very least I owed you.

"No. You won't," I said. "That's my promise to you."

I had daily sessions with him at first. I couldn't get out of them. If I dragged my feet then Joy would literally carry me, uncomplaining and uncritical, wearing the same placid smile she always did. They couldn't make me talk, though, so I didn't. I might have tried if he had at least admitted what he was doing, holding me captive, away from you, but he kept insisting you were dead, that I was imagining you, that, in short, I was crazy. That – more than the locks on the doors or the strength in Joy's back muscles – was what he felt gave him power over me. If he strayed from it, he was weakened.

So, at ten every morning, *every* morning, I went to his office, and sat in silence on the same chintzy armchair listening to the mantelpiece clock chip fragments off our life together.

Time became strange. I started out keeping track of the days with tally marks, first on paper, which they took away, then on the bathroom soap, and then finally on the skin on the inside of my upper arm with a thumbnail. But as weeks stretched to months, it became too painful. Not physically, but I knew I was missing milestones: around about now your vision would be perfecting itself, your world becoming sharp and defined; this was the time you might be sitting up; you might be trying food for the first time today. I measured my own life by yours, the one I was missing, and I couldn't handle it. So I stopped.

As a result, I don't know how long I'd been inside when I met the unlikely individual who led me, eventually and indirectly, back to you. It was a bright spring day, and I was taking a walk around the garden. It was a pretty garden, with wide lawns and tall trees clustered in the middle (though none by the walls, of course). Word in the cafeteria was that when the summer leaves came in, the bushes all but hid the fifteen foot-high walls, and then it was like being in a park.

There was a boy standing looking at the peonies. He was skinny and pale and pimply, but he was about my age; and anyway, I liked peonies, always had done, so I wandered over.

"Hi," I said. "I'm Cat."

He flinched immediately, and then said, "Will Jenkins, of the Beaconsfield Jenkinses."

"Huh. Well, I guess I'm Catherine Canczuk of the

Tooting Canczuks, although I've never run into enough other Canczuks to make me feel like I needed to clarify."

He flushed. "Dad said I should introduce myself that way in here so people know who they're messing with. Or who they didn't ought to mess with, rather. Or..." He squinted at me. "Have you heard of the Beaconsfield Jenkinses?"

"I can't say I have."

He flushed deeper – this kid could give me a run in the blushing stakes – and then pulled his shoulders up protectively around his neck, bracing himself like he was expecting a punch.

"If it's OK with you, though, I'll refrain from messing with you anyway."

He looked reassured. The shoulders descended. "Thanks," he said.

"No problem. I'm sure your family's very famous and scary."

He made a face. "Not really. Dad's a lord and owns a big building supplies company so everyone does what he tells them, but he's not a gangster or anything. What brought you over here?"

"I just wanted to look at the flowers. I like peonies."

He grinned suddenly, and I saw he had braces. "Me too. They're like, *spooosh*." He mimed an explosion with his hands. "Like a frozen fireball."

I looked at the flowers. The petals were red and yellow, and layered into their big spherical heads. I could see what he meant.

"What are you in for?" he asked.

"I had a pop star's baby and they took her away, and now they're keeping me here so they can pretend she died." I'd had the same conversation a half-dozen times since I'd been in here. There was no harm in telling the truth, since no one believed you anyway. "You?"

"I tried to blow up Parliament," he said.

For a moment, the only sound was the ticking of the leaves in the wind.

"Wait ... seriously?"

"Well, I didn't get very far," he admitted. "I mean, I'd done a load of research: architectural drawings, modelling different explosive yields, chemical make-up analysis, you know, the basics; but before I could buy any of the actual materials, our cleaner found all the plans on my bedroom floor while I was having a pee. She called the police and they called Dad, and because he's Lord Beaconsfield – he's descended from Disraeli, or at least he says he is – they called a psychiatrist rather than the anti-terror squad, and here I am." He sighed, like he was talking about the love of his life who got away.

"Here you ... sorry, I'm still stuck on you wanting to blow up Parliament?"

"Yeah."

"Like Guy Fawkes."

The smile on his face became blissed out. "Yeah."

"Guy Fawkes, who has been burned in effigy annually for four hundred years and counting."

"Well, sure, people get tetchy about it, but at least they know his name. All my life, I've only ever been a Jenkins of the Beaconsfield Jenkinses; it's all I've ever been going to be. I just wanted people to know who *I* was." He came over all misty-eyed.

"It's overrated," I told him. "Trust me."

Despite myself, I liked Will Jenkins of the Beaconsfield Jenkinses, with his runny nose and cuffs he chewed when he was thinking. He drew me a (really good) picture of the peonies and I asked Joy for tape so I could stick it to my wall. We met again and again in the garden over that endless summer. He listened, enthralled, to my stories of being flayed alive on the Internet, and in exchange he geeked out to me about explosives, enthusing about the differences between anti-personnel and anti-structural like he was comparing the powers of his favourite superheroes.

And I talked to him about you. I had to talk to someone or it would have chewed its way out of my chest, and since I wouldn't talk to Smith and didn't trust Joy, he was it. I told him about all the love I had for you, bottled up behind my ribs and turning hour by hour, day by day, to acid. I swore blind to him that the moment I got out of that place I was going to find you and cherish you and be the best mum in the world to you.

And then one day – it was autumn by then; the brown leaves whipped around us in vortices, the wind was vicious and we were the only two outside – he turned to me. "You know they won't let you out of here while you keep talking about her like that, right?"

"I don't talk about her to them," I said.

"I know. But still, they know. They know she's all you think about, and they won't let you go until you let her go."

"Which means they won't let me go, ever." I sighed, and felt a kind of settling. I'd known it was true for a while, but it was the first time I'd said it aloud. "Which means it's time for plan B."

I reached into my jacket and pulled out a folded piece of paper. Puzzled, he took it and opened it out. It was his picture of the peonies, the tape still stuck to its edge because I hadn't wanted to tear it.

"Other side," I said, and he turned it over and read the notes I'd taken in tiny careful handwriting, and which – if everything he'd told me was true – outlined an explosive which could be made from chemicals used on the premises, and was powerful enough to blow through the locks on our doors.

I squeezed his wrist; his spit-soaked sleeve was freezing against my hand.

"Can you make this?" I asked.

A siren-shriek from outside brings me back to myself. My heart lurches up to speed like an outboard motor. I cast about myself. I'm slumped against the door frame of the kitchen, but I don't know how long I zoned out for.

Where are you? Where are you? Are you still here? Have you left me, like I left you?

The world sways and swims around me as I head down

the hallway. I can't remember the last time I slept.

You're not in the downstairs loo, or the spartan bedroom that was Evie Simms's last resting place. Increasingly frantic, I mount the stairs. I push on the door to your room, and there you are, on your side on your bed. Knees tucked in like when I carried you. Duvet rucked around your feet, eyes closed. You never even knew about my lapse of attention downstairs. A pang of longing seizes me, to put that pillow more fully under your head, to tuck that pretty winter-tree-patterned duvet up under your chin, to...

Stop, I plead silently with myself. *You have to stop.*

I swore I wouldn't do this. I *swore.* I renounced you. It hurt like cutting out my own heart, but I did what I told them I'd never do. I gave you up.

I told myself I'd made peace with the fact I'd never see your first steps, hear your first words, that you'd never call me *Mama.*

I didn't come here for you. I said it over and over, a mantra inside my head. I clung to it when you first rounded the kitchen door and saw me, and my heart lurched towards you. I had to tense every muscle in my legs not to run to you, every sinew in my neck and mouth not to beg you to remember me. I knew that if I did, you would reject me – a certified madwoman you'd never seen before claiming to be your mother, of course you would – and that rejection would destroy me.

And I will not be destroyed. I promised myself that over and over too, back in that prison with its perfumed garden and its smiling nurses and its needles and its lies. I will not let them break me: not your father, not the woman who made herself your mother.

Not even you.

I am here to find proof of what was done to me: that is enough. That *has* to be enough. I can't hope for more.

And yet, you stir, and your face shifts towards mine, and all the feelings I so carefully tamped down and sealed off pour back into me like gunpowder towards a fuse. It feels like no time has passed since I held you in my arms, like my heart has just now begun to beat again.

Oh God, what have I done to you? What am I *going* to do?

Your eyes snap open then. And I freeze, my blood thundering, because I can see *him* in them.

You stretch your back, like you've woken from a trance, holding my gaze the whole time, and I'm so afraid of what you're going to say to me that it's all I can do not to flee, out of the house and down the path and into the waiting crosshairs of the police marksmen.

I will not be destroyed.

You open your mouth; every muscle in me seizes up.

You say, "It doesn't make sense."

CHAPTER TWENTY-SEVEN

Amy

"What doesn't make sense?"

She blurts it out, awkward and off-balance, a guilty expression on her face, like she's been caught in the act of something embarrassing. Though what could embarrass her now is anyone's guess, given that she's already openly threatened to blow up her own ...

Say it, at least to yourself.

I clench my jaw; my mouth is full of too much spit and I swallow hard.

... her own daughter.

My head feels like a wasps' nest, vibrating, buzzing, angry.

"Why?" I ask.

I stand, slow, unsteady, but I stand. I can just about focus on the gaunt, frightened-looking woman in the bomb vest, but the world around her is fuzzy.

"*Why* would Mum do all this to you, trap you in a mental

hospital, blackmail the staff, why would she take that kind of a risk, why expose herself like that, just to have *me*?"

"She..." She hesitates and her expression hardens, but she forces the words out. "She loved you."

"Yes," I say. "She did. After weeks and months and years of feeding me and changing my nappies and reading to me at bedtime and driving me to school and making packed lunches."

Polly winces with each word, each maternal detail, and I'm not sure why I'm dwelling on them. I don't want to hurt her exactly, but it's a kind of defiance and a kind of loyalty. *I might not have been her daughter*, I'm saying, *but she* was *my mother*.

"But that love had to have a beginning, and to trap you in that place the way you say she did, she would have had to make *preparations*. What, you think you just happened to land in the care of a shrink who had a dick pic out there she could burn him with? Mum was methodical in this, just like she was in everything else. She was precise, she did *research*. And while she did all that, I was just a bag of cells in your uterus. So, why? Why do all this for *me*?"

Polly winces. "She ... she didn't do it *for you*. She did it *to me*. She hated me. Evie was..." She barks a short bitter laugh. "She was the best friend I've ever had. She was kind and smart and generous, but she was also a true believer. So much of her, her world, her status with her friends, her sense of herself, was wrapped up in her belief, in her *need*, for Nick to be Ryan's lover."

She recites it calmly, fluently. The past seventeen years have clearly given her a *lot* of time to think about this.

"But he wasn't; I was. She couldn't believe that, but in the end she couldn't evade it either. So she had to *make* it not true. She had to destroy me."

I try to reconcile that kind of insane jealousy with my logical, methodical, *kind* mother, and my brain just rebels. I can't see it. But then, seventeen years is a long time, and what has this whole endless, impossible day been if not proof that I didn't know her the way I thought I did?

"OK," I say slowly. "But even if that's true, what about … the father." I still can't make myself say *my*. "He just ignored me all my life? He *let* all this happen?"

"Ryan…" Her mouth shapes the words three times before sound comes out. "He never wanted you in the first place. It took me a long time to see it, but he didn't. He wanted you to go away."

"It's a pretty big step from *wish I'd been a bit more careful with my penis* to *I'm OK with abandoning my baby to the care of a psychopath and conspiring to falsely imprison her mother*," I object. "Especially with seventeen *years* to dwell on it. He was a rich guy with no problems paying child support. He must have had some other reason than just not wanting to give up partying. He must have…"

I tail off as the thought clicks into place. I walk straight past her and down the stairs. I hear the steps creak behind me as she follows, but I don't look round.

The kitchen is dim, sunlight barely bleeding through

the blinds. Is it just me, or is the hubbub of activity out on the street – the purr of engines and the crackle of voices – a little louder, a little more urgent than it has been?

The big flat screen is dark and I have to scrabble around under the table, sticking my thumb with a shard of Mad Hatter teapot, before I find the remote.

Polly arrives at my shoulder. I suck my injured thumb and switch on the TV.

It's still on the BBC news. A skinny dude in a suit and turban speaks to camera backed by stock prices, but the ribbon at the bottom of the screen reads: *Heartstream hostage situation enters twentieth hour – terror link confirmed.*

Terror link confirmed. I feel my throat narrow. I hit *rewind.* The coverage cycles back. It's not long before I see an aerial view of my house, spinning slowly clockwise on the screen like it's floating on a freshly poured cup of tea, then the picture cuts to footage of the street outside. Police cars, high-vis tape, reporters, stragglers, bunches of flowers and hand-drawn cards taped to nearby trees like I'm already dead. A close-up of my driveway, where fragments of my living-room window still glitter, and my stomach clenches at the rust-coloured stains among them.

I rewind further back to yesterday's programmes; and yes, there he is.

Pause.

London's mayor. Adrian R. Rijkaard stares belligerently down the lens. I've frozen the picture on him brushing his hair out of his eyes, and his right shirt cuff has ridden up, showing a thin sliver of darkness that might be the beginning of a tattoo. I hear a hissed breath at my shoulder. I look at my gouged thumb, remembering how the teapot became shattered.

I haven't ruled terrorism out of your face, *you duplicitous little shit.*

My phone still lies on the table, beside Mum's secret one. I gather it, and Polly does nothing to stop me – I'm not even sure she notices. Her gaze is still locked on the screen, her nostrils pinched and lips pulled back like she's staring at a scorpion. I open Wikipedia.

> Adrian Ryan Edgar Rijkaard is a politician, author and musician who is the eighth and incumbent Mayor of London.

I scroll down, and hit

Musical Career, 2016-2026

> *Main article: The Everlasting*
>
> Under his stage name, Ryan Richards, Rijkaard was a founding and continuous member of boy band The Everlasting until they went on permanent hiatus in April 2026. Along with other founding members Nick Lamb, Dion Butterfield and Stefan Wilhelmsen (Stef Williams), Rijkaard recorded six albums, all of which were certified multiple times platinum...

It started in the US, I remember Mum telling me, with Reagan. Then Schwarzenegger, then Trump. It was only a matter of time before it showed up here. Fame as the passport to power, to everything. She'd found it hilarious and terrifying. "People think you must make a good leader, just because they happen to know your name," she'd snort. "They'd probably vote for Mickey Mouse if he pinned a rosette on."

I'd vaguely known that the mayor used to be a pop star; I might even have heard some of his songs, although I couldn't be sure. I'd never paid much attention; it was old, stuff my parents would have listened to...

I let out a long breath to steady myself, and then study that face. I look left to the still snarling woman next to me. Yes, it's there if you looked for it. He's become pouchy and his hair has gone grey early. The life Catherine Canczuk has been forced to live has eroded her face almost beyond recognition. You can't see it if you only look at one or other of them, but if you *mix* his face with hers, you get something like a beaten-up version of the one staring back at me from my Heartstream profile pic.

An illegitimate kid with a vulnerable teenage fangirl isn't exactly the must-have accessory for every budding politician, and people on the news keep saying he wants to be prime minister one day. Yes, I can see why our mayor might've decided he didn't want anything to do with me.

Polly's lips are moving. She stares at the screen through a film of tears and it almost looks like she's praying, but then I make out the words:

"*I dreamed last night I rode a white horse, rode a white horse to the ocean...*"

I have no idea what she's on about. Maybe it's a poem.

I get to my phone to google it, when a subheading on the mayor's still-open Wiki stops me cold.

Political Career

Anti-Terror Controversy

I stab it with my thumb.

> Immediately upon entering office, following the Tulse Hill bombing, Rijkaard made several changes to the Metropolitan Police's anti-terror strategy, local policing powers having been substantially devolved to the so-called big three city mayors in June 2026.

> This new strategy included rules of engagement for terror scenarios that gave much greater latitude for the use of force, as well as guidelines on the use of new technology (particularly intra-limbic transducers) in the interrogation of terror suspects. Rijkaard received backing for these changes from Home Secretary Julia Ogunawa and widespread praise from the British media; however, some human rights organizations expressed concern that the use of the transducers was a breach of suspects' human rights.

Intra-limbic transducers, I think, putting my hand to the back of my head where the burred hairs are tipped with sweat. *We just call them patches.*

There's a link to a main article. I thumb it, and the story it tells is one I already know by heart. All streamers do.

There was a man, Ibrahim Karimov, who was rounded up in the Tulse Hill aftermath, but Ibrahim was a plumber, who just happened to share a name with one of the bombers. When it became undeniable that he had an unbeatable alibi, they had to release him, and when they did, he went on TV and told his story.

They'd stuck patches to his head, he said. And they'd made him stream, first off an advanced appendicitis patient, then off a guy on suicide watch, then off some woman with end-stage cancer. The mayor went on TV too, and admitted it, but said it wasn't technically illegal, since no "incremental harm" would have been done.

That statement became famous among us streamers. A punk band even called themselves Incremental Harm and got popular with people who used Heartstream, even though they were, in my opinion, shit.

"*And the white-crested waves, they crashed in the caves...*" Polly's still singing to herself. She's picked up the remote from where I left it, and she hits *play*.

"*We haven't ruled out terrorism,*" he grates, playing tough for the cameras. Is that what he has lined up for her?

"*... but there was never a sound of you.*"

She hits *fast forward*. Cops tape off cordons and footballers score goals and celebrities dance under spotlights at dizzying speed, until there's the mayor again, and she hits *play*.

"*We have identified the hostage-taker,*" he's saying. "*She is considered extremely dangerous, has significant diagnosed mental health conditions and has been known to associate with terrorists, including a man who plotted a foiled attack on the*

300

Palace of Westminster."

"Mayor Rijkaard, does this change your strategy for dealing with her?"

"We are still working for a peaceful resolution; force is always a last resort."

Fast forward.

"I rode my white horse to a secret city, the streets were paved with stars..."

Rijkaard's back on screen. I stare at him. *This man is my father.* As I try out the thought, the kind, placid face of the man I've always thought of as *Dad* appears in my mind. Did he know? Obviously he must have known he wasn't my father, but did Mum tell him the rest? *No*, I think. I don't know what story she sold her husband to pretend to be my biological father, but it had to be less risky than *she's the mayor's kid and I've got the real mother jammed up in a mental ward.*

Polly keeps rewinding, playing, rewinding again, seeking out every instance of his face, but wincing each time she sees it. It's like she's jabbing her tongue into a mouth ulcer, over and over again.

Play.

"...as I previously announced, the woman holding Amy Becker is a highly unstable individual who was until recently being treated for delusional psychosis. Moreover, the police have received evidence that she was radicalized while in hospital, and we cannot rule out that this kidnapping may be the start of a coordinated terror attack on our great city. All

301

options are on the table to bring this situation to a speedy res-
olution, and I shall be working with Commissioner Khan to
do just that."

The screen goes blank. Polly's shrunken features look
back at me in the reflection of the dark glass. *"All options
are on the table,"* she echoes softly. She sounds hopeless.
"They're coming in, then."

I wheel to face her. "What do you mean, *coming in*? They
can't come in. What about the bomb?"

"Oh, once the word *terrorism* starts getting thrown
around, all the rules change. There might be other bombers. There might be a conspiracy. That justifies them trying
bridges, shunts, radio-jamming the detonator, all manner of
risky, finicky ploys to get in here and grab me. That's why,
I imagine, my dear old ex brought it up."

She almost laughs, but tears glimmer in her eyes. "Tell
me, Amy, how many terror attacks can you remember on
London?"

"What has that got to do with—"

"Humour me. Please."

"Four." A little spike of adrenaline jabs through me at
how close her hand is to the trigger of her bomb vest. "Tulse
Hill, Tufnell Park, Paddington and Greenwich."

"Four, yes, very good. And for any of those four, can you
remember the mayor going on TV three times in less than
twelve hours?"

"I don't … I don't know. I don't remember. I don't think so."

"No, it's always the Met commissioner, or the officer

in charge. But our Ry's taken the lead on this one; in fact he seems to be taking a rather hands-on role, doesn't he? I wonder why?" Her finger and thumb toy with the little silver cap on one of the flasks of explosive on her vest.

"From *haven't ruled out terrorism* to *confirmed terrorist contacts* to *start of a coordinated terror attack* in under half a day. Just like *I have some concerns* to *she's very problematic* to *she should go die in a fire.*"

She makes a sound in the back of her throat; her mouth twists like she tastes something nasty. "Next thing you know, they're burning your house down. Bless him, Ryan never could *act* without working himself up into a total state first. *Force is always a last resort,*" she snarls. "Yeah, well, last resorts are where fuckboys end up when they don't have the guts to take responsibility for anything. I bet dear old Dr Smith thought keeping me locked up and drugged up was a last resort too."

She's stumbling over her words; her eyes are staring, feverish. My stomach cramps up with fear. Her fingers flicker at her bomb vest.

She's going to do it, I think. *She's really going to do it.*

"I misjudged you, Ry," she murmurs. "I thought you'd be too weak for this. I should have known. It's always your weakness that's hurt me. I should have been more afraid of your weakness than your strength."

Her gaze seems to clear and settle on me. "They're coming in. If they can, they'll take me. If not, oh well, they'll shoot me and probably shoot you too and say I did it."

303

"Polly." I reach out towards her. "*Cat, please.*"

"Well, *fuck* them." Tears are streaming down her face now. She howls it. "Ryan, Ben, Evie, all of them. I'm not going to let them take me. I won't go back; I won't let them take me. I won't let them, Amy, I won't let them I won't let them…"

Her hand tenses on the bomb vest and every muscle in me seizes up with the premonition of the blast.

"I WILL NOT BE DESTROYED!"

CHAPTER TWENTY-EIGHT

Cat

As my fingers tense on the vest, a smell pricks my nostrils, a smell from memory, the one time in my past when I triggered an explosive.

Smoke pouring from a keyhole, the acrid stench of paint, peeling as it burned, the clunk of the door handle falling to the floor. The leap in my chest as I skidded out into the doorway, my shirt flapping around me. I didn't have a plan. I was too lost for plans; the only thought in my head was seeing you again.

I made it sixteen feet up the corridor before I felt Joy's meaty forearm on my back, bearing me back to earth. I cried and howled and clawed at the floor. Twenty minutes later, I was in another room that looked identical to the one I'd blown up. Nothing had changed, except that for two months my meals were brought to me in my room, and when they let me out into the garden for twenty minutes once a day, a nurse shadowed me to make sure I didn't infect anyone else with my escapee fervour.

Will Jenkins of the Beaconsfield Jenkinses got moved to a different clinic, or maybe prison, where perhaps he's still chewing his cuffs and dreaming of blowing up Parliament. I didn't see him again, but I never forgot what he taught me about bombs.

"Don't!"

I blink.

"Please." You're stretching out an imploring hand towards me. "Polly, Cat…" You swallow hard and force the syllables into your throat. "*Mother*, please."

"*Don't. Call me. That*," I snap, and you recoil. Oh God, you look so frightened. Guilt and self-disgust flood through me. I fight to gentle my voice. "Please, Amy, don't call me that. Not when you don't mean it. I can't bear it."

My promise to myself whirls through my head. *I won't let them destroy me. I won't let them destroy me. I won't let them destroy me. I won't I won't I won't.*

But I already have. I thought I'd endured, but – I pluck at the vest I made with the scraps of what Will taught me – how much of the Cat Canczuk they locked up in that place survived?

I roll my gaze hopelessly around the room. Evie's kitchen. Evie's tasteful lighting. Evie's elegant Swedish furniture. Evie's drawers upended, Evie's fancy cutlery scattered all over the floor by me, Evie's pricey health food stamped into the floor by me. Despair mounts in me like a wave. She was always so ordered, so careful, so in control. I'm a ball of chaos and undirected rage. I couldn't even break out of the hospital she put me in; I had to wait for her to die so they'd let me out. I've never done anything right. How could I ever have expected this to work?

And now I've got you, my child – *my only child* – cowering away from me.

"They've already won," I say softly.

I look down the hallway, at the four glass panels set into Amy's front door. I look at the heavy latch stamped BANHAM and imagine the wood around it splintering under a police battering ram, the way our locks splintered, the way our boundaries shattered on that night more than seventeen years ago when that hilarious Internet prankster called in the raid.

I remember my face ground into the familiar patterned carpet of my old living room, friction burns springing up on my cheek, my arm bent around to breaking, men's voices screaming at me "DON'T MOVE! DO NOT MOVE!" I remember feeling a cold metal ring pressed into the back of my neck and knowing it was the muzzle of a gun because I could see the same thing jammed into Mum's back. I remember the pain of the pressure as my swollen abdomen was forced down. How easy it would be now, as it would've been then, for a pumped-up scared shitless twenty-year-old boy in a flak jacket to let loose a stray round.

The vest is suddenly stifling. My head is pounding and I'm parched. I feel like I haven't had a drink in years. I look down. Two switches gleam greyly where they emerge from the nest of gaffer tape that fixes them to the old cigar tin I've drafted as a control box. The blink of the green light is oddly soothing. My hand strays towards my chest without me even meaning it to.

"Don't!"

You utter a little frightened mew, and I look up sharply. Slowly you come out of your defensive crouch. I want to curl up and weep at the fear I've put on your face, but despite it, you take one step towards me, then another. Your eyes, the same shade as his, hold mine. You stretch out a hand towards me.

"Please. You don't have to. Walk out of here, with me. Give yourself up. Tell your story."

Your voice is high-strung, desperate. Judging by your expression, the sour laugh that bubbles up out of my chest shocks you as much as it shocks me.

"And who'll believe me? A confirmed mental patient who claims the mayor of London fathered her baby?"

I put my hand back to my chest. You scream and tense to jump, but there's no time for your muscles to unwind as I pull one of the bottles from my vest.

I unscrew the cap. "It's only water," I tell you, and to prove it I take a long draught. "See?"

You gape at me. The silence makes me feel guilty and embarrassed and I spill on into it, trying to explain.

"I had to make it *look* like a real bomb, because I knew they would have caught me on some camera coming in here,

308

and *you* had to believe it, because I knew I couldn't watch you the whole time *and* search the house, and if you sneaked out and ran to the cops, they'd kick down the door in thirty seconds flat and I'd lose my one chance to find the proof that..."

I'm gabbling, desperate to ease the terror I can still see on your face. I take a deep breath, let it out, drain and then drop the bottle. You flinch, but all it does is bounce.

"It doesn't matter. I failed. There *is* no proof."

I stand aside to give you a clear path to the hallway and, beyond that, the front door, your fans, your life and ... your family.

"Go."

You don't move.

"Amy, *go*. Judging by the way our dear mayor's sounding off on TV, they're about to come in shooting. That really *would* put you in danger, and what kind of a mother would I be if I let that happen?"

It's a weak attempt at humour, and I can't make you smile. I guess I've given up that privilege. I go around behind you and gently push you towards the hall.

"I said *go*. Don't say anything about your mother, or the mayor or anything else. If Ryan knows you know, I don't know what he'll... Look, just tell them I was an obsessive fan of yours, OK?"

And finally, mercifully, you begin to shuffle over the tiles.

"Amy?"

You look back, your eyes wild and frightened.

"I'm glad I got to see you again."

CHAPTER TWENTY-NINE

Amy

When I try to walk, I find I can only manage a kind of zombie shuffle. My limbs are full of pins and needles; I feel like I've been tied up. My head is a cloud of static. Ahead of me, through the kitchen doorway, I can see the hallway, the front door with its bubbled glass and, through that, the milling vagueness of the police and the news cameras and the gawking crowd. Out there is safety, only a few steps away if I could just walk properly. Out there are Dad and – my heart flickers in my chest – Charlie.

I feel her eyes on me as I leave, and, despite myself, I look back from the threshold to the hall. Her eye sockets are like pits. She looks desolate, but in a way almost relieved, like she's even more glad that this is over than I am. There's something familiar about the expression, but in my dazed state it takes me a second to place it. It's the exact expression that stared back at me from the bathroom cabinet the morning after Mum died. The face you wear when someone you love has been suffering, and you've been suffering with them, and you hate yourself that you didn't do more for them, but at least it's over now.

My tongue feels like it's stuck to the roof of my mouth with glue and sawdust, but I prise it away to ask, "What about you?"

She looks startled. "Oh, don't worry about me." She flaps her hands at me, waving me away. "I'll be *fine*."

"Seems like," I say, "I've been told a lot of lies by a lot of people, not least you, and apparently I've swallowed most of them, but even I can spot that one."

She laughs. "Fair enough."

I wait for her to say more, but she just smiles at me sadly, mouthing *go*.

"Well?" I press her.

"Do you really care?" she asks.

"No." I shake my head. "I don't know. Let's say for the sake of argument that I do. What are you going to do when I walk out of here?"

"Well, Ry's already branded me a terrorist, and I suppose you know what he does with them." I swallow and nod. "Well, don't worry." That sad, relieved smile stays on her face. She reaches behind her vest and pulls out the little snub-nosed pistol.

"I'm not going to let them take me back."

We stand there for long enough for me to become aware of the ticking of the kitchen clock.

"Amy," she says gently. "Go. Please. There's not much time."

I don't move. I don't know why not. I feel like everything inside me was thrown up in the air when I saw her drink from that bottle, and it hasn't landed yet.

"You ... you could still come out with me," I say. "There are press out there; you could tell them your story."

She just laughs at that. A shocking, deep laugh, from the roots of her belly.

"A freshly released lunatic who's already been branded a terrorist on national TV?" she scoffs, tears running down her cheeks. "Oh, I can definitely see them taking my word for it. I need *proof*, Amy."

"There's ... there's Mum's secret phone."

She snorts. "Even assuming I can convince them I didn't plant that, all it shows is *someone* leaned on Dr Smith to do *something* and that a dead woman was *somehow* involved. I need proof that indisputably connects me to Ryan and Evie, and there isn't any."

She raises the gun and I flinch hard, but she's only using the back of it to wipe the tears away.

"Go. Don't worry about me. What happens to me isn't your problem. Go see your brother."

Charlie. I turn and make my way into the hall, the parquet slats creaking under me. The hubbub outside grows louder. My legs feel like they could run now. In seconds I could be out there, with him, looking after him, like I so desperately owe him.

What happens to me isn't your problem.

Into every life a little rain must fall, Mum liked to say, *and sometimes more than a little.* And now the Internet can pipe every drop of it into our front rooms until we feel like we're drowning in it, and what on earth is the point if we don't sometimes *make* it our problem?

I look back at her. She's smiling, but braced rigid as though for a blow, waiting to be abandoned one last time.

"There is," I say softly, and as I speak, I realize I've decided.

"What was that, Amy?" she asks.

"You said there's no proof, but there is; there has to be."

The resigned smile vanishes instantly. Now there is only anxious, barely daring hope. I fight not to look away.

"W-w-w-what do you mean?" Her gaze is so vulnerable it's painful, like looking at a naked bulb.

"When I was thirteen," I begin slowly, still working through it in my head as I speak, "and Mum was first diagnosed, I went into a proper moody, rebellious phase. Wouldn't leave my room, wouldn't clean it either. Mum would yell at me to get off my arse, to do *something*, anything, that wasn't doodling or dicking around on the Internet. 'This isn't an excuse,' she'd say, and then point to herself. 'I'm going to be fine.'

"Then, one day, I came home from school, dropped my bag on the floor by the door like I always did, stomped my way up the stairs like I always did, and she was standing in my bedroom doorway with her arm across it like a tollbooth pole. She was holding up her phone; it had one of those email coupons open on it for something called Jazzercise – it's as awful as it sounds.

"'We're doing this,' she said. 'The docs say I need to stay active, and they've got a two for one offer.' I looked at her like she'd just sworn undying loyalty to Satan, because I was thirteen years old and, like an idiot, I said I could think of literally nothing that would be more embarrassing than tap-dancing sweatily in a leotard next to my middle-aged mother.

"And then Mum got this victorious smile on her face and said, 'I can.' She swiped right on her phone, and there was a photo of me from Easter a few years before, wearing this fluffy yellow chick outfit. Come to think of it, it's still on there – you saw it earlier. 'Think of it this way,' she said. 'You wouldn't be seen dead at a Jazzercize class with your aged parent, correct?' 'Correct,' I said.

"'Then I imagine none of your school friends would either. Which means they won't be there to see you. On the other hand, if I hear another word out of you that isn't *Yes Mum, what a lovely idea, Mum; we'll get some exercise and spend some quality time together* then this *adorable* photo of you might just become the new banner image on your school intranet site, maybe with some of your baby shots as well, I haven't decided yet. Might put a bit of a dent in your image, that. Mightn't it?'"

"You remember it word for word?" Polly puts in. She sounds sceptical, like she thinks I'm trying to con her. She's

314

sat down and put the gun on the tabletop, but her hand is still only an inch or two away from it. "Four years later?"

"I…" I grimace. "She'd just been diagnosed for the first time and all I heard was the word *cancer*. I didn't understand that it can take years to work through. So, just for a couple of weeks, in the evenings I took to writing down everything she said, all our conversations that I could remember, like I had this idea I could keep her alive that way. Since she died I've been reading them back."

Polly winces, and sways a little on her feet like she's been hit. "I see," she says. "So what's your point?"

"My point is, how did Mum get your shrink to do what she told him? She threatened to post his junk where people would see it. She blackmailed him. Same as she did to me."

I think of her going through the house, straightening plates and stacks of paper. *Making right.*

"Mum liked order. She liked patterns. She liked habits and routine. She had her ways and she stuck to them."

"A place for everything," Polly says. *"And everything in its place."*

"Exactly. So we have a woman with form for blackmail, who founded a cybersecurity company, who engaged in a conspiracy with the father of your child and current mayor of this city to illegally imprison you in a mental hospital and steal your baby to raise it as her own."

I thought I'd have trouble getting that out, but my voice doesn't even waver. I pronounce it with all the emotion of a supermarket checkout robot. It's amazing what you can assimilate when you're trapped in a house with an armed and very, very wronged woman.

"She knows this man's darkest secret, this man to whom every copper in London reports, and what's more she knows that *he knows* she knows it. Are we supposed to believe she didn't have blackmail material stashed away on him in case he ever turned on her?"

She stares at me; for a moment hope lights her face, but then her brow creases.

"But there's nothing!" It comes out of her in a frustrated, doglike cry. "I've looked everywhere; I've torn the place apart looking for it. She must have thrown it out or deleted it."

"But you said it yourself: she never threw anything away. Not if she thought it was useful. She had drawers full of old birthday cards in case she needed something to shove under a table leg. She even kept old wrapping…"

I tail off and Polly gapes at me. "Amy?"

"Yeah?"

"You didn't finish your…"

"Yeah." I push past her through the narrow kitchen doorway, close enough to smell the terror sweat soaked into the hem of the fake bomb vest, and run headlong up the stairs.

"Amy? *Amy!*" she shrieks in alarm behind me and I hear the clump of her feet on the steps as she follows.

I shoulder my way into Mum and Dad's bedroom, and in my memory I'm doing the same five years ago, with the same urgency, only then it was born of eagerness, not fear. I'm hot on Charlie's heels, because it's Christmas Day and we have our stockings clutched in our hands. Mum and Dad are awake and alive, smiling, and soon we're surrounded by a lunar landscape of crumpled wrapping paper, and Charlie and I both have chocolate smeared around our mouths like clown lipstick, and then we head downstairs, to the tree where the big presents are, and my chest is swelling with hope and anxiety because I bought Mum's from Charlie and me this year, and I really *really* want her to like it.

And there she is, opening it the way she opens all her presents, with the flat blade of a kitchen knife under the tape, lifting it away as precisely as a surgeon, unwrapping the paper and then carefully folding it away, and then she gasps and her face glows with genuine pleasure and I glow too as she holds it up and looks it over.

It's slim, in a velvety grey slipcase with the Tenniel illustrations inlaid in beautiful gold foil on the front: a folio edition of *Alice's Adventures in Wonderland*.

I look at it now, lying open on the floor amid the chaos Polly has wreaked in my parents' room. The discarded bolero lies in front of it, rucked up and twisted like a fallen ghost, and I step over it to reach towards the book.

"I already looked at that," Polly says plaintively. She's hovering in the doorway again; I wonder if she knows she does that. "There's nothing in it: no paper slipped inside it, no secret cavity cut into it or any of the other books. I *looked*."

I glance back over my shoulder at her. "This woman wouldn't even throw away greetings cards – you think she'd mutilate her books?"

I reach past the book itself, for the discarded folio case.

"Just before Mum died," I start, and I feel tears clutch at my throat like an infection, "like, five minutes before, she said she wanted to read this; she asked me to go and get it for her. I thought she was being kind, because it was a gift Charlie and I gave her, a thing we shared."

I thrust my hand inside the slipcase, probing with my fingers, my knuckles distending the cardboard, and ... *yes*. Something's there, right at the back; she must have put it there with tweezers: a slick smoothness like plastic, gummed flush to the case's surface. I find an edge and scratch and it comes away under my nail. Polly's hovered closer; she peers over my shoulder at my hand as I pull it out.

"Now I think she just wanted to get rid of the evidence in case someone found it after she died."

Stuck to the nail of my index finger is a square of brown packing tape, no bigger than a stamp. Stuck to the tape is a removable memory card. All those years I took the piss out of her for being a Neanderthal, the tech consultant who was also the only person since the last ice age to use a phone without a built-in memory.

Wordlessly, Polly produces Mum's old phone from her pocket. Using the post of one of Mum's earrings in place of a paper clip I pop the old card out, replace it and switch it on.

The screen lights up and I delve into the archive. It takes me a handful of moments to find the folder, and then I let out a low whistle.

"What?" Polly barks. "What is it?"

"It's … it's all here. From the beginning. Even the Mad Hatter emails. It was a burner account; she only ever sent those two messages from it."

"And Ryan? The mayor, is he in there?"

But I don't answer. I've scrolled down to the very earliest file in the folder. It's an email from seventeen years ago.

From: TeenagePetrolhead@Bextel.com
To: RyanRichieRichards02@me.com

Dear Ryan,
I'm so, so sorry you've had to deal with that plague of lies about you having had a kid with some skank fan. I, and all of your other true fans know that you've done no such thing, and I know Nick knows that too. I just wanted to tell you I've taken care of it. You don't need to worry about Wild White Horse any more.
All my love,
A fan

"Who's Kevin Kordechevsky?" I ask Polly.

She replies immediately. "He was one of Ryan's managers, why?"

But I'm already reading the response.

From: Kevin.Kordechevsky@GlobalFireTalentMgmt.com
To: TeenagePetrolhead@Bextel.com

Dear Sir or Madam,

My client, Ryan Richards, does not know how you came by his personal email address, and he has no idea what you refer to in your previous email. Please desist from contacting him again.

Sincerely,

Kevin Kordechevsky

As far as I can tell, Mum did as she was asked, and for almost two weeks that was that. Maybe that's how long it took for a busy pop star to check his own email, because the next email was from someone calling himself Vreigeiter 66.

From: Vreigeiter66@gmail.com
To: TeenagePetrolhead@Bextel.com

To the individual who emailed Ryan Richards claiming to have "dealt with" the rumours surrounding an illegitimate child, I'm an associate of Mr Richards, and would like to enquire precisely what you meant by that. Please respond as soon as possible.

Ryan Richards may have had a good voice and a flair for politics, but a talent for digital smokescreens he did not. Attached to the email where it's filed in my mother's inbox are a series of screenshots of a hack into the Vreigeiter66 account, including one showing that the recovery email was RyanRichieRichards02@me.com, and, if that wasn't enough, another shot from another hack, this time on the phone company's servers, showing that the mobile number listed for two-step verification was registered to one Adrian Rijkaard and giving his home address.

I feel a sudden stab of recognition, and it doubles me over, winded. Sometimes it feels like all Mum left behind in this house is relics of her sickness; but this, this is her in her full strength – neat and meticulous and devastating. I can almost hear her pitying sigh at how easy it was to shred this weak man's threadbare cover.

If she'd Photoshopped herself into the screencaps flicking V-signs she couldn't have been more present, or having more obvious *fun*.

From: TeenagePetrolhead@Bextel.com
To Vreigeiter66@gmail.com

Hi Ryan!
This is such a thrill! Probably shouldn't discuss this over email, though. Grab me on Signal on the number below and we'll have a good chat.
Exx

The Signal messages are in the next file down. Once safely encrypted, Mum gleefully outlines the "gift" she's given her favourite pop star – adopting his "fake" daughter and squirrelling her mother away in a mental home.

Oh, she added, as an afterthought. *I know what you're*

thinking: why would the shrink play along? But don't worry, I've got that covered. Love to Nick. Exx.

And Ryan? I feel a little lurch in my stomach as I read his replies.

Ryan went along with it.

His messages were nervously solicitous. He seemed caught between not wanting to admit I was his, and worrying that the arrangement for my care wasn't sustainable.

Do you need money or anything? he asked once.

Mum's response was sharp. **Why? You don't owe her anything.**

That shut him up for a while. Later, his conscience seems to have been needling him. How long will that girl be stuck in the hospital?

Why?

I'm just concerned for her, that's all.

> **You're a sweetheart, but don't worry about her, Ry. Honestly, it's the best place for her; she was a real mess before she went in. She'll stay until she gets her head back in order, and admits you aren't the father. I'm sure it won't take long.**

After a two-day delay, Ryan's response was two letters long.

OK.

"He just…" I'm aghast. Disgust grips my throat like

nausea that this man is my father. "He just went along with it."

Polly snorts. "Of course he did. That's all he ever did. Went along. Never made a fuss, never disagreed. He could never bear to *confront* anyone. He needed everyone to love him, all the time. He was terrified that if he turned one person against him then that would be the beginning of the end; we'd all leave him. So he told everyone what they wanted to hear – me, his bandmates, his fans, his management, even when what we wanted were completely contradictory. He could never bear to disappoint, so he betrayed instead. Of *course* he became a politician. I should've seen that coming."

A murmur of voices from outside the house rips my attention away from the screen. I go to the window and peel back the curtain. The afternoon sunlight glints off the silver tape on the frame as I peer through the glass.

The crowd's still gathered on the street, the same mix of crow-shirted streamers, ordinary passing rubberneckers and media types with shoulder-mounted cameras, but they're being hustled and jostled back over the road by bobbies in uniform and the media types in particular aren't taking kindly to it. "Freedom of the fucking press!" I hear one squawk.

Why are they… But I don't even get to finish the thought before I see the van.

It cruises silently up the street, lights dark and sirens silent. It's painted blood red and I don't even need to read the markings on the side to know who's riding in it. The reporters have seen it now, a shout goes up, and like a troop of robotic meerkats I see the cameras swing towards it. It pulls to a stop and I feel my stomach hollow out. If Mayor Rijkaard sent the Vreigeiter66 emails – and we know he did – then he probably realizes we've got them.

Polly's voice echoes back to me. *They're coming in.*

The van's rear doors swing open. I can't see the faces of the figures that jump out; their helmets and masks and flak jackets are all black. My eyes are drawn to their guns.

"Is it..." Polly's hopping nervously from foot to foot. "Is there enough there to prove it? To nail him?"

I hold the phone out behind me. "Read it for yourself if you want," I croak, because all the moisture's fled my throat. "But hurry."

CHAPTER THIRTY

Cat

I take the phone with nerveless fingers. I stare at you, uncertain.

"Hurry!" you bark at me again. The skin's drawn tight around your eyes and your knuckles are pale where they grip the curtain. I lower my eyes to the screen and start to read.

I am wrong-footed by my emotions, just like I was when I first realized I loved you, six months before you were born.

I expected triumph; I *should* feel triumph. Here in my hand is the proof I searched for. I was betrayed. I am not crazy; I am wronged. But all I feel is a deadly weariness. I want to let the phone slip from my fingers, walk over to the bed of my enemy, crawl into it and pull the covers over myself until I hear the bang of the rifle, feel the instant's percussive impact, and then pain, and then nothing, as one of Ryan's emissaries ends me.

I hadn't realized how much I was still hoping I was wrong, that he somehow didn't know, that he wasn't involved, that he was a coward, yes, too cowardly to acknowledge you as his own, but not cruel enough to do what was done to me.

"Well?" you demand, and my gaze snaps up to meet yours. When you're scared, your cheeks go dark the same way mine do.

I gape. I try to give you an answer, but there are no words in my throat.

"I … I … I … let me finish." I keep scrolling down. After the initial flurry the thread goes cold; and then, almost two years after the first message … my breath stalls in my throat.

Vreigeiter66 I'm not kidding, Evie, pick up the phone.

>**TeenagePetrolhead** Anything we have to say to each other can be done where we have the protection of end-to-end encryption, thank you.

Vreigeiter66 Why am I hearing Cat's still in that mental hospital?

>**TeenagePetrolhead** Oh, it's Cat now, is it? Since when are you two on first-name terms?

Vreigeiter66 Answer the question.

>**TeenagePetrolhead** Perhaps she's finding it therapeutic.

Vreigeiter66 Don't fuck about with me.
We agreed she'd only be kept in there
until she could get back on her feet.

> **TeenagePetrolhead** She'll
> be kept there as long as Dr
> Smith deems it necessary.

Vreigeiter66 And how long is that going to be?

> **TeenagePetrolhead** As
> long as it takes.

Vreigeiter66 As long as *what* takes?

> **TeenagePetrolhead** As long
> as it takes for a mother to let go
> of the child she bore, to accept
> she'll never see or hold her
> again. So, y'know, a while.

Vreigeiter66 What the fuck, Evie? This
wasn't the agreement. You said you'd let her
out when she admitted I wasn't the kid's dad.

There's an almost prim offence in Evie's reply.

> **TeenagePetrolhead** That
> was two years ago. I'm Amy's
> mother now. I'm not going to
> hand her over to some psycho
> straight out of mental hospital.

Vreigeiter66 We can't leave her there for ever.

> **TeenagePetrolhead**
> Why do you care?

Vreigeiter66 Because she's the mother
of my child, you psychotic bitch!

I wonder how Evie reacted to that. Did she reel away from
her phone in horror? Or had she already begun to suspect?
Did she take some perverse satisfaction in being the secret
adopter of her favourite pop star's baby? I guess I'll never
know her feelings now, but whatever they were, she got
them under control fast. It only took her forty-five seconds
to reply.

> **TeenagePetrolhead** In case you've
> forgotten, the agreement was that
> I take Amy off both your hands, for
> ever. And I'm sorry to disillusion you,
> but that can't happen if we let poor
> Catherine roam the streets, because
> she won't roam them, she'll *stalk*
> them, for us. She'll break laws and
> windows and bones and careers
> and anything else she has to get
> her daughter back. It's what I'd do if
> my daughter was stolen from me.

Vreigeiter66 I'm going down there.

> **TeenagePetrolhead** To do what?
> The doctor belongs to me, not
> you. He wrote me, not you, into the
> paperwork as Catherine's nearest
> relative. I have all the legal rights.
> What are you going to tell him?

That you spunked a few millilitres
of fluid into one of his patients
a handful of times three years ago
and on that basis you *demand*
he overlook his own professional
judgement and let her out?

Vreigeiter66 I'll tell him I know he's
being blackmailed. If he doesn't let her
out, I'll go to his bosses.

TeenagePetrolhead Think very
carefully, Ryan. I just told you
what I would do to protect my
relationship with my daughter.

TeenagePetrolhead Do
you really not understand
that I can destroy you?

Ryan didn't reply after that, but I know what his answer
would have been, because he never turned up at the hospital,
never hammered on the desk demanding to see me. I would
have heard. Wouldn't I?

I try to scroll for more, but my fingers are slick with
sweat and the screen doesn't respond. Minute droplets of
water hit the glass and fragment, spraying over my hands.
I realize I'm crying.

"Polly? Polly? *Cat!*"

You look at me and speak to me like I'm a wild animal
you're trying to gentle. I can see the cords in your throat
move like piano strings as you fight to keep your voice even.

You're standing by the window, holding the curtain an inch from the wall.

"Please," you say. "We have to go. They're getting ready to come in." I can hear the panic bubbling under your words, and I know you understand. If Ryan's riot cops come in we could both die here. I know you're right. I know I should be raising my hands, hollering surrender, trying to get myself in front of every camera I can find.

But…

"Did you read this? All of it?"

"Yes," you say. "I don't understand. What's wrong? We have to go!"

But I shrink away from you, the very way you did from me.

I just told you what I would do to protect my relationship with my daughter. Did you feel the fierce heat of her love for you coming off the screen when you read those words?

"I … I can't," I whisper.

"Why *not*?" Tears of frustration glimmer in your eyes and for a crippling instant I'm back in the hospital bed with you, so tiny and alive, crying in my arms. "You have your proof."

"It doesn't matter. They won't listen. He's powerful. *You're* powerful. Even with this, you'll find a way to bury me again."

"But … but…" The hurt, confused innocence on your face is just the way it would have been on hers. "I won't. I'll help you. I'm on your side."

I want to believe you – I *long* for it; I feel wrung-out with that longing. But the part of me that needs to move is like

330

stone. What would I do, if I were in your place? I picture my own mother with her lonely, exhausted smile and my guts twist.

"You know it wouldn't stay private." The words march out of me, relentless and unforgiving. "He's the mayor of London; it'd be a huge scandal, *huge* news. And that's before we get to you. You built an empire, an entire *identity*, on her memory. On how you feel about her, how your followers feel about her. Are you really ready to tear that memory to shreds? For a stranger who turned up in your kitchen saying she had a home-made bomb stuck to her chest? You could do that to her? I couldn't, not to my own mother."

You hold my gaze, and very slowly you say, "I thought you said *you* were my mother."

A laugh of pure despair pulls itself out of my chest. "No, you see that's just it. I'm not. It was *her* voice that taught you to speak. *Her* finger you followed as you learned to read. She fed you, clothed you, kissed you when you were hurt, cuddled you when you were sad and yelled at you when you broke her rules. Don't you see? That's the horror of what they did to me. They didn't just steal away my child; they made it so that I never *had* her."

The tears are running hot and free down my face now, but I can still see you clearly enough to see the way you half crouch, almost like you're going to spring at me.

"I would give anything, everything. Everything I ever had, to be able to trust you, to know you. But you're a stranger to me. The one thing I really know about you is that the

331

woman who raised you is the most manipulative human being I ever met."

You straighten, a confused little tuck of skin appearing on your forehead. "What?"

"I said you're a—"

"No, I heard. Sorry. It's been a long time since *anyone's* called me a stranger. What about when you streamed off me – do you not feel like you got to know me then?"

I bark a brief laugh. "Streamed off you? They didn't even let us have phones in the hospital, let alone those patches you're so attached to. I've never touched Heartstream. Everything I know about you I found on the Internet since I got out."

"But…" You gesture to the back of your head, where your hair's as close-cropped as mine.

"This?" I flush. "Oh, they shaved my hair off in the hospital."

"Why?"

"Because I was pulling it out." I blink, and for an instant my hand's full of rust-coloured curls, blood on the roots like paint on brush tips.

You gape at me for a second, and then something flits over your face, a decision, a resolution, but it's gone so fast I wonder if I imagined it.

"If I could prove it to you," you say quietly, "if I could *show* you could trust me, would you look?"

I gaze at you, frozen, desperate for some way out of this paralysis.

Gently, you take my arm with one hand, and put the other around my waist, and I find myself walking. I feel so weak I can barely support my own weight. It's muscle memory with you; you've had so much practice easing broken people into motion.

"*Quick!*" you whisper.

A murmuring outside swells into a shout, creeping in through a flaw in the window glass. I can hear voices raised, barked in what sounds like orders. A muffled cheer. Then a voice through a loudspeaker.

"*To the woman holding Amy Becker; this is the Metropolitan Police. You are surrounded and your detonator circuit has been jammed. Release your hostage. Send her out of the building ahead of you, and come out with your hands up.*"

You guide me along the landing into your room. We're surrounded by charcoal drawings of birds. You dive flat onto your stomach and I drop to a crouch, expecting bullets or a blast, but you're only scrabbling under your bed. You pull out a slim black box.

"Do you trust me?" you ask.

My throat is so parched I can barely answer. "N-no."

"You will."

You pull the lid off the box. Sitting in the bottom, nestled in plastic, sucking all the light out of the world like black holes, are three oval fabric patches.

CHAPTER THIRTY-ONE

Amy

"Today's not too bad," Mum said with an anxious smile. "I think I could do today."

"You're sure?" I asked.

The smile stayed in place, but it crumpled at the edges like paper starting to burn.

"I don't know if it's going to get any better than this, to be honest."

So I put the word out. That special stream I'd been trailing for weeks now was finally here. Clear out if you don't want to be part of it, because at 8 p.m. GMT, for one hour only, like a guest DJ, my cancer-riddled mother is taking over my feed.

"I'm not sure I can do that for you," she'd said, when I'd finally sucked up the courage to ask.

We were having our traditional tea and toast, relocated from the breakfast table to her bedside because the twenty-three steps to the kitchen were about half a day's worth of energy for her at the moment. Well, technically *I* was having it. Her toast was untouched, and instead of English breakfast tea she had some kind of herbal monstrosity that smelled like it had been distilled from old women's underwear drawers, but she said it helped with the nausea. But still, tea and toast. Rituals are important, especially at the end.

"I want to spare you that."

"I understand," I'd said. "I do, and it's completely your call, but…" I'd hesitated. "If it's me you're worried about, I genuinely think I'd find it easier to know, rather than spend the rest of my life wondering, you know?"

She'd thought about it for a few days and I hadn't pressed her, until finally she'd agreed.

"On a good day," she'd stipulated. "If you want to know the depths, we can talk about that later, but for now I ease you in. You might be the one handling the kit, but I say when it starts, and when it stops. Agreed?"

I had. She'd hesitated then.

"Amy?"

"Yes, Mum?"

"You know, all the people who … follow you?"

"Yeah?"

"If it'd help you to know, do you think it might help them too?"

And so there we were, a week and two days later, in that hateful bedroom, with two and a half million people on six

335

continents standing by anxiously to receive. I pressed the patches to the base of Mum's skull, and tried not to think about how papery the skin felt.

"At least we haven't got to shave my head," she said. "Not with the osteosarcomb-over here."

I laughed. "Suits you – you've got the bones for it."

"Why thank you."

"I wish you'd passed the bloody things on."

She smiled a little sadly, but didn't answer.

"You ready?"

She nodded.

"Just say if you want to stop."

"I will."

I picked up her phone, thumbed the newly installed little blue heart, scrolled to the top, and hit *broadcast*.

I remember gasping as the exhaustion hit. I just felt so *heavy*, like my skin was suddenly made of lead. It was hard to lift my arm, and when I did I cried out. Nausea swelled in me and my stomach bucked, but Mum had warned me not to eat for the last twelve hours and I came up empty. There was a bone-deep ache in my shoulder, another in my chest, and it rose to a shrieking pitch when I moved. Tears sprang into my eyes, blurring her face.

"It's OK," she said, and I felt her sympathy for me throb through the link. "You get used to it."

"Really?"

"Yeah," she said, and even connected as we were, I couldn't tell if she was lying. "People can get used to

336

anything. It's the best and worst thing about us."

I closed my eyes. She didn't try to hide anything, not the fury, the acid humiliation at being stuck in this godforsaken bed, not the fear, not the desperate, needle-tipped guilt she felt at leaving Dad and me and Charlie, especially Charlie, so young. But also, how deeply and implicitly she trusted me, not just Dad, but *me* especially, to look after him. And alongside that was love. I was staggered by the sheer weight of her love and how proud she was of me.

"If we're going to do this," she said, "let's do it."

I picked up my own phone (and my hand felt like a boulder on the end of my wrist) and hit *broadcast* there too.

I remember the messages as they came in.

♟ Holy shit.

♟ What the fuck, Amy?

♟ Christ, I never knew.

The numbers dwindled fast, from 2.5 million, to 1.8, to 1 million, to 700K, as the tourists got out. But then they stabilized and, astonishingly, started to grow again.

And then something amazing happened.

♟ Oh my God, this is exactly how I feel.

Other *patients* started to log into the feed. I couldn't believe it. I didn't understand, how, when you were living with this, you could want *more* pain. But more and more of them were.

All of them said the same thing, more or less.

♟ I don't feel alone any more.

Twenty-three minutes in, the first parallel feed came

online, then another, then another, spreading like echoes in a cave system. When Mum finally nodded to me, and we killed her feed, there were more than two thousand of them, broadcasting not just to us, not even mainly to us, but to one another. A Fundarella account someone in Kuala Lumpur set up raised more than nine and a half million dollars for research into the rare and obstinate kind of bone cancer Mum had.

With all the follow-up takes reverbing her story around the Internet's various echo chambers, her name trended on every major social site for two months.

I press the patches to the back of Polly's head. The scalp between the bristles is slick with sweat and I have to press them down three times before they'll stick. I think of how I did the same for Mum.

Her old phone, sitting on my desk with its secret memory card and its cargo of poison, catches my eye.

Can you really go public with that? I don't know. Didn't she suffer enough? She was my *mother*, for God's sake. And Charlie's. Can I do that to his memory of her? Can I do that to *him*?

I grapple with it, fighting to make the woman I read in those texts and the woman who made me tea in the mornings fit into the same space, but I can't. She was different women to different people, at different times. The seventeen years between then and now changed her. *I* changed her. I have to believe that.

But she never told you, a voice inside me retorts. *And she never let* her *out.*

Her. I look at Polly, and she looks back at me with huge, frightened eyes, shrunken like a starved animal inside the fake bomb vest that is far too big for her, her hand clutching her gun to her breast like a kid with a stuffed toy rabbit.

She's so stuck, so crippled in every synapse by constant betrayal, that she can't trust me without proof.

In the end it always comes down to who you trust.

The robotic voice rattles the windows in their panes. *"This is your final warning."*

"Amy," she says, "you don't have time. Ryan can guess what I've told you. They have orders to kill us both for all I know. Just go, before they come in."

I thumb my phone, ignore the Heartstream icon – odds are there are coppers following my stream now, and I don't want them picking this up – and instead scroll over the basic one-to-one app that comes with the patches.

Establish private transduction loop? I hit *yes.*

Boots crunch the gravel below my window. Polly emits a frightened mew.

"Think of Charlie," she begs me. "He needs you. Go to him."

In my memory, Charlie is falling towards me in a glittering spray of glass, the echo of the shot still in the air, the panicking crowd scattering around him like shrapnel from a grenade, and the concentrated force of their emotion slamming me into unconsciousness.

Enter partner transducer serial no. I dash tears from my eyes as I stab it in.

"I've let you go," she pleads. "Why won't you just *leave* me?"

I flinch from the misery etched in her face. *That's what people have always done,* her expression says, and part of her, the part gripping that gun so tight the veins stand out on her knuckles, can't believe that I won't do the same. I have to show her.

"You won't read my mind, exactly," I tell her. "But you'll feel how I feel towards you. You'll know I mean you no harm; you'll be able to tell if I'm lying to you."

More boots crunch gravel. Through the crack in the open window I hear clicks that could be safety catches being flicked off.

Just run, a voice in me urges. *Drop the phone and run. Think of one of those coppers putting a bullet in your brain. Think of Charlie. Think of him losing his mother and big sister inside of a week. Now RUN!*

But my feet stay rooted to the floor. Sweat drips from my forehead onto the phone. I stab at the screen, but the wet glass won't answer. "FUCK!" I scream, and Polly starts hard. I wipe it clear on my hip and thank Christ it works again.

Leave her. You don't know her. So what if you started out in her uterus? That doesn't make her your mother. Your mother's the one whose memory you're about to destroy. The one who raised you and loved you your whole life.

I look up at Polly. She stares back, baffled, frightened, frozen.

And lied to me my whole life, too.

"Amy," Polly says quietly. "Leave me. It's what I deserve."

"No," I say simply. "It's not; it never was."

I hit *broadcast*.

For the first two seconds, it's like a normal stream. I feel the ghost of her heartbeat in my own chest, tripping even faster than mine. I feel the drag of her sleeplessness at the corners of my eyes. I feel her confusion, her guilt, her desperate, paralysing fear of betrayal, and under that, as quiet as the sound of breathing under rubble, hope against hope that *this* time, someone is being true to her.

Trust me, I'm begging her. I stretch out a hand towards her, and she stares at it. Then I feel her in my head. She thinks of Mum, the happy, smiling pictures of us she found on her phone, and as she does my mess of feelings for my mother surface in front of her. She picks at the strangled knot of them, brushing up against my love and grief and anger and confusion as one by one they come loose from it.

Trust me. Hesitantly, she reaches towards my hand.

And then the feedback comes in like a tornado.

The dampeners! I think frantically. *They're only default in Heartstream. I forgot to set them…*

But then the thought's gone in a blizzard of images and emotions.

Mum's body, cold and waxy under my hand.

Ryan slamming the door in my face.

All my pain and fear and hopelessness spins through her and through me and back again, growing each cycle, feeding and feeding and feeding and feeding, louder and louder and louder and LOUDER AND LOUDER AND LOUDER AND LOUDER—

My baby's heartbeat echoing through the ultrasound.

Charlie's face, dark with betrayal. You promised!

My legs go out from under me, my jaw is slack and drool runs freely from the corner of my mouth. I'm going to pass out. Polly crumples against the wall, eyes glazed. My stomach clenches. Oh God, this could *kill* her. I try to touch my phone, to end the stream, but I can't even make my thumb twitch.

I slide down the edge of the bed, flat on my back, staring at the ceiling.

A girl, just like me. In love. Trembling with excitement as she kisses him.

Watching the flames eat her home, her life, her family.

Cradling her baby in her arms.

I will not be destroyed I will not be destroyed I will not be destroyed.

I feel her will to survive in her like a pulse.

Darkness creeps in at the edge of my vision. I'm going to pass out. Polly's now flat on her back, her eyes like marbles. I feel her heart breaking.

I won't … let … them.

And then, just like that, it's gone.

I'm gasping, spit and air rasping in my throat. I flop like a fish, until I manage to get my elbow under me. My head feels anvil-heavy as I drag it far enough off the floor to look down at my hand, but my phone's not there.

With a gurgling groan, Polly pulls herself into a sitting position. Her left hand holds the gun. Her right holds the phone.

I couldn't even lift my thumb, and she, on her *first* ever stream, dragged herself across the room and took it from my hand. If she hadn't, we both would have died.

I won't let them destroy me. The sheer power of that impulse devastates me.

"You really aren't going to leave me?" she asks. Tear tracks claw her cheeks.

I shake my head and the throb in my temples makes the room blur. "No. I couldn't; you're—"

A crash from downstairs cuts me off, the sound of splintering wood. Boots drum on the floorboards. Someone shouts *"Clear!"*

"They're in the house." Somehow, I clamber to my feet. My legs feel like overwarm butter but they're under me. Now I'm pulling her up. She clings to me like *she's* the child.

"Stay close to me," I breathe. "Whatever you do, don't give them a clear shot."

I hesitate for a fraction of a second, then sweep up Mum's old phone from my desk and hand it to her. "You're going to need this."

"Downstairs clear!"

The boots are like thunder on the stairs. Polly's fingers twine through mine. With my free hand, I wrestle with the window sash, and for a moment it won't budge, but then it slides and the tape gives way with a sucking noise and air rushes over my face. Shouts of surprise and alarm carry from the crowd across the road. Cameras flash like distant gunfire. I look down. The roof of the porch slants away, barely two feet below.

The door bursts inwards under a boot.

"Stop! Police!"

I yank Polly into my arms; she's as light as a sparrow. With a last shove from my wrecked legs I bundle us out into the night.

"Aaaaaaaaaaah!" Burning erupts along my spine as I slide down the tiles, and then we hit the gravel with a crunch.

A single shot cracks the night, and tiny pebbles fly beside my head.

I lurch to my feet, dragging Polly with me, hauling her around in front of me, desperate to keep my body between her and them. We break into a shambling run.

"The cameras," I gasp to her. "We have to reach the cameras." I slip my hand into my pocket and open a stream, but that won't be enough. For this we need to be *seen*.

The grass is cold and dew-slick under my bare soles. If I slip we're dead. If I stumble we're dead. We stagger out across the lawn, and onto the harsh asphalt of the road.

"Stop! Police!"

With every step I expect a bullet. An end. And with every step it doesn't come and I take another. I can't give them a shot.

"Amy? *Amy!* Are you all right?"

A familiar voice. *Dad.* I jerk my head up. Somehow, we've reached the cordon. Bodies press in all around.

"Ame?"

"Charlie?" I gasp.

And there he is, his hand clasped in his dad's, bandages pressing pads against his eyes. He turns his head, searching for the source of my voice.

For a moment I quail at what he's about to find out, at how he's about to feel. But then I remember holding him outside Mum's bedroom, whispering, *You shouldn't have to see her like that.*

No, he shouldn't. But it's the truth, and I can't protect him from it. I never could.

"POLICE!" The bellow deafens me, just as I feel a shove in my back and we sprawl forward. Polly grunts as she hits the pavement. The asphalt grazes my hands. Gun barrels hem us in like the branches of a thorn thicket, but camera lights are flashing; people are recording.

"Don't point those things at my daughter!" Dad's struggling through the press, trying to reach me.

"Don't SHOOT!" I scream it hard enough to tear my throat, begging the microphones on all the phones pointed at us to pick it up. "WE SURRENDER!"

The rifle barrels twitch. Camera flashes gleam off their masks and their ID badges. I feel the cops' hesitation. Muscles screaming in protest, I shove myself up on my forearms and throw myself across Polly's prone form. I cling to her, my head sideways, covering hers, her breath warm against my cheek. My ribs are pressed to hers; I can feel the outline of Mum's phone in her pocket, pressing into my side. I can feel the swell of her breath, the tremor of her pulse, and with every beat of it, I know we're still alive.

My heart beside her heart, where it began.

ENJOYED *HEARTSTREAM*?
WE'D LOVE TO HEAR YOUR THOUGHTS.

🐦 #Heartstream
@WalkerBooksUK
@WalkerBooksYA

📷 @WalkerBooksYA

ACKNOWLEDGEMENTS

This was a weird one. Written in bursts over seven months as the subject matter constantly evolved around it. I wouldn't have got it done without the dedication and consistent professional excellence of all at Team Walker. Most especially my brilliant editor Frances Taffinder (suffice to say the edit on this one was detailed, complex and you just read a much better book for it), as well as publishing's wisest human Denise Johnstone-Burt, publicity supremos Rosi Crawley, John Moore, Becca Oram and Kirsten Cozens, typesetter par excellence Anna Robinette and cover art legend Maria Soler Canton ...

... who never would have had a chance to work on it at all if it hadn't been for my heroic agenting team. First and foremost, Nancy Miles, who not only has my back, but my sides and my front as well, Caroline Hill-Trevor, Alice Natali, Clemmie Gaisman and Emily Hayward-Whitlock for their relentless enthusiasm and skill in pushing my stuff at people in all places and in all media.

Three friends in particular were invaluable in helping me land this one: Emma Trevayne, Emily Richards and Amy McCulloch. Legends one and all.

My family I rely on for basically everything, so Sarah, Dad, Matt, Jasper, Barbara, Robin, Moira, Sally, Livs, Chris, Aislinn, Toby, Arijana, James and Rachel, love and gratitude, for being there.

And finally Lizzie, my rock, lover, tolerator-in-chief, without whose commitment to the best and worst the internet has to offer, this book would certainly not exist: I love you with all of my everything. Thank you.

TOM POLLOCK has been described as "a powerful new imagination" by the *Guardian*. He is the author of five novels, including the critically acclaimed *White Rabbit, Red Wolf*. *Heartstream* is his second novel for young adults. He is also an ambassador for *TalkLife*, the peer support network for youth mental health. Tom lives and works in London and can be found on Twitter: @tomhpollock